MURDER AT
MABLETHORPE
CASTLE

A HARLOWE & FITCH HISTORICAL MYSTERY
ELIZABETH ROSE

OLIVERHEBERBOOKS

Cover art by Dar Albert at Wicked Smart Designs

Published by Oliver-Heber Books

0 9 8 7 6 5 4 3 2 1

Chapter One

Mablethorpe Castle, Late 1300's

Trouble seemed to follow Lady Vivienne Harlowe wherever she went, and tonight would be no exception.

Vivienne let out a deep sigh, standing at the top of the stairs inside Mablethorpe Castle, dreading her uncle's gathering of arrogant nobles. All she wanted was to be anywhere but here right now. These needless events seemed a waste of time to her, not to mention, boring. But Lord Gilbert Irvine liked to keep up appearances. He tried hard to make alliances with just about any noble he met as long as it boded well for him. Since he was her guardian and she owed him greatly for taking her in when she had nowhere else to go, she really couldn't object to attending his pompous feast.

"Oh, Rosina, I am not looking forward to this at all," she told her handmaid, who stood at her side.

"Why not?" asked the girl. "I'm sure you will have a wonderful time, my lady."

"Nay, I doubt it. My stomach is in a knot already, and that always seems to happen just before there is trouble of some kind. I have a bad feeling about this."

Rosina giggled. "Oh, my lady, what could possibly go wrong? The castle is filled with nobles, and the cooks have prepared a feast like no other. When I was in the kitchens earlier, I watched them putting the feathers back on a cooked peacock. You'd be surprised how alive it looks!"

"But it's not alive, Rosina. It's dead." When she said the word *dead*, it brought a flood of emotions coursing through her. Vivienne didn't want to think about death right now. The knot twisting in her gut felt the same as the night she'd seen both her parents murdered. "Let's get this over with as fast as possible," she told her maid servant, trying to gather up enough courage to walk down the stairs. Why couldn't she shake this awful feeling of dread? What was it that made her want to turn around and run back to her chamber and hide her head beneath her pillow?

"Everyone is waiting for you, my lady," Rosina reminded her.

"I know," she answered in a half-whisper. Vivienne had finally agreed to attend the gathering, but was honestly only doing so for her dear aunt's sake. Purposely wearing her cloak over her gown even though she'd be indoors, it was Vivienne's intention to make a quick appearance in the great hall and then sneak out to the mews or the kennels to have some time alone until the event ended.

Holding up the hem of her green velvet gown, Vivienne slowly started to descend the stairs. Her soft, embroidered slippers didn't make a sound as she walked. Her cloak swished over the stairs, the rich cloth trailing after her, following in her wake.

"Listen, my lady," said her handmaid in excitement. "The music has already started."

Sure enough, the sounds of music and conversations floated up to them from the great hall. Mablethorpe Castle seemed to always be bustling with life. Sometimes so much so, that it made Vivienne long for solitude more than ever. Tonight the castle was filled to the brim with those who lived here, as well as her uncle's many guests from near and far. Lords and ladies strutted around with their noses in the air, every move aloof and planned. For once, she'd love to see any one of them do something out of the ordinary. Predictability was something Vivienne could live without. She prided herself on acting at the spur of the moment. Life was too short not to have adventures. And if anyone knew how precious life was, it was she.

Each step she took brought her closer to the nobles who always seemed to try to outdo one another with their tales of bravery or their continuous bragging about their holdings and extraordinary wealth. Servants hurried to and from the kitchens, tending to the nobles' ridiculous needs. Kitchen maids carried trays loaded down with pewter tankards filled with ale, as well as wooden goblets of heather wine that came all the way from Scotland. For his gatherings, Vivienne's uncle spared no expense. The new large stone statue of a dragon just inside the door of the great hall was proof of her uncle's usual need for attention as well as items that served no purpose whatsoever.

The minstrels were playing cheery tunes, just as Rosina had said. From Vivienne's position she could already hear the sound of harp strings being plucked by a musician who was perched in the minstrels' gallery that bordered the high walls of the great hall. A drummer banged out a beat in perfect time on the long tabor. Lutes, fifes, and bells blended together to add to the plethora of sounds that created a pleasant symphony. Vivienne enjoyed and appreciated music, wishing she had the talent to play an instrument of any kind. Her intentions were to learn to do so someday soon. What she wasn't fond of, however, was dancing. She supposed it was because her uncle always forced her to dance with men of his choosing, but ones that she didn't like.

"Did you see the jongleur who arrived here three days ago?" asked her handmaid excitedly, having the habit of continuous chatter. "He is wearing parti-colored clothes of blue and yellow, much like those of a jester."

"Yes, I saw him," Vivienne answered. She had noticed the jongleur who had been passing through the land and arrived at their castle looking for work. The traveling minstrel had been welcomed to stay for the gathering and feast by Vivienne's Aunt Ellen, who could never turn anyone away.

All these people crowded together inside the great hall anticipating the elaborate feast that was about to be served. Uncle Gilbert had told everyone earlier that he had an important announcement to make, but wouldn't reveal it until after the meal. Well, whatever it was he had to say, it didn't interest Vivienne at all.

As she neared the bottom of the staircase, the aroma of roasted duck, savory venison, fresh bread, and the tangy scent of cinnamon and ginger-spiced tarts filled the air. Cook, the large man who was in charge of the nearby kitchen, was also making his famous stew tonight. Everyone looked forward to it, since the man seemed to have the touch of gold, able to turn a bland pot of simple pottage into an intriguing specialty with the spices he used. Vivienne loved growing herbs, and offered anything from her garden to not only the cooks, but also the castle healer. As far as she was concerned, herbs were magical when it came to providing flavor or aiding the injured.

"I am so hungry that I cannot wait to eat," Rosina rambled on from behind her.

Vivienne had personally requested rosemary-encrusted white bread tonight for the nobles, since that was her favorite, and something her mother used to make on occasion. The scent alone brought back fond memories of Vivienne's childhood, growing up with her little brother, Adrian. Her heart suddenly ached thinking of Adrian and how much she missed him. Even so, she needed to cling to the good memories, since the bad ones constantly haunted her each night in her sleep.

"I wonder what Lord Mablethorpe's announcement will be," commented her handmaid, never at a loss for words. Rosina was a young woman of twenty years, and always talkative and over-curious about anything and everything. While she tended to Vivienne's needs with excellence and care, on more than one occasion Vivienne had caught the girl gossiping with the other handmaids as well as the alewives. Usually it was only about the other servants, and nothing to be considered harmful to a noble's reputation. Therefore, Vivienne had refrained from reprimanding her. She decided that Rosina was just lonely and hungry for friends. Vivienne tried to be a friend to her, but sometimes the girl's chattering could become very annoying.

"I am not sure what his announcement is, and neither do I care." Vivienne didn't feel like making conversation at the moment. She'd felt that anxious twisting in her gut all day and it concerned her greatly. In the past when this feeling engulfed her, it was always when something bad was about to happen. It was almost as if Vivienne could somehow sense trouble. Now if only she had the means or the wisdom to avoid it, that would be a true skill indeed.

"I've heard through the rushes that Lord Mablethorpe is going to try to match you up again with one of the noblemen, just like he did last month," Rosina told her, anxiously spreading the word of wagging tongues.

"Now, how could you or anyone know that?" asked Vivienne. "My uncle made it clear he would tell no one his announcement until after the meal."

"I am just telling you what is being said, my lady." The short, plump woman had only been in Vivienne's service for six months now as her handmaid, having worked in the castle's kitchens for a few months before that. Rosina was likeable and a good worker. That's why when Vivienne's last handmaid, Justina, suggested her when she left, Vivienne gave her the position. No one could compare to Justina, and Vivienne missed her dearly. But she let the girl leave to live in town with her new husband and raise a family together.

Family. Vivienne's stomach clenched again at the mere thought of the word.

It had much meaning to her at one time, but for the last seven years, the word only held grief and pain.

"Rosina, I'll remind you once more, just like I constantly tell my aunt and uncle–I am not interested in being married. Not again. Ever." Vivienne hoped this would end the conversation, since the knot in her stomach continued to tighten like pulling a bowstring taut.

"Now, now, Lady Vivienne, it is every woman's dream to marry and have children. I know it's mine. I hope to someday be able to marry a man I love and have his babies. I want to be a perfect wife." Rosina sounded as if she really meant it.

"I thought that way at one time too, but not anymore," she sadly told her handmaid. "I am done with marriage and babies, and actually quite content just the way I am."

"Really, my lady! The way you say that makes me think that you must have had a bad experience with your late husband." Rosina continued to pry. "God's eyes, he didn't beat you, did he?"

The woman was sometimes too meddlesome for her own good, even if she meant well. However, Vivienne had no intention of talking about her past with anyone today or ever. She was a person who liked to keep to herself, and rarely offered information about her life to anyone at all. Stopping abruptly at the bottom of the staircase, she turned to speak to her handmaid, hoping to douse any wild gossip in the making before it grew to a disproportionate size. After all, everyone already whispered about her behind her back, since she wasn't a proper well-bred lady.

Vivienne had a mind of her own and didn't like to be told what to do. Therefore, instead of using a ladies' saddle, she rode her horse astride. She'd learned how to wield her late father's sword, having practiced with the squires in secret until her uncle found out. By then, there was nothing he could do to stop her. Sometimes Vivienne even wore breeches and scaled walls and climbed trees just for the fun of it.

She had learned at a young age how precious life could be and not to take it for granted. A hunger deep inside made her eager to learn all that she could in every aspect. She wanted to embrace life and live it fully at every minute. Waking up tomorrow wasn't a promise, and one never knew how long they had on this earth. Vivienne discovered that much too early in her life. She wished she could change the past, but sadly she couldn't.

"Rosina, I understand that you are only trying to know me better, and I appreciate your friendship as well as your attempt to urge me to confide in you. However, I prefer not to talk about my past."

"Oh." She frowned and lowered her head as if she felt she'd done something wrong. Brushing back a stray dark strand of hair from her eyes, she quickly tucked it back under her wimple. "I understand, my lady. I am sorry for asking such a thing," she answered softly, seeming as if she felt ashamed or mayhap shunned. "I can understand your wishes. I don't like to talk about my past either."

Vivienne smiled and reached out to touch her on the hand, feeling bad to have reprimanded her. Rosina had always been such a sweet girl. Vivienne supposed she'd been a little too harsh with her just now. Rosina didn't seem to have much confidence, and Vivienne usually tried to build up the girl's spirits whenever she could. "I assure you, we will have more time to chat later, as I would like to be good friends with you. However, right now, we have a feast and celebration to attend."

"Of course, my lady. I didn't mean to pry." A smile spread across her face. "I would like nothing more than to be considered your friend. I hope someday to be just like you."

"Your attempt at flattery doesn't go unnoticed. But believe me, you don't want to be just like me. Not unless you want to be the focus of those wagging tongues." This made both of them giggle, breaking the tension.

"Nay. I wouldn't want that, my lady."

"Why hello, Lady Vivienne Irvine. You are looking quite fine tonight in that comely gown," came a voice from behind her. Vivienne spun on her heel to see that pompous fool, Lord Dinadan Knapp from Gainsborough, staring up at her from the bottom of the stairs. Dressed in his gaudy clothes as usual, he wore too many rings, as well as silly shoes with pointed toes that were so long that the ends had to be tied up to his legs or he'd trip when he walked. His beady, dark eyes drank her in, as he made no effort to hide the fact he was perusing her from head to toe. That hungry, lustful look in his eye made her feel as if he wanted to eat her. As usual. It was no secret that Lord Gainsborough liked all women. He'd had more than a nobleman's fair share of mistresses through the years, most of them being commoners and servants. He was older than Vivienne's twenty-three years, by at least a good decade. He was also married, even though he'd never acted as if he cared. Having a wife didn't seem to stop his wandering eye in the least.

"I am Lady Vivienne *Harlowe*, not *Irvine*, Lord Gainsborough," she said, referring to him by the town from whence he came. She politely curtsied as she greeted him. Rosina stayed silent and hidden behind her, most likely scared of Lord Gainsborough, since he had such an overpowering personality. "I chose to keep my father's surname instead of taking that of my uncle, as I am sure you already know."

"Ah, yes," he said, snapping his fingers. "Your *dead* father, that's right," he pointed out, as if he'd just discovered the fact, which he hadn't. "He was married to your mother, who is dead as well." His calling her parents dead aloud only managed to create a shiver that bolted up Vivienne's spine. Why did he have to say that? What on earth would cause the man to act so insensitive and uncaring to her when she'd lost her entire family? God's eyes, how could her uncle even have befriended such an intolerant fool?

"If you'll excuse me, Lord Gainsborough, my uncle is awaiting me in the great hall and he is not a patient man." She hoped he wouldn't mention her parents again. Or for that matter, ask her any questions about them.

"Don't worry about that," he said with a low chuckle. "Your uncle is busy talking to the other nobles. There is time. Besides, he knows I want to talk with you."

"Talk to me? About what?" The last thing she wanted was to talk to the cur any longer than she had to.

Once again, his gaze swept from her head all the way down to her toes, making her feel ravished. "Take a walk with me, my dear. We'll go out to your personal herb garden where we can speak in private." He held out his beefy arm. Vivienne silently groaned. Did the fool actually think she was going to go anywhere with him? Especially alone? "The air is fresh and cool so you can clear your head without the chance of anyone disturbing us."

Vivienne usually went through this little game every single time Lord Gainsborough visited. He'd try to get her alone and she'd object. Then she'd walk away, and it would all be over.

Well, she didn't have time for this kind of foolishness tonight. All Vivienne wanted was to make an appearance in the great hall and silently slip away when no one was watching. She needed to rid herself of the man, and suddenly had an idea.

"Well, what a nice thought, I'd like that," she said, feigning a smile, almost laughing aloud when she saw the shocked look upon his face that she'd answered in this way. She glanced over his shoulder spying his wife stretching her neck from the entrance of the great hall, trying to see them. Their son, Wilfred, who was about Vivienne's age was with her. "Since it's such a beautiful evening, I'll just motion to Lady Gainsborough and your son to join us. I am sure they'd like some fresh air to clear their heads as well." She held up her arm and waved them over.

"Nay!" he spat. "Never mind." Gainsborough quickly lowered his arm to his side. He scowled at her and turned around so abruptly that he knocked into the jongleur who had just walked up playing his lute. The force caused the musician to drop his instrument. The lute went crashing to the floor, landing in the rushes. "Watch where you are going, you fool!" the nobleman bellowed, and stormed off in a huff.

The young musician quickly bent over and retrieved the lute. Standing upright with the neck of the instrument in his hand, he wiped the stray rushes away to inspect the damage to his precious piece. His thick brows dipped and a frown turned down the corners of his mouth. Vivienne realized the rough encounter with Lord Gainsborough had resulted in a broken lute string for the musician.

"I'm so sorry about that," she apologized for the rude lord, knowing that Gainsborough wouldn't think twice about running over a commoner. Neither would he have any feelings of remorse. Musicians were poor and had very little in life. They made their living by the music they played. Without the lute, the boy would have nothing. Lord Gainsborough should have apologized and also offered to buy the boy a new string. However, Vivienne knew it would never happen.

"Thank you, my lady." The boy's eyes stayed focused on the broken string.

Vivienne believed everyone deserved respect, no matter how low they were in status. Unfortunately, most nobles did not think the same way as she. Her heart went out to the young musician, and she wanted to help him however she could.

"What is your name?" she asked.

"I am Leif, my lady." He looked to be about ten-and-six years of age. That is how old her brother Adrian would be right now. If he had survived that awful night, which she sincerely doubted. Her heart went out to the jongleur, mainly because she missed her younger brother. Vivienne couldn't accept Adrian's disappearance, and neither could she accept the fact that he might be dead, since she hadn't been able to find him for the last seven years. Her head told her if her brother was still alive, he would have contacted her by now. Her heart told her she would never see him again.

"Hello, Leif. I am Lady Vivienne," she introduced herself. "Mablethorpe Castle is my home. Welcome."

"Thank you, my lady. However, I don't feel very welcome here." Leif continued to brood. "That nobleman broke my string and now I can't play. If I cannot play, I won't get paid. And with no money, I won't eat. Mayhap I should be on my way now." The jongleur shot a daggered look toward Lord Gainsborough's back, and Vivienne couldn't blame him. She watched as the nobleman entered the great hall, brushing right past his wife and son without even acknowledging them.

"Nay, Leif. Please stay. I will make sure your string is replaced and it will not cost you a penny. You are welcome to partake of the meals until you are back on your feet again."

"Thank you, my lady. That is ever so kind of you. I appreciate your generosity." This was the first time she saw the boy smile since he'd been here. He was very polite for being nothing more than a traveling vagabond. Vivienne realized how important it was to always help those in need. She was more than happy that she could do it. If only more nobles felt this way, life would be so much better.

"My lady, my lady," called out a young page boy, running up to her as the jongleur trudged back to the great hall with his broken instrument in hand. The child's wide eyes told her something was wrong.

"What is it, Martin?" she asked, being fond of the little blond boy. She'd taken him under her wing ever since his family had sent him to Mablethorpe to be fostered. He was seven years of age, which was the same age her own son would be right now. In her heart, Vivienne never gave up hope that her missing child would someday still be found.

"Cook is fightin' again with the kennel groom. They are starting to push each other," the boy announced, his hands waving wildly in the air as he explained the situation.

"Why? Whatever is the problem now?"

"Cook doesn't want to give Grunt a bone, but the kennel groom says he has to do so."

"Oh, no! Has my hound followed his nose and ended up under Cook's feet again?" asked Vivienne, knowing this meant trouble. Cook didn't like anyone underfoot or even in his kitchens at all if they didn't belong there. Especially not dogs. "I'll handle this." She headed off to the kitchens with Rosina hurrying right behind her.

Vivienne's bloodhound, Grunt, seemed to always have a nose for trouble, even if he was the one usually causing it. In a way, her pet was not unlike herself, she realized. That made her smile. Her dog was a limer, taken on a leash to find the hart or boar before it was chased by the rest of the hounds on a hunting expedition. Grunt had a great nose for sniffing out a trail. Once he even helped the sheriff find a robber by sniffing the scent of the thief from a piece of torn clothing they'd found. If only she would have had a dog like this seven years ago, mayhap he could have helped the sheriff find her missing baby and brother.

Cook was a big man with a short temper. Vivienne had to hurry before he took his cleaver to Grunt just for wanting a soup bone.

"Cook, put down the blade at once!" Vivienne shouted, running into the kitchens to find the sweaty man waving his knife in the air. "Grunt, come here, boy!" she called, patting her thigh, urging her dog to listen. Grunt was standing on two legs, trying to get a bone that the cook held high in his other hand. Both the cook's hands were over his head. Grunt pawed the air and continued to bark. "Adam," Vivienne called to the kennel groom who had been spatting with the cook. "Please collect Grunt before he causes any more trouble." She hurried across the room, making her way to them, carefully dodging the many servants carrying trays of food on their way out to the great hall. The meal was about to start and things were disorderly. The nobles liked their food hot and prompt. Just the smallest issue and they became unhappy, yelling and bringing even more chaos to an already bad situation.

As if matters could not get any worse, Lord Gainsborough strutted into the kitchens, making his way directly over to Cook.

"Oh no," mumbled Vivienne, seeing the troublesome man. The servants noticed too, all staying well clear of him. Rosina dodged behind Vivienne's skirts to hide. Vivienne wished she could hide away from Lord Gainsborough as well.

"What is taking so long?" Lord Gainsborough demanded to

know. "I am famished." He snitched a cooked carrot off the tray of a passing kitchen maid whom Vivienne knew as Maria. He popped the root vegetable into his mouth, then proceeded to reach out and pinch Maria on her ass.

"Oh!" gasped the girl, nearly dropping her tray, but managing to save the food from hitting the floor at the last second.

"Where is my meal, wench?" snapped the nobleman. "I want you to serve it to me personally." His wife hurried into the room after him, probably to make sure he didn't go after the kitchen wenches, but it was already too late for that. If she had been half a minute sooner, mayhap Lord Gainsborough would have stilled his roaming hand and not pinched Maria after all.

Their son Wilfred shuffled along with his head down, silently following his mother. Wilfred was about the same age as Vivienne, and the only child of Lord and Lady Gainsborough. In Vivienne's opinion, he was also the saddest excuse for a man that ever existed. Since Wilfred wasn't looking where he was going, he knocked into Rosina who was still standing half-hidden behind Vivienne. Wilfred looked up with wide eyes, reminding Vivienne of a deer in the torchlight.

"Oh!" he said, covering his mouth with his hand and then quickly stepping away from her handmaid. He hurried back to his mother with his head down once again.

"As soon as this bloody hound is out of my hair, I'll get the food on the table, my lord," promised the cook, still holding his cleaver in one hand over his head and the soup bone in the other. Grunt continued to dance on two legs trying to reach the bone, barking wildly.

"You don't even have any hair," Gainsborough said to the bald cook. "You are an incompetent fool! I'm going to have a word with Lord Mablethorpe about dismissing you at once." After Gainsborough threatened the cook, he kicked at Vivienne's dog. Grunt whined, losing his balance, but landing on all four legs. "Someone put this mutt out of his misery and shut him up. He is making my head hurt with all his barking." Grunt turned around and snarled at him, then bit at his elongated shoe. "Ow! Nay!" The nobleman stumbled backward, knocking into the kennel groom, sending Adam sprawling across the floor, face down. The cook cursed under his breath. Adam lifted his head and glared at Gainsborough from his prone position. The dog continued to bark, sounding as if he were going to attack the man now. Vivienne couldn't blame Grunt, and wouldn't reprimand her dog for his actions. Lord Gainsborough was obnoxious and deserved to be bitten after kicking at a helpless animal for no reason at all!

"This is unacceptable," sniffed Lady Gainsborough, speaking up for the first time since she'd entered the kitchens.

"Yes. Unacceptable," echoed Wilfred, reminding Vivienne of a child mimicking his parents' words.

Lady Gainsborough grabbed on to her husband's arm. Vivienne wasn't sure if the woman was speaking of her husband or the servants when she'd said *unacceptable*, but it didn't matter, since either way she was right. This entire incident never should have happened.

"Let go of me, Avice," growled Lord Gainsborough. "You have no right to talk to me this way."

"I can say the same for you," she answered, her eyes flashing over to the buxom maid, Maria. Maria stood there with her tray of food balanced on her shoulder, never having left the kitchens. Lady Gainsborough directed her glare over to Vivienne next. Wilfred watched with wide eyes but didn't say a word.

"Come on, Grunt. You are causing too much trouble." Vivienne reached down and pulled her dog to her.

"You are the only one who is true trouble, and everyone

knows it," spat Lord Gainsborough. As he passed her he mumbled '*bastard child*' under his breath before leaving the kitchen. His wife trailed after him. Wilfred stood there by himself looking lost. He glanced over at Vivienne and almost seemed to stare right through her. Then he backed up slowly, but knocked into Maria, causing her to drop the entire tray of food after all. Without saying a word to the kitchen maid or even trying to help her clean up, Wilfred ran out of the room and didn't look back.

"God's eyes, what did you do?" screamed Cook.

"I'm sorry," apologized Maria, hunkering down to pick up the food. "It was that nobleman's fault. He knocked into me."

Cook had a bad temper and was in the habit of yelling at the kitchen help. Vivienne expected him to go crazy, but instead he surprised her when he didn't. He even lowered his voice. "Well, clean it up, Maria. We are behind schedule."

"I will," promised the girl.

"I'll help her," offered Rosina, rushing over to assist her fellow maid.

Vivienne's stomach twisted to the point of making her sick, having heard Lord Gainsborough call her a bastard child. Quickly scanning the room, she hoped that no one had heard what he'd said. It was bad enough that he'd called her *troublesome,* when she was just really curious at times, and had the knack of being in the wrong place at the wrong time. Vivienne was about to go help the girls clean up when the outside door to the kitchens burst open, taking her attention next.

"Fire!" yelled the page, Martin, as he rushed in from outside. The back door slammed, hitting hard against the wall. A spring breeze blew into the room, smelling like smoke. The cook fire flared from the breeze and a dust of flour from the breadmaker's table lifted up into the air.

"Shut the damned door!" screamed Cook. "The food will be cold before I even serve it."

"Martin, did you say fire? Where?" Vivienne released her hold on her dog and ran over to the young boy with her heart beating rapidly in her chest. "I don't see a fire." She continued to look around the kitchens, but everything seemed in order.

Kitchen fires were not uncommon in castles, but through the years Vivienne had made certain that her cooks were careful. One unattended spark could end up putting the entire castle at risk.

"The fire is not in here. It's in the kennels," the boy yelled.

"God's eyes, nay!" Vivienne knew how fast fire could spread if they didn't extinguish the flames quickly. Especially since the kennels was filled with straw. The entire castle could go up like a lit torch along with it.

"Fire in the kennels?" Adam jumped to his feet when he realized the dogs were in danger. "Are you sure, boy?"

"Aye, I'm sure. The kennel is burning," cried Martin, pointing at the door. "The flames are reaching all the way up to the sky." The little boy lifted his hands over his head to show the height.

"Adam, fast!" cried Vivienne. "Get to the kennels and save the dogs. Cook, have the servants collect buckets of water to help douse the fire." Vivienne took control of the situation at hand, removing her cloak and throwing it down. There was no time to lose. "Save the hounds, Adam!" she called after him as he ran out the door. "I'll inform my uncle and get more help at once." Vivienne ran into the great hall to look for her uncle. Rosina was instantly at her side.

"This is awful, my lady, just awful," cried Rosina, wringing her hands together. "Those poor dogs will die."

"Not if I can help it, they won't," Vivienne promised. She

looked up at the crowd in the great hall and shouted loudly so all could hear. "Fire in the kennels!"

"Fire?" someone called out.

"What? The great hall's on fire?" yelled someone else, having misunderstood her message.

"Run for your life!" screamed a man in the crowd. "We are all going to burn to death!"

Vivienne realized immediately that she should have been more discreet about this announcement. Everyone panicked at hearing there was a fire, having missed the part about it being in the kennels and thinking the fire was inside the castle instead. They all started running around the room in a frenzy, not knowing where to go. It took all her might just to push through the chaotic crowd, finally managing to make it to the main door.

"Wait, my lady! Where are you going?" her handmaid shouted after her, getting pushed back into the crowd.

"I've got to help Adam save the dogs," Vivienne called out to Rosina. "Get to the kitchens and tell everyone there to come help put out the flames." She turned and ran to the kennels, seeing the flames shooting through the roof as soon as she got outside. The fire lit up the sky, making the silhouette of the wooden building glow in the darkness of night. "Quickly, everyone. Bring more buckets of water to the kennel from the well. Use the water in the horse troughs as well," she shouted to no one in particular. Thankfully, the chain of water buckets had already begun. With any luck, the fire would be put out before the building burned to the ground.

Without a care for herself, Vivienne ran closer to the kennels, seeing Adam rushing out of the burning building with three dogs on leads.

"Adam, did you save all the hounds?" she asked him.

"Nay, my lady, not yet. There are two left in there but the

flames are too hot to reach them. I'm afraid they will die before I can go back to try."

"Nay! I won't let that happen. Take these dogs to safety. I'll get the others." Quickly looking around, Vivienne spied a horse trough of water. She ran over and jumped into it, soaking her clothes and hair entirely. Pulling herself out, she headed toward the fire. Her shoes squished with water and her heavy gown weighed her down, but she didn't let that stop her. The air became thick and hot, making it hard to breathe. Ripping off a long tippet, a sleeve from her gown, she tied it around her nose and mouth. Then she removed the other one as well, putting it under her arm. She rushed into the kennel to look for the remaining two dogs.

Vivienne bravely entered the burning building, using the wet tippet to beat out the flames along the way. She had to find the poor, helpless hounds! Time was running out quickly. The fire was getting too hot, just like Adam had said. She wouldn't be able to stay in here much longer. Glancing over the top of the enclosures, she saw only empty stalls. Then she heard barking from up ahead, and made her way to the far end of the kennel. Ripping open the furthest gate, she managed to set the last two hounds free. The animals ran from the kennel with Vivienne following right behind them. Just as she exited the building, the roof caved in behind her. The force of hot air pushed her, knocking her to the ground.

"My lady!" One of the castle guards threw down his bucket and hurried over to help her up.

"I saved the last two hounds, Richard," she said, calling him by name. Slowly, she removed the wet sleeve from her face, coughing, trying to catch her breath. "Where is Adam?" She looked through the crowd, but with the smoke and because of the darkness of nightfall, she couldn't tell one person from the next.

"I'm not sure, my lady. It is hard to see with all this smoke." The guard covered his mouth, coughing as well. Then he helped her to stand.

"Vivienne! Vivienne, what are you doing?" Vivienne's aunt ran over, holding a handcloth to her nose and mouth. "Are you all right?"

"I'm fine, Aunt Ellen," she replied. "Where is Uncle Gilbert?"

"I suppose he is heading the water line for the fire."

"This fire is horrible. I am just glad the hounds were saved," Vivienne told her.

Her uncle came pushing through the crowd next, mumbling profanities with each step he took. Vivienne expected him to at least be carrying a bucket of water, but he wasn't.

"Uncle, how are things going with the water line?" she asked him.

"I put my men in charge. I was needed to calm down this frantic crowd."

"I see," she answered, thinking a guard or two could have handled that just as well.

Vivienne heard another dog barking. Her ears picked it right up and this time it seemed like it came from inside the castle. "That sounds like Grunt barking." She stretched her neck, trying to see through the horde of people running around the courtyard. "I hope Grunt is all right. He might be frightened by the fire. I need to go to him."

"Hurry up with those buckets of water before I lose everything I own!" shouted her uncle, finally taking control of the water line himself. Knights rushed forward to help organize putting out the fire. "Vivienne, once again, you have managed to embarrass me in front of the other nobles," her uncle scolded, shaking his head as her perused her appearance.

"Embarrass you?" She released a puff of air from her mouth, using the back of her hand to wipe soot from her face. "Uncle, I saved two of your hunting hounds that were trapped inside the burning kennels. They would have died if it wasn't for me," she pointed out, only managing to get a disgruntled look from the man.

"Yes, well, that's a good thing," he said, clearing his throat. "But you should have left that to my men. It is too dangerous for a woman to be running into burning buildings." He turned and headed away, shouting more orders to everyone now.

"Just once, I'd like him to show me a bit of gratitude," she mumbled.

"Your uncle is right, Vivienne." Her aunt spoke without moving the piece of cloth from over her nose and mouth. "It was too dangerous and such a risk for you to take. You could have been killed!"

"But I wasn't," she pointed out. "And the dogs escaped, alive and I believe unharmed, because I did something that no one else had the courage to do."

"Yes, you were brave, my lady," said Richard. "I only wish more ladies were like you." He excused himself and went back to helping fight the rest of the fire.

Lady Gainsborough seemed worried as she approached them, holding a cloth over her nose too. "Who could have done such a thing?" she cried, staring at the burning building. Vivienne was surprised to see the woman out here by herself without her husband or son at her side. She didn't normally go anywhere without them. Her gown was blowing in the breeze, the front of it already covered in soot from the flying debris in the air coming from the kennels.

"I'm not sure why you say someone did this, when we don't know how it happened," said Vivienne, wringing out her wet hair that had come loose during her rescue attempt.

"Well, it's highly unlikely the dogs started a fire," sniffed the woman. "And everyone was inside the great hall at the time."

"I suppose you have a point," she answered, never even entertaining the thought that this fire could have been started on purpose. Once again, she heard the barking of a dog and it seemed to be getting frantic. "I hear Grunt barking. I need to find him to make sure he is all right. Excuse me." She nodded to the women and ran off, following the sound of her hound.

She almost bumped into Wilfred running from the keep.

"Ah, there you are, Wilfred."

"Have you seen my mother?" he asked. "I seem to have lost her in the frenzied crowd. She was in the great hall, but now I cannot find her. I even checked the kitchens but she wasn't there. I am worried."

"No need to worry, she is fine. I saw her just now, over by the kennels," said Vivienne with a nod, continuing on her way. "Grunt?" she shouted, looking for her pet. "Where are you, boy? Don't worry, you are safe from the fire." Vivienne made her way toward the sound of her barking dog.

Once she got outside the entrance of the great hall, she was greeted by Grunt, who ran up to her, still barking like crazy. There was no doubt in her mind that something was wrong. He was usually a calm dog and only acted this way when they were on a hunt and he wanted her to follow him to the kill. Or when he wanted a bone. "Show me," she instructed her hound, following the dog as he led the way. She glanced inside the kitchens as they passed by, noticing Cook talking with Maria. Their heads were together and they seemed to be speaking in hushed tones. They both looked upset. Neither one of them were working. Cook looked up and his eyes met with hers. As soon as he saw Vivienne, he turned the other way and started stirring a pot of food. Just like Cook to not even help put out the fire with the rest of the servants, since he probably didn't want to leave his kitchens unattended.

"My lady! I've been looking for you." Rosina ran up behind her from the great hall, holding Vivienne's cloak. "I fetched your cloak from the kitchen where you left it. I figured you'd need it to keep you from the night air." Her eyes settled upon her and an odd expression crossed her face. "My lady? Why are you all wet?"

"I dunked myself in the horse trough and entered the burning kennels to save the dogs," Vivienne explained through ragged breathing, as Grunt continued to bark.

"You did what? There were men out there to save the hounds. You didn't need to put your life in danger." She scowled at the dog. "Hush," she told Grunt. "You are making too much noise." Rosina never seemed to care much for Vivienne's dog, or any of the hounds, actually. She didn't like the sound of barking and often scolded Grunt. "Put this on before you catch your death of cold," said the handmaid, placing the cloak around Vivienne's shoulders.

"There were lives at stake, Rosina. I wasn't about to wait for any man to step up and offer to run into a burning building. I did what needed to be done. Besides, since when have I ever thought a man could do something that I couldn't?"

"My, you are brave, my lady."

"I only wish everyone were as brave," she replied. "I just saw Cook and Maria in the kitchens talking when they should be outside with the rest of the servants, trying to fight the fire."

"I tried to get everyone outside like you instructed," said Rosina. "Most everyone went out to the kennels. I was just going outside to help as well."

"Don't bother. The flames are probably almost out by now. My uncle is controlling the water line, and you know he won't put up with anyone slacking."

"If you're certain," said Rosina.

"I am."

"Let's go to your bedchamber then. I will help you change into dry clothes before you become ill from the night air." Rosina always doted over Vivienne like a mother hen over her chicks, even though the girl was younger than she. Rosina started to walk away but Vivienne didn't follow. "Is something the matter, my lady?" asked Rosina, her voice barely able to be heard over Grunt's continuous barking.

"Yes. Something is wrong," Vivienne told her. "Don't you hear the way Grunt is barking?"

"How can I not? He's always barking, my lady. Grunt, be quiet!" she told the dog.

"He doesn't usually bark like this," Vivienne told her. "Something has him upset tonight, and I don't believe it is just the fire. He won't stop."

"I'm sure it's just the fire upsetting him, and rightly so. Two dogs from the kennels ran through here just a short while ago looking very frightened. It would make sense. Mayhap Grunt can pick up the feelings of fear from the other hounds."

"Those were the two dogs I set free. I am glad they are seeking shelter inside the castle. I will be sure to let Adam know, since he'll be looking for them. Rosina, I think Grunt wants me to follow him. Something is wrong, I tell you."

"If you say so, my lady." Rosina held her hands to her ears, trying to block out the barking of the dog.

"Take my word for it, something is not right." Vivienne held her hand to her aching stomach, and followed Grunt through the corridor. Rosina trailed right behind. They stopped at the foot of the staircase that led to the second floor. A shiver swept up Vivienne's spine as she made her way over to her dog who was sticking his nose under the stairs, sniffing at something. She had a bad feeling about this. Somehow she knew

Grunt wasn't just hunting down rats this time, like in the past. This was more of an anxious bark combined with odd behavior. The feeling in Vivienne's stomach that she had right now was the same way she always felt when trouble arose. And by the way her dog was barking, she highly expected the worst.

"Are you after a rat again, Grunt?" asked Rosina. "That is a job for a cat, not you."

Vivienne joined the dog. She bent down to calm her hound, and that is when she noticed something sticking out from under the stairwell in the dark. She slowly stood and removed a nearby burning torch from the iron sconce on the wall. Then, with her heart beating in her throat, she walked back and stuck the torchlight under the stairwell to see what had her dog so upset. It didn't take time to figure out that it wasn't a rat after all. There, lying prone on the floor, was Lord Gainsborough! His eyes were bugged out and his mouth opened wide. In his hand he clutched his dagger which was sticking out of his chest. He wasn't moving. Neither did he blink or seem to be breathing at all. Blood soaked his tunic in the color of deep crimson from the stab wound to his heart.

Vivienne's eyes closed and she swayed momentarily, feeling as if she were going to vomit. Visions flashed through her mind of a very similar time, seven years prior. That is, the night she lost her entire family. With her eyes closed, she started to relive that horrible, deadly night all over again ...

Lying in the back of a wagon filled with trunks and hay, sixteen-year-old Vivienne held her newborn baby boy close to her chest. Her nine-year-old brother, Adrian, was asleep in the hay next to her. Her parents drove the team of horses pulling the wagon down the bumpy road. They were heading north from Somersby. She watched the positioning of the stars in the sky above her, on their way to Mablethorpe where her aunt and uncle lived.

They'd left their home in a hurry after packing most of their belongings. They were going to live with her aunt and uncle in Mablethorpe this time, not just visit. She'd overheard her parents talking about it earlier.

Her mother was a noble, but her father was a commoner. He was a foot soldier in Somersby, and was being sent overseas to fight for the king. He was about to join an army of others, boarding a ship that would take them across the Channel to France. She had heard him tell her mother that he would be gone for months this time, or possibly never even return.

With the new baby and her young brother as well, Vivienne and her mother were going to need all the help they could get, since her father would be gone. Vivienne realized she was actually the reason they had to leave their home. She was to blame, and could only hope that someday they'd be able to return to Somersby with her entire family.

Vivienne lay in the hay of the wagon too exhausted from giving birth earlier that day to even sleep at all. She smiled down at the newborn, who had a tuft of blond hair, the same color as hers, and clear, bright blue eyes. He was a cute little baby. Everything was perfect about him. Well, almost everything. Opening the blanket, she ran her fingers over the brown heart-shaped birthmark on the bottom of her son's left foot. Her mother said he'd been kissed by an angel. Vivienne smiled, wrapping him back up, knowing that indeed he was an angelic child. She had been blessed to be given a son, and she just wished her late husband could have seen him before his untimely death.

Suddenly, Vivienne felt her stomach twist into a knot. She couldn't help feeling that something was horribly wrong, or perhaps about to happen. The twisting feeling inside her gut felt like the sharp blade of a dagger, such as the one she had strapped to her side. The last time she felt this way was six months ago when she'd lost her husband, George, after he was kicked by a horse and died. She reached down to touch the hilt of her blade, feeling odd. The thought flashed through her mind that she'd need it tonight for protection, although she had no idea where this thought came from. The feel of the cold, sharp metal in her hand was so opposite the warmth of new life from her baby pressed up against her.

"My lady? My lady? Are you all right?" Rosina's voice dragged Vivienne from her daze, causing her eyes to open. Her head snapped around. In a flash, the nightmare of her past had diminished, although it was never really gone for good. Right now, she found herself pressed with the matter at hand.

"I'm fine," mumbled Vivienne, shaking her head to clear away her hauntings of the past.

The page boy ran up to join them by the stairs. "My lady, I heard the dog barking. Is Grunt harmed?"

"Nay, Martin. Grunt is fine," she assured him. Martin had taken a liking to the hound, and never seemed to leave the dog's side for long. He liked all the hunting dogs, and even told Vivienne that one day he hoped to have his own. "Unfortunately," she continued, "I can't say the same about Lord Gainsborough." She leaned in and held the torch up higher to bring light to the dead man's body so they could see what she meant.

Rosina glanced down at the floor and gasped. Her eyes opened wide and a blood-curling scream escaped her lips.

Vivienne let out a deep breath, holding back her own cries of terror. What started out as a celebration feast ended up in fire, and now death.

"Lord Gainsborough killed himself!" cried Martin, the little boy's eyes focused on the body. Even though he was only seven years of age, he didn't scream. His bravery at a time like this was admirable. Martin's gaze held sadness as well as intrigue, mayhap dashed by a little fear.

"Now, Martin, we don't know that Lord Gainsborough took his own life," she told him, already envisioning the gossip that would occur from this. Especially with Rosina present.

"We don't?" Rosina squeaked out. "But the man has his dagger in his hand and the blade is sticking out of his chest." She pointed at the corpse, her eyes wide with fright.

"He killed himself," Martin said once again, nodding.

"Nay, we don't know that," Vivienne told the other two, feeling the same way she'd felt when she'd encountered her murdered parents. It was a gruesome sight, to be sure.

"What do you mean, my lady?" asked Rosina, looking as white as a sheet.

"I'm not sure how I know he didn't commit suicide, but I just do. You see, I've had this feeling inside me before. My instincts tonight, I am sure are right."

"Your instincts?" asked the boy in question.

"What do your instincts tell you now?" Rosina spoke to Vivienne, but could not drag her eyes away from the corpse. She looked frightened enough for her legs to buckle.

Vivienne spoke the words she hoped she would never have to say again as long as she lived. "I am not sure, of course, but my instincts tell me that Lord Gainsborough did not take his own life, but instead was murdered!"

Chapter Two

"Murdered?" gasped Rosina, making Vivienne curse herself inwardly. Why had she mentioned her suspicions aloud? The gossip would be even worse now than everyone thinking the man had killed himself. If Vivienne hadn't been so engrossed by her feelings of the past, she would have known better than to say anything aloud at all.

"Martin, run and fetch Lord and Lady Mablethorpe and bring them back here at once," Vivienne instructed the page. "Please don't say anything about him killing himself or possibly being murdered in front of the others. Just say a man has died, but don't say who it was."

"I will tell them," said the boy, taking off at a sprint.

"Oh, this is so horrible!" cried Rosina, covering her mouth with her hand. Her body shook now, her knees knocking together so hard that Vivienne wasn't sure the girl wouldn't fall down. It was clear that her handmaid had never seen a murdered man before. Vivienne wished she hadn't seen this one now either. No one should have to face such a gruesome sight. She remembered how frightened and horrified she had been seeing her parents' murdered bodies when she was just a little younger than Rosina was right now. It was something not easily forgotten. "My lady, I cannot bear to look upon his bloody body any longer." Rosina squeezed her eyes closed and shuddered. "I am sorry, but I feel as if I will retch or perhaps faint if I do."

"Yes, you're right. It is not easy. Leave at once," Vivienne instructed her handmaid. "Go back to my bedchamber and wait for me there. Try to relax and stop your shaking. I promise, I will join you soon."

"But I don't want to leave you here with a ... a dead man." The handmaid's eyes slowly opened and once again she was staring at Lord Gainsborough's lifeless body as if in a trance.

"I will be fine, Rosina. Really. Please go." Lady Vivienne put her hands on the maid's shoulders and slowly turned her around.

"Thank you, my lady." With tears streaming down her face, Rosina ran up the stairs, leaving Vivienne alone with the dead Lord Gainsborough and just her dog.

Vivienne hunkered down to inspect Lord Gainsborough's body. The sight of blood always made her queasy. Especially when it was seeing the life drained out of someone that one knew or perhaps even loved. Memories of her mother and father's lifeless bodies crept into her mind again, but she tried to stay strong and push that away. The murder of Lord Gains-borough was her concern now. No one deserved to lose their life this way, not even this man, although Vivienne had never even liked him.

Still holding the torch in one hand, Vivienne stared down at the stab wound in Lord Gainsborough's chest. The blade was sunk deep and directly into his heart, but on a slight angle. He most likely had died quickly, she surmised. But why would anyone do this, if it truly was murder? Then again, she still wondered the same thing about her own parents' deaths, never giving up looking for answers.

Wanting to know more about the matter at hand, her curiosity gave her the courage to explore the body before everyone else arrived. With one shaking hand, she reached out and touched Lord Gainsborough's neck, just to verify that he had no pulse. He didn't. However, there were scratch marks on his neck that could prove there was a struggle. He also smelled strongly of whisky. Not able to stand the corpse's hollow, beady eyes staring up at her, she reached over and quickly closed his eyes with a gentle touch to his lids.

"That's better," she said, releasing a breath she had not even been aware that she'd been holding. Grunt whimpered and lay down at her feet, putting his nose between his paws. She then used the torch to light up Gainsborough's body, starting at his head and moving toward his feet.

If she could only find a clue, perhaps then she could find the killer and bring about justice for this man's death. It was something she had wished she could have done for her parents. But to this day, not even with the help of the sheriff, had she been able to find a single clue of who murdered her mother and father. Noticing a white mark on the nobleman's shoes, she ran her finger over the powdery substance, rubbing it between her fingers and bringing them to her nose to smell it.

"Flour," she said, sure of herself. She supposed it wasn't surprising, since Lord Gainsborough had been in the kitchens earlier when the breadmaker was kneading dough. Next, she found short brown dog hairs on the dead man's breeches. They were most likely from Grunt, she realized. After all, Lord Gainsborough had kicked at the dog earlier in the kitchens and Grunt had bit his shoe in retaliation. She picked up the man's free hand next, laden down with oversized jeweled rings. If this had been murder, then why didn't the killer take the man's riches? Perhaps her instincts were wrong after all, even though she didn't think so. She noticed red stains on the tips of his fingers and tunic that weren't blood. Rubbing her thumb over his tunic, she realized it was dry. Wine, she decided after sniffing his hand as well. Odd, since there didn't seem to be a goblet on the floor with him. She looked over at her dog who was watching her with wide eyes and she got the distinct feeling of disapproval. "Well, you use your nose to sniff out things, so why can't I?" she asked Grunt.

"My God, what has happened?" Her uncle ran up, out of breath, stopping when he saw his good friend's lifeless body on the floor, covered in blood. He threw his hands in the air and then grabbed his head. His eyes became glassy, and a frown turned down the corners of his mouth. Her uncle's clothes were covered with soot and his shoes were filthy, his breeches soaked with water. "Nay," he mumbled. "This cannot be true."

Vivienne's aunt walked up behind him with Martin. The page held on to her hand.

"Lady Vivienne thinks someone killed Lord Gainsborough," the little boy blurted out. "He's covered in blood and was stabbed through the heart."

"Thank you, Martin, they can see that," Vivienne answered in a calm voice, hoping not to scare the boy or make him feel scolded. "Mayhap you should go now." Vivienne stood up and dismissed the boy, wishing he hadn't said in front of her aunt and uncle that she thought it could be murder. Not at a time like this. But the damage had already been done. Her uncle was surely going to reprimand her for even suggesting such a thing. Her body tensed as she waited to hear his disapproving words raining down upon her. "Take Grunt back to my chamber, Martin. Tell Rosina I will be there soon."

"Aye, my lady," said the boy, releasing Lady Mablethorpe's hand and grabbing the dog by the collar. "Come on, Grunt. You don't want to see this." The small boy dragged the big dog along with him. Grunt whined again and looked back at Vivienne.

"Go on, Grunt. You were a good boy to lead me here. I'll make sure Cook gives you a bone later as your reward."

"Give me that torch," instructed her uncle, grabbing it from her and holding it over Gainsborough's body. "God's teeth, he is bleeding like a stuffed pig."

"Oh, this is horrible," cried Aunt Ellen, holding her hand to her mouth. "Is he really dead, Gilbert?"

Gilbert hunkered down and put his fingers to the man's throat and then to his wrist. He also wet his fingers and held them under the man's nose. "Yes. I'm afraid so, my good wife. It seems my silly friend has taken his own life." Vivienne wanted to correct him, but for now she held her tongue.

"Why would he ever do such a thing?" asked her aunt Ellen. "He had everything going for him in life. He had a wife, a son, a castle, and plenty of wealth. This doesn't make sense at all."

"Nay, it doesn't," he agreed.

"Pardon me," said Vivienne, interrupting since her aunt and uncle hadn't even seemed to hear Martin when he announced Vivienne's thoughts about the death. "If you ask me, Lord Gainsborough did not take his own life. I believe he was stabbed to death."

"Murdered?" asked her aunt in shock.

"Yes. I think so," she answered.

"Vivienne, that is nonsense. How can you even say such a thing?" growled her uncle. "God's eyes, look at him. He is gripping his dagger having plunged it through his own heart. Are you blind that you cannot see that?"

"Could it be that someone wrapped his fingers around the hilt of the dagger after they stabbed him to death?" she asked. "I mean, to make it look like he killed himself?"

Her uncle slowly shook his head. "Don't even suggest such a thing, Vivienne. You are always stirring up trouble." He stood up, his feelings about her instinct no secret. She could see the anger and disappointment in his eyes. "How did you even find him? He is so well hidden under the stairwell and it is dark."

"Grunt led me to him," she explained. "He kept barking, wanting me to follow him."

"The dog showed you?" gasped her aunt.

"Yes. Yes, he did," she answered, proud of her pet.

"It must have happened while everyone was trying to put out the fire," said Lady Mablethorpe. "There was so much commotion, that it must have gone unnoticed."

"I have a thought on that as well," said Vivienne, holding up one finger, feeling nervous to voice her opinion aloud at all. Still, even her uncle's glare did not stop her from doing so. "Aunt Ellen. Uncle Gilbert. I think the fire was naught but a well thought-out distraction so the murderer could kill Lord Gainsborough without anyone noticing."

"You know nothing of the sort, so stop voicing these thoughts aloud," snapped her uncle. "It is most unappealing." His gaze swept the area, probably looking for others and hoping that no one had heard her. He raised his hand in the air, getting the attention of his steward, who hurried over to join them.

"My lord?" asked his steward, running up and coming to an abrupt halt when he spied the dead body. His mouth fell open. "Is that ... is that Lord Gainsborough?"

"Yes, John, it is," her uncle answered.

"Is he ... is he ..."

"Yes, he's dead," Vivienne spoke up.

"How did it happen?" asked the steward, taking a step closer to inspect the dead body.

"Stay back," instructed Gilbert. "I don't want everyone gawking at his body."

"So sorry, my lord." John took a few steps backward.

"Please send for the sheriff immediately," Vivienne's uncle instructed his steward. "We'll let Sheriff Fitch decide what and how it happened."

"Aye, my lord. I'll send for him at once," said John with a bow, hurrying away.

Gainsborough's wife and son came running down the corridor next, followed by several guards. Vivienne knew this was going to be hard for them to see. Still, they deserved to know what happened.

"We heard that something horrible happened," said Lady Gainsborough, holding up her skirts as she ran. "My husband's name was mentioned. Please tell me he is all right."

"Calm down, Mother, I'm sure it isn't Father," said her son, as they came to a stop in front of the group.

Lady Gainsborough laid eyes on her dead husband and screamed. Lady Mablethorpe pulled the woman to her, and they hugged each other, crying. Wilfred peeked out from behind his mother, being shy as usual, not saying another word.

"God's teeth, get the women out of here!" Gilbert looked up, giving the command to his guards. One of Gainsborough's guards was there as well, and he stepped forward to protect Lady Gainsborough and her son. "Someone find a blanket to cover the dead man's body." Gilbert paced the floor, running a hand through his hair. "We also need to move him before everyone shows up and starts asking questions. I don't want that. Not during my feast and celebration. If so, chaos will arise."

"Chaos has already arisen from the fire in the kennels," Vivienne pointed out, not knowing why her uncle was making such a fuss. It was almost as if he was trying to keep this death quiet.

"Well, this news will spread quickly as well," said her uncle. "And when it does, it will ruin me."

"Ruin you?" Vivienne thought that was an odd thing for him to say. "Uncle, how can you think about yourself at a time like this?" Disgust washed over her, thinking that her uncle wasn't showing more remorse for his dead friend. Especially since the dead man's wife and son were standing right there! How insensitive of a man was he? Vivienne took matters into her own hands as she usually did, removing her cloak and spreading it out over the corpse to hide the dead body from sight. "Lady Gainsborough, we offer our condolences to you and your son. We will do all we can to find out how this happened, I assure you."

Lady Gainsborough still clung to Vivienne's aunt and they both wailed loudly.

"Take them away, anon," commanded her uncle with a wave of his hand. "All this crying is unnerving me and I cannot think straight."

"Yes, Herman, take me away," agreed Lady Gainsborough, speaking to the guard she brought from her castle. "I cannot bear to look at him anymore."

"Come, my ladies." Herman stepped up to escort the women. "We'll go to the great hall and await word there."

"Yes, we'll await word there," echoed Wilfred. "It would be better that way." The milksop wasn't one for thinking on his feet. Vivienne had always known Wilfred to be one who needed to be given orders, rather than to be the person giving them. She despised this in a man. Lord Wilfred should act more like a knight, being brave and strong and protecting women without having to be told to do so. Sadly, she was sure he needed women like his mother protecting him instead. How in heaven's name would any woman ever want him for her husband if he continued to act as meek as this?

"Thank you, Herman." Vivienne nodded as the little group left, with the women still wiping at their eyes and crying. Wilfred started to follow them, but Vivienne stopped him. "Lord Wilfred? Don't you want to stay with your father's body and wait for the sheriff to arrive?"

"Oh. Aye. I suppose I should." The man shifted from one foot to other, seeming uncomfortable being there.

"Nay." Her uncle finally stopped his pacing. "There is no need for you to stay, Wilfred. It wouldn't make a difference. It would be better if you were with your mother to comfort her during this trying time. She is taking the news badly."

"Of course, my lord. I will do that." Wilfred bowed and hurried away to follow orders. Vivienne watched him go.

"That is one odd man," she commented aloud, her gaze fastened to his back as he sidestepped servants in the corridor when they should be moving out of his way instead.

"You would have gotten used to him once he was your husband," said her uncle, rubbing both hands over his face.

"What?" Her head snapped around in surprise. "What are you saying, Uncle?"

"Vivienne, I had made an alignment with Lord Gainsborough. You were to be married to Wilfred. I was going to make the announcement later tonight."

"You didn't! Uncle, I told you, I will never marry again." Hearing this filled her with fury.

"This celebration was for you, Vivienne. I only had your best interest in mind. I figured if you were married, all the gossip about you being odd, troublesome, and unruly would end. That is, once you were the wife of a respectable Gainsborough man."

"Hah!" she spat. "I can hardly call Wilfred respectable, or even a man, for that matter."

"Vivienne, watch that sharp tongue of yours," her uncle warned her. "You are speaking of the son of a dead man."

"I know. But what did you mean by *all that gossip?*" she asked, knowing what he meant since she'd heard it too. Still, she wanted to know what her uncle had to say about it.

"People are saying things about you."

"What kind of things? And why do you even care? I don't." She meant this in a way, but still there was a little part of her that wanted people to like her and not judge her. But she'd learned early on in life not to live by the expectations of others. Instead, she chose to be true only to herself, and to never be unkind or do something that she wasn't comfortable with doing. That, to her, included ever being married again.

"My dear niece." Gilbert reached out and put his arm around her shoulders, pulling her closer. "I know you don't believe it, but I do care about you and what happens to you. I really do."

"I should hope so. You are my guardian!"

"I have no living children, and you are like a daughter to me."

"Thank you."

"I made a promise to keep your little secret and I swear I have, but it is hard. When I hear the gossip about you, I want to shout out who you really are. Then people would treat you differently."

"My secret," she repeated, her hand covering the ring hanging from a chain around her neck that was hidden beneath her clothes. She kept it close to her, but had never showed it to anyone other than her aunt and uncle. "So you've really never told a soul?" she asked, still wondering how Lord Gainsborough knew about it.

"Nay. But sometimes I think we should let others know."

"Why should we? What would it really matter?"

"It would matter," he assured her. "Like I said, people would see you differently if they knew the truth. The gossip would end."

"Or possibly get worse," she pointed out.

"Now, now, Vivienne. I know what's best for you. You need to trust me."

"You and Aunt Ellen gave me your word," she reminded him. "It was a request from my dying mother. No one else will ever know my secret. I shouldn't even have told you or Aunt Ellen. Sometimes I wish I hadn't."

"I know, I know. But you were distraught and needed to confide in us. You did the right thing. Don't worry. We will keep the promise we made to you, my dear. But tell me, don't you think it would be better if people knew the truth eventually? It would make things so much easier for you."

"Easier?" she asked. "How is claiming I am a bastard child supposed to make my life any easier?"

"Being a bastard to ... him ... is something to be respected, my dear. I should think you'd want to shout it from the rooftops."

She dropped her hand to her side, releasing the ring she coddled, even if it was hidden and she couldn't show it to anyone. Still, she knew it was there. She supposed she shouldn't care who knew, since what people thought of her wasn't important to her. But what *was* important was the promise she'd made to her dying mother. Even if she didn't understand her mother's last request.

"Now that Lord Gainsborough is dead, will my betrothal to Lord Wilfred be called off?" she asked, to change the subject.

"I suppose it'll have to be delayed," her uncle answered. "Until Wilfred signs the papers for the alliance. You should really consider it. After all, he is Gainsborough's heir now. Wilfred would be a good match for you, Vivienne. He will be rich and inherit everything from his dead father since he is Gainsborough's only son, and only child. However, no wedding can take place until things are settled. With the dead body and all, I mean."

"Did Wilfred know about this betrothal, or were you going to surprise him the same way as you did me?" asked Vivienne.

"Yes, he knew. I believe his father took him out to the garden earlier to tell him. Right before this all happened," answered her uncle. "Gainsborough didn't want his son acting too surprised when we made the announcement tonight after the meal, so he decided to tell him first."

"What about me? When were you going to tell me? Or weren't you going to do so at all for fear if I knew I wouldn't make an appearance in the great hall tonight?"

Her uncle hesitated before answering. "I admit, I wasn't eager to tell you ahead of time since I knew you'd object and hide away. However, Gainsborough thought that you needed to be told. Actually, he offered to tell you for me himself. So, he didn't mention it to you at all then?"

Suddenly, things made sense to Vivienne. "That's why he wanted to take a walk with me alone to the herb garden. I didn't go, so no, he never told me." Obviously Gainsborough wasn't as awful of a man as Vivienne thought him to be. He actually cared enough to tell her about the betrothal. That was more than she could say about her uncle. Vivienne had thought the man had other intentions when he said he wanted to be alone with her. Improper ones. Now, she felt horrible for judging him in this manner. She had acted no better than all the people who gossiped about her. Even so, she felt disgusted with her uncle for not having the courage to mention it to her before everyone showed up for the celebration.

"I only want the best for you," her uncle told her once again. "Gainsborough acted cheap, but he has a lot of money and many holdings. That would have all been yours someday if you had married Wilfred. Actually, it still can be, if you'll only reconsider marrying him after all." His eyes trailed down to the corpse. "It is what I want, and I am sure what my good friend, Lord Dinadan Knapp, wanted as well."

"I am so upset with you right now that I cannot even talk to you anymore, Uncle," she spat. "I am going to my chamber. Please send a page to fetch me once the sheriff arrives. It is important that I talk to him."

Vivienne turned and hurried to her room, not waiting for his answer. She felt frustrated. Not only because of the murder of a man tonight, but because her uncle seemed more upset that he'd lost a good alliance rather than lost a good friend.

She pushed open the chamber door to be greeted by the slobbery tongue of Grunt licking her hand. Rosina was across the room, keeping her distance from the dog as usual. "Hello, boy." She bent over and pet her hound.

"My lady!" Rosina jumped up from her chair and hurried across the floor. "What happened? Did they find any answers about Lord Gainsborough's death?" She wrung her hands together.

"Nay, not yet," said Vivienne, sinking atop a chair, using both hands to pet Grunt who had his front paws on her lap already. "We are waiting for the sheriff to arrive first. We'll know more once he has inspected the body."

"I see," she said in a soft voice. She was still shaking.

Vivienne looked up to see Rosina staring off into the air, slowly sinking down atop a chair. "Are you all right, Rosina? I know that was hard for anyone to see."

"I—I think I am all right, my lady. Although, every time I close my eyes, all I can see is that bloody dead man." She shivered. "I don't like the sight of blood. I never did. Even when I worked in the kitchens, I had to have the boys kill the chickens. I plucked the feathers instead."

"Try to sleep now," she told her handmaid, closing her eyes and resting her head back against the chair. She heard Grunt lie down at her feet. "I am sure justice will be served eventually. Lord Gainsborough's murderer will be caught and tried."

"How can you say that, my lady? We don't even know yet that the man didn't take his own life. I mean, he had the knife in his grip. Surely that should prove he was the one to kill himself."

"Mayhap he wasn't plunging the blade into his heart but perhaps trying to pull it out after his murderer left him there to die."

"Oh, I never considered that!" Rosina stopped breathing and her face froze. "Do you really think that could be true?" she asked, in a voice no louder than a whisper. "That there is a murderer here at the castle?"

"I don't know for sure," she answered. "But what I do know is that if it was a murder, I am going to do everything in my power to hunt down that killer and make him pay for taking the life of an innocent man. It is something I wish I or someone would have been able to do for my own departed parents."

Chapter Three

Despite finally settling into her bed, Vivienne remained restless all night. Unfortunately, the horrific events of the day only brought about her own terrible nightmare again. The one that had haunted her since she had lost her entire family in one night.

Holding her newborn baby boy to her chest, Vivienne stretched out in the hay along with her younger brother, Adrian. It was hard to sleep, since the baby's crying kept her awake.

"Vivienne, allow me to rock your baby to comfort him," offered her mother, Flanie, from the bench seat of the wagon in which they traveled. "Mayhap then you can get some rest."

"We should be at Mablethorpe soon," her father, Abiathar Harlowe, assured them. "Once there, you'll have plenty of people to help you with the baby."

"All right, Mother. You take him for a while," agreed Vivienne, handing the newborn to her mother over the side of the wagon and to the bench seat. "Perhaps you'll have the calming touch that I have yet to learn."

"My grandson is so precious." Her mother smiled down at

the baby in her arms, giving him a kiss on the forehead. "What have you decided to name him? Will you name him George after his father?"

"No, Mother. I won't do that," Vivienne answered with a yawn. Her husband, a stablehand at Somersby, had died by being kicked by a horse shortly after they'd married. George had been a kind lad even though he had no money. Vivienne's family, although they were poor as well, strangely always seemed to have whatever they needed. It broke her heart when George died, but she promised herself she'd stay strong for their baby. She had to be strong now, since her poor child would grow up without a father. "I don't want to curse my baby by using the name of his dead father. I'm afraid if I do, my baby might die as well."

"That's nonsense," scoffed her mother. "No name is cursed. I'm sure your baby would love being named after his father."

"My baby's already cursed since he'll be growing up without a father," she told her parents. "I cannot even imagine how awful it will be to never know the man who sired him." Her parents became quiet all of a sudden, and Vivienne thought it was an odd thing for them to do in the middle of a conversation.

"He'll need a name, sweetheart," her father finally spoke up from the front seat. "You should give him one before much longer."

"He'll get a name," she promised. "Mayhap I will name him Abiathar after you, Father. That way he can follow in his grandfather's footsteps instead." Once again her parents became quiet.

"Nay, I'm not sure that is a good idea," her father finally answered. The clip clop of the horses' hooves on the road was the only sound in the night, now that her mother had managed to get the baby to sleep. She'd swaddled him tightly and placed him into a wicker basket she carried at her side, using it like a crib after she'd removed the food. "I am sure you could name your son after someone more honorable and respected than me," her father continued.

"What do you mean? You are the most honorable and respectable person I know," she told him. "Besides, I don't know anyone else who fills those qualifications, do you?"

"Oh, I don't know. How about … the king?" asked her father.

"Abiathar," scolded her mother. "Hush."

"Edward," Vivienne said the king's name aloud, pondering the suggestion. "I kind of like the name, actually. Still, I'm not sure. I will decide soon, but right now I am just too tired to think straight."

"You get some rest then, sweetheart," came her mother's beautiful voice from the front of the wagon. "And don't worry about a thing. Your baby is sleeping safely in my care. He seems to think that basket is a cradle and he likes it. I will protect him, I promise. Sleep now, and save your strength, Daughter."

Vivienne had finally dozed off, but was abruptly woken after too long. What roused her was the sound of neighing horses and the jerk of the wagon as it halted, coming to a complete and sudden stop. She heard voices, and they sounded menacing if she wasn't mistaken.

"Off the wagon," commanded a gruff male voice.

"Nay. Leave us alone. We just want to pass," her father replied, doing all he could to protect his family, she was sure. Vivienne's heart sped up. She realized these roads were filled with bandits and perhaps they were about to be robbed. Her fingers closed over the hilt of her dagger strapped to her side. She would fight to help protect her family if need be.

The next thing she heard sounded like a sword being drawn from a scabbard, followed by the sounds of a struggle. Slowly, she pulled her blade from its sheath and rolled over in the hay, trying to see what was happening.

"Abiathar!" shouted her mother. "Nay!" she screamed and started crying.

Before Vivienne could get to her knees to look over the back of the bench seat, she heard the sickening sound of a body hitting the ground.

"Kill her, too!" commanded another man.

"Nay," Vivienne mumbled to herself, pushing up to a half-sitting position to see what was happening. She saw her mother struggling with a man as he pulled her off the wagon and to the ground. The basket with her baby in it was still on the bench seat. Vivienne started to panic. She needed to get to her baby as well as to help her poor mother. Since her father was so quiet and not protecting them, she was sure he'd been killed.

"Sister, what's happening?" Her brother rubbed a sleepy eye, looking up at her from under the hay.

"Adrian, stay down," she warned her brother in a hushed voice. "We're being attacked by bandits. Keep quiet, so they don't know you are here."

"Who won't know?" he asked, and she silenced him with her finger to his lips.

"Mother is in trouble. I have to help her, as well as to protect my baby." Not wanting to be seen, Vivienne quietly flipped over the far side of the wagon, letting her feet silently drop to the ground. She hoped to be able to sneak up to the front of the wagon and grab the basket with her baby, without the ruffians noticing her. It was night and very dark, so that would give her cover. Only a partial moon lit the sky, but was mainly hidden by clouds.

Gripping her dagger tightly, she crept around to the front of the wagon, scared because she knew she was still weak from giving birth. How would she fight off a full-grown man? Especially in her condition? Her toe hit something on the ground. When she looked down she saw the bloody, lifeless body of her *father lying in a crumpled heap. Biting her tongue so as not to cry out, she quickly hunkered down to check for signs of life. His throat had been slit and there was no hope he could survive such a heinous act. He was no longer moving. It was too late for her father, but mayhap she could still save her mother and her son. She was their only hope now. Slipping her dagger back into her waist belt, she reached down and took her father's sword from his hand. Since he was only a foot soldier, he didn't own one of the longer, heavier swords mainly used by knights. His was a shorter, lighter blade, devised for closer, hand-to-hand combat. Therefore, Vivienne was able to lift it, having even learned from her father how to use it, at her insistence. Holding it in two hands, she stepped around the front of the wagon, ready to strike down whoever killed him.*

"MY LADY, WAKE UP."

Vivienne's eyes popped open as she was dragged from her nightmare into her waking world. "W-what did you say? Where am I?" It took her a moment to realize she was no longer that sixteen-year-old girl in the back of a wagon and scared out of her mind. Nay, she was grown now and at Mablethorpe Castle, speaking with her handmaid.

"You are in your bedchamber, my lady," said Rosina. "It is morning and I was trying to wake you up." She walked over to open the window. Sure enough, the first signs of daylight spilled into the room, making Vivienne realize she had slept much longer than she'd intended.

"Oh, yes. I suppose I should get out of bed." She actually wanted nothing more, since every time she slept she seemed to drift back into her recurring nightmare.

Rosina crossed back and reached out, touching Vivienne's brow. "You are perspiring, my lady, and can barely catch your breath. I think you are feverish. Dunking yourself in the horse trough has made you ill, just like I knew it would."

"Nay, Rosina, you worry about me too much. I am not ill. I am fine," she answered, hearing pounding at her door. "Please answer the door."

"Of course, my lady." Rosina hurried across the room and opened the door a crack, peeking around to see who was there. After some soft and muddled conversation, she heard her handmaid say, "Thank you, I'll tell her at once." Rosina closed the door.

"Who is it?" asked Vivienne, standing up and straightening her gown. Her hand went to her head to smooth back her mussed hair. She'd never meant to sleep in her clothes. Grunt got up, stretching his legs and then his back.

"It was Martin the page boy, my lady. He said the sheriff is here and that your presence is requested downstairs in the great hall anon."

"The sheriff! Of course." It all came back to her now. She suddenly remembered she'd been waiting for him since last night. The kennels had burned down as well as a murder had taken place. "I'll go at once."

"I will come with you, my lady," offered Rosina.

"There is no need for that," she replied. Vivienne stopped at the door and looked back at the woman. Worry creased her brow and she still looked pale. It was apparent that seeing the murdered man earlier was still affecting her, even now.

"Are you sure?" asked the handmaid, being loyal to Vivienne as always. "I want to do my duty."

"I'm certain," answered Vivienne. "But thank you for the offer. Stay here for now and rest. You've been through a harrowing experience. We all have. Unless the sheriff wants to talk to you, there is no need to subject yourself to that awful sight again." She headed out the door.

"Did you say the sheriff might want to talk to me?" Rosina called after her, rushing over to the door and looking out into the corridor. "Why would he want to do that?"

"I'm not saying he will, but there is a possibility that the Sheriff of Mablethorpe will want to question everyone who was at the castle when Lord Gainsborough died, to find out if they saw anything or perhaps anyone suspicious. It might shed light on what really happened to Lord Gainsborough."

"Oh, I understand. Of course." She released a breath and seemed to calm down. "In that case, I will be happy to help in any way I can."

"Thank you, Rosina. You are always so accommodating. Come on, Grunt," Vivienne called her hound. "I might need your nose."

Vivienne hurried down the corridor and descended the staircase, noticing when she got to the bottom landing that the dead body had been moved and was no longer beneath the stairs. She hurried off into the great hall where there was still commotion as many of the occupants spoke softly about what had happened last night. Some of the servants and guards were sleeping on the floor near the fire. The hall smelled strongly from acrid smoke, a reminder of the kennels that had nearly burnt to the ground. As she headed toward the group of people at the far end of the hall, she noticed the sun breaking the horizon out the open window. The sound of singing birds floated in the air, promising that everything would be all right and back to normal soon.

"Vivienne, over here," called out her uncle, looking up and waving to her, having seen her approach. Vivienne joined the group which was composed of her uncle; Gainsborough's son Wilfred and his mother; Vivienne's aunt; the kennel groom Adam; Richard the guard; John, the castle's steward; and Herman, the guard from Gainsborough.

Zachariah Fitch, Sheriff of Mablethorpe, was there with them.

"Uncle, I'm here now," said Vivienne, nodding slightly in greeting to the others. Grunt hurried over to the sheriff and sniffed his leg.

"Hello, Grunt," said the sheriff with a chuckle, smiling and reaching down to pet the hound. "I'm sorry I didn't bring you a treat this time, but I promise I will next time we meet."

"Vivienne, you already know Sheriff Zachariah Fitch," said her uncle.

"Yes. Hello, Sheriff," she answered with a nod and a smile.

"Hello, my lady." The sheriff strolled over to her and reached out for her hand, as was proper. She didn't hesitate to give it to him, since he was a friend. "Good to see you again, as always." He kissed the back of her hand, his dark brown eyes never leaving hers as he half-bowed.

Zachariah Fitch was a handsome man, mayhap three years older than she. His hair was thick with a slight wave to it, and he usually always wore it tied back in a queue so it wouldn't fall in his eyes when he was working. It was dark brown, almost black. The color reminded her of the bark of the mighty oak tree that she and he used to climb together as children when she'd come to visit her aunt and uncle. The sheriff had a short and trimmed beard and mustache, as well as craggy brows.

He released her hand and stood upright, his tall form towering over her. She had known Zachariah for most of her life. She and Grunt had even helped the sheriff track down a thief last year. It was not something a normal lady would do, but then again, Vivienne was anything but normal. It was only once, and Grunt had been beneficial in sniffing out the perpetrator, but Vivienne liked the adventure. It had been mysterious and exciting in a raw sort of way. It made her feel alive and as if she had a purpose. That purpose being to help others when all hope seemed lost.

SHERIFF ZACHARIAH FITCH was happy to see Lady Vivienne Harlowe join them. Secretly, he was pleased to see her again under any circumstances. She'd proven to be ever so helpful during a past investigation of a robbery. Her skills of observation were sharp, her instinct strong. And that bloodhound of hers seemed to be able to sniff out trails easily. But this time was different. This time, a murder had been committed. That would hit too close to home for Vivienne. He was sure it would bring many emotions to the surface for her, and he didn't want to see her so upset again. When she'd first moved here seven years ago, she had lost all hope and didn't even want to live after losing her entire family. He'd stayed by her side and held her hand, did everything he could to make her feel safe and secure. He wanted his friend back with all the life and excitement that used to make her the amazing girl he always knew her to be. It had taken a long time to bring her back to that point, and he hoped this murder wasn't going to set her back again.

Lady Vivienne was a beautiful woman with long blonde hair that she seldom braided or wore tucked away hidden under a hat. Zachariah tamped down a smile. Lady Vivienne's choice to display her hair so freely was just one of her highly unusual attributes. Sometimes startling even him, she often claimed she 'liked to be independent,' and resented the constraints placed upon women of her status. Too often, he didn't know what to think of her outrageous views. But he did know that he enjoyed her company. Perhaps even too much.

Mischief danced in her bright blue eyes today, just like it had when they knew each other as children. He'd always found that refreshing. It made him enjoy being around her. Tall for a lady, she still held all the elegance of a noble, even when she was acting out-of-sorts, which was basically all the time. Often when he visited the castle, he'd witness her in the practice yard with a sword in her hand, sparring with all the squires. Her skills were impressive. Especially for a woman. Most women wouldn't be able to even hold a sword in one hand let alone wield it through the air. Yes, Lady Vivienne was amazing, and so unlike anyone he had ever met.

"I am sorry it took so long for me to arrive," he apologized to the group with a bow of his head. "I was assisting my constable down on Rotten Row. It took longer than expected."

"Rotten Row?" Vivienne's head snapped up. "Did something awful happen there as well?" she asked him.

Zachariah chuckled softly. "Not more than usual, I suppose. That is, besides the normal brawls in the taverns, trouble with jealous whores, theft, and now a madman who seems to think he is the Pied Piper and is giving the townsfolk trouble."

"The Pied Piper?" Vivienne looked up at him and blinked in confusion. "What do you mean by that?"

"The Pied Piper of Hamelin," he said, but she didn't react. "The man who played the flute to lure the rats?" Haven't you heard that old story?"

She silently shrugged. No one answered, and that told him that they didn't know of this event that took place in Germany over fifty years ago. It had been retold so many times through the years that it became folklore. Or at least to some.

"I am talking about a rat catcher," he explained, finally getting a reaction.

"Oh, I see." Vivienne flashed a smile.

"There are so many rats on Rotten Row that the town pays for each one collected and killed. There is a man there now who either likes killing rats or is just going crazy doing it because he likes the money he gets for it."

"Mmmph," grunted her uncle. "Can we get on with this, please? A good friend of mine died last night and some of us suspect he was murdered. I want to know what you are going to do about it."

"Since I've only just arrived, Lord Mablethorpe, I cannot give you an answer to that question yet. I will have to view the body first and determine the facts."

"My father's body is back here," Wilfred said in a soft voice, walking over to a screen that had been set up in the great hall to block the view of the dead man from the other occupants. Zachariah had met everyone in the group as soon as he had arrived and while they were waiting for Lady Vivienne to come downstairs. Actually, it was he who had suggested she be present, even though her uncle insisted she didn't need to be here and that they did not need to wake her. But Vivienne Harlowe was observant and might be able to tell him something that others wouldn't have noticed. She was also wise and cunning. Yes, she truly had a nose for trouble, and wasn't bad at solving puzzles that stumped the average person. Zachariah hoped Vivienne had possibly seen something last night that could aid in his investigation. With his insistence that she be present, Vivienne's uncle had finally sent the page to fetch her.

"If there are no objections, I will take a look at the body now." Zachariah walked behind the screen with the others following.

Sure enough, a dead man in bloodied clothes was lying flat on his back atop one of the trestle tables. His fingers were wrapped around the hilt of a dagger that was embedded in his chest. "This isn't where the man was found," he commented, seeing immediately that the body been moved.

"Nay, it wasn't," said Lord Gilbert Irvine. "I had my men

move the body here, where you'd be able to view it in better light. Also, to keep prying eyes off of him."

"It is always best not to touch the body before I've arrived, and especially not to move it." He reached out and turned the man's head to one side and then the other, noticing red marks on his neck that looked like they could be from someone's fingers. Then he surveyed the man's hand gripping the dagger.

"Did my husband take his own life?" asked Lady Gainsborough, sobbing.

"I can't believe that Father would do that," said her son, Wilfred, putting his arm around his mother.

"I cannot answer that at this time, my lady." Zachariah was careful with his words, needing to surmise the situation to gain facts before even making a guess as to what happened. "I have a lot of questions I'll need to ask, but first tell me, who found the body?" He continued looking over the corpse for clues.

"I did, Sheriff," Vivienne spoke up, pushing to the front of the crowd.

"I see," he said, looking at her, not surprised in the least that it was she who had discovered the dead man. After all, trouble seemed to always cling to Lady Vivienne everywhere she went ever since she was a child. Finding corpses wasn't new to her, since the deaths of her parents. "Where did you discover him, Lady Vivienne?"

"Under the stairwell. I can show you the exact spot. It is in this direction." She motioned with her head and started to walk. The group began to follow.

"There is no need for everyone to come with me right now," said Zachariah with his hand in the air. "Lady Vivienne and Lord Mablethorpe will assist me and that will be sufficient. I will talk to everyone else in turn."

"Of course," said Lady Mablethorpe. "John, spread the

word to the others that the sheriff will be talking with them all," she instructed the steward.

"Aye, my lady." John hurried away to carry out his orders.

"I'll be out in the kennels, seeing what I can save," Adam announced.

"I'll join you with my guard," said Wilfred. "Mayhap there's a way we can help."

"Thank you," said Adam, heading outside.

Grunt led the way to the stairwell with Vivienne right behind her hound. Zachariah and Gilbert walked together talking softly amongst them.

"Sheriff Fitch, I want the murderer of Lord Gainsborough found and imprisoned immediately," commanded Gilbert.

"That is my intent," he answered. "However, first I need to determine if it truly was a murder, or simply a disturbed man taking his own life."

"Lord Gainsborough was a good friend of mine and I assure you he was not disturbed. The man never would have taken his own life. He was happy, as well was I. We just planned an alliance between us, but sadly that may never transpire now. Everything is ruined by this, I tell you. I want his killer executed for what he did!" Lord Mablethorpe seemed to be getting emotional, now that they were away from the others.

"What kind of an alliance are you talking about?" asked Zachariah curiously.

"He planned on marrying me off to Lord Gainsborough's son," Vivienne answered before her uncle could respond.

"Really?" That surprised Zachariah since he knew Vivienne too well to believe she'd ever agreed to be married again. Not after the trauma she'd been through. "Do you mean Lord Wilfred and you were to be ... husband and ... wife?" he asked, still in shock to hear this piece of information. He remembered the timid man in the great hall and couldn't see him and Vivienne together. He knew that Vivienne would never marry or agree to marrying anyone again. And if she did, he was sure she'd want a man who was as least as strong and as skilled as she. He'd heard the gossip that Lord Wilfred Knapp of Gainsborough was a milksop and a disgrace to the family name. The thought of him marrying a strong woman like Vivienne almost made him laugh aloud.

"Yes, Lord Wilfred. He's the one," said Vivienne, with a puff of air from her mouth. Then she mumbled softly, "As if I'd ever really marry him."

"Ah, I see," said Zachariah with a nod, being right about Vivienne after all. "Then you disagreed with this marriage alliance," he said, as they came to a stop by the staircase.

"Disagree? I didn't even know about it. But yes, of course, I disagreed and I still do," snapped Vivienne. "My uncle knows I will never marry again, yet he keeps on trying to trick me into it. Your actions, Uncle, are unquestionably improper, immoral, and disgraceful, if you ask me."

"I didn't," came her uncle's deep-voiced reply.

"Sheriff, I want you to realize that no one bothered to tell me about this betrothal until Lord Gainsborough was murdered," Vivienne continued.

"Is that so?" Zachariah looked over to Vivienne's uncle for an explanation. "Why didn't you tell your niece your plans, Lord Mablethorpe? I do find that a little odd."

Gilbert shook his head. "I am her guardian and do not need her permission. I will marry her off to anyone I choose. I will do what I feel is best for her."

"I see," said Zachariah. "But the fact remains that you didn't tell her about it."

"She was going to find out last night at the celebration. I don't see what difference it makes."

"You didn't think it was important to tell her ahead of time?"

"Nay. Why should I? She'd only object to it the way she fights me about everything else. There was no need for her to know ahead of time because it would have only caused trouble."

"No need?" Vivienne's hands went to her hips. "If something involves me and my life, then it certainly does mean I have a need to know."

"Agreed," said Zachariah, taking a torch from a wall and heading over to the space under the staircase where he spied a puddle of dried blood on the floor. "I am guessing this is where the body was found?"

"It is," said Vivienne while her hound sniffed around the floor. "It was actually Grunt who found him. He barked to get my attention, and then he led me right to the ... to Lord Gainsborough." It seemed Vivienne had a hard time just saying the word corpse or dead body. He felt her pain, knowing the horrible experience she'd been through with her parents.

Zachariah hunkered down, using the torch to light up the floor. Coming from the puddle of blood which was mostly dry now, were some footprints. They were in several sizes. Some were larger, looking like boots with heels on them. Some were smaller, seeming to be flatter shoes. Besides that, he couldn't see anything that would give him an idea as to who would have done this. "I really wish you wouldn't have moved the body," he told them.

"Well, we weren't going to leave the poor man here for all to see while we waited for you to arrive," answered Gilbert.

"There are quite a lot of footprints in the blood," he said, still studying the area.

"Yes. Probably from me and also from the men who moved

him," said Vivienne, picking up her foot and looking at the bottom of her shoe. "We should have been more careful."

"Did anyone have a disagreement or argument with Lord Gainsborough recently?" Zachariah continued to study the footprints, hoping to be able to figure out if there had been a struggle. However, it was too hard to tell, since so many people had walked through the blood when it was fresh.

"Who hasn't had a disagreement with Lord Gainsborough?" commented Vivienne, shaking her head.

"What do you mean?" he asked.

"It is no secret that he wasn't well liked," Vivienne relayed the information.

"Did you argue with him before he was murdered?" he asked.

"Nay. However, he wanted to walk alone with me out in my herb garden, but I refused," Vivienne told him.

"He wanted to be alone with you? Why?"

Her cheeks reddened and she almost seemed hesitant to tell him at first. "Well, at the time I thought he wanted to get me alone to possibly make improper advances toward me."

His head snapped up, not liking to hear this. "Is that so?" Damn it, he didn't want any man pushing himself on her. She deserved better than that.

"She is wrong about that," Lord Mablethorpe interrupted. "Lord Gainsborough was going to take Vivienne aside before the announcement to explain to her about the betrothal."

"Is that true?" Zachariah looked up at Vivienne from his position hunkered down on the ground.

She bit at her bottom lip and nodded slowly. "Yes, I suppose it was," she admitted. "Although I didn't know it at the time."

"I see. Do either of you know of anyone else who could

have been angry with Lord Gainsborough? I mean, angry enough to want to possibly kill him."

"I'm angry at him now that he died," said Gilbert. "His son was going to marry my daughter. We had an agreement. An alliance in the works." His hands waved in the air and he acted as if he thought Lord Gainsborough had died on purpose just to ruin his plans.

"Your daughter?" Vivienne's eyes narrowed as she stared at her uncle. "I am not your daughter and you know it. I'm your niece," she blatantly corrected him.

"Vivienne, you wound me with your words," her uncle answered, holding his hand to his heart. He truly looked hurt. "You are my ward. Your aunt and I consider you to be the daughter we never had. I would have hoped you knew that by now and felt the same way about us."

"Of course, I do, Uncle. I'm sorry," she apologized. "I truly meant nothing by it."

"Sheriff," said Gilbert with a yawn. How long will this take? Most of us have been awake all night and we are all very tired from putting out the fire."

"A fire?" This took his interest and he stood up. "Ah, yes, I did see the smoking kennels when I arrived. How did it burn?"

"We are not sure yet how the fire in the kennels started," explained Vivienne. "However, in my opinion, I believe it was a distraction so the murderer could kill without being seen."

"I see." Zachariah realized that what Vivienne was saying could very well be true.

"Do you think that is what happened? That the fire could have been set on purpose as a distraction?" Gilbert asked Zachariah. "Who would do such a thing? Especially with the lives of my hunting hounds at stake."

"I don't know. It's too soon to tell." Zachariah replaced the torch on the wall. "I'll have to inspect the kennels before I can determine that. I'd like to have another look at the body, too. I'm sure Lady Gainsborough will want to take the body back home and bury her husband as soon as possible. I don't want to miss anything."

"Aye. Be my guest," said Gilbert with a yawn.

"With your permission, Lord Mablethorpe, I'd also like the body moved into a smaller room for viewing purposes. A place that is closed off from the others where I can continue my investigation in private, would be good," said Zachariah.

"Of course," answered the lord. "Whatever you need."

"Also, no one is to leave the castle until I question them first."

"No one at all is to leave? Is that what I just heard you say?" Lady Mablethorpe walked up with Lady Gainsborough, their arms interlinked. They both looked tired and their eyes seemed sunken in their faces from crying.

"That's right, my ladies. Everyone is to stay put for now."

"But I'll need to get back to Gainsborough to tell everyone what happened to my husband and that my son Wilfred is their new lord." Lady Gainsborough sniffled, clutching a handcloth, using it to dab at her eyes.

"I'm sorry for your loss, Lady Gainsborough. I understand how you feel but I can't let you leave just yet," Zachariah told her. "You see, if this truly was murder, then the murderer could still be inside the walls of Mablethorpe Castle. If so, we are all in danger. At the same time, I'm sure you wouldn't want the killer escaping, would you?"

"Of course not," said Lady Gainsborough with a shudder. "For all I know, the crazed murderer might decide to follow me home. Mayhap my son and I should stay here where we will be well protected, until we know it is safe to return."

"Good idea. I think that would be best." Zachariah let her

think it was her decision, when in truth, he wouldn't have let her leave at will right now.

"But Sheriff, we have many guests here and they will want to be heading home as well," added Vivienne's aunt. "After all, some of them came from afar for a celebration that never took place."

"Then I will question those who live the farthest away first," he explained. "I will speak with those who live at the castle, as well as the Gainsboroughs and their traveling party, when I am finished. Once I am satisfied that someone is not a suspect in this death, then I will allow them to leave, but not until then."

"Suspect?" asked Lady Gainsborough. "Then you truly believe my husband was murdered."

"Like I said, it is too soon to tell," he told her. "I am only being cautious, which I am sure you can appreciate, my lady."

"Yes." Lady Gainsborough dabbed at her eyes again. "I appreciate all your work, Sheriff."

"We all do," added Lady Mablethorpe. "Don't worry, no one will leave until you give them permission to do so, I assure you."

"I suppose with so many people to question, you'll be staying here at the castle for a while as well, Sheriff?" Vivienne asked.

"I think that is in order. I will do whatever it takes to solve this. It is my job."

"Sheriff Fitch, we will gladly offer you a bedchamber during your stay," Lady Mablethorpe told him. "You are welcome to all the food and drink you'd like as well."

"Yes, of course," agreed her husband. "It is the least we can do."

"Thank you," he answered with a nod.

"If there is anything else that we can help you with, please let us know," said Vivienne's aunt as she and Lady Gainsborough left.

"I have a lot of work to do, so I guess I'd better get started." Zachariah looked over to Vivienne and her uncle. "Is there a free chamber where the body can be stored in the meantime, and another chamber that I can use to question everyone?"

"Of course," said Gilbert. "I'll call for my steward at once to accommodate you in whatever way possible. Will your bedchamber serve as a sufficient place to question the others?"

"That will be fine. Thank you," said Zachariah, rubbing his hands together, ready to work. "And is there a room to store the body for a few days until it starts to rot and needs to be incinerated or buried?"

"Well," said Gilbert, scratching his head. "I'm not sure. I don't really want to keep the corpse inside the castle, because of the stench."

"What about the smokehouse, Uncle?" asked Vivienne. "I don't believe Cook has it in use at the moment."

"Yes, the smokehouse would be perfect to store the body if that is possible," Zachariah agreed.

Vivienne's uncle slowly nodded. "I suppose that'll be fine. I'll let Cook know your intention so he doesn't plan on using it. My men will move Lord Gainsborough's body at once."

"That's perfect," said Zachariah. "I don't want anyone tampering with the body, so please post a guard at the door as well. I will send a page to collect those I need to question as soon as I am ready."

"Uncle, I will tell Martin to help the sheriff," suggested Vivienne.

Zachariah was familiar with Martin. He was a young boy brought to Mablethorpe about six months ago for fostering. Nobles usually sent their sons to another noble family to be pages when the children were around seven years of age.

Martin was a cute yet responsible child who seemed to be wiser and more responsible than most boys his age.

"Fine, fine," mumbled Gilbert, turning and walking away.

"Sheriff, I'd also like to help you in any way that I can," offered Vivienne. Her dog was at her side. "Grunt and I have assisted you in hunting down a thief in the past. We'd like to assist you with this case as well."

"Yes, you and Grunt have been a help to me in the past," he agreed. "I must admit, you have a keen sense of observation." Grunt barked happily and Zachariah chuckled, reaching down to pet the dog. "You too, Grunt. I didn't forget about you, don't worry. Your nose is the best tool of all."

"I'd like to help you find Lord Gainsborough's murderer," Vivienne blurted out.

"What?"

"I want to be more of a help than just hunting down common thieves."

"Nay, Lady Vivienne. Not this time. I don't believe it's a good idea." Zachariah spoke, still petting the hound on the head. He looked down at the dog rather than at her when he gave her his answer, which she was sure not to like in the least.

"Why not?"

"I think this case might be a little too much for you, my lady. If there truly is a murderer on the loose, it could also be very dangerous for you."

"Not any more dangerous than what I've already lived through. Give me the chance to prove it to you. I know I can do this."

His gaze lifted to see the look of determination in her bright eyes. Mixed in with it was a tinge of sadness or mayhap it was desperation, he wasn't quite sure. This was a hard situation to be in because of his past investigation that had centered around her parents' deaths. That is, the case he wasn't able to solve. It pained him for the last seven years that he hadn't been able to get her answers to all the questions about her murdered parents and missing baby and brother.

"Vivienne, I'm sorry I was never able to discover who murdered your parents," he said in a soft voice. "God knows I tried. I was young and inexperienced at the time. I had just taken over as sheriff after my father's death." It felt like a knife twisting in his heart that he couldn't help her. He'd known her parents for years, and they were some of the nicest people he'd ever met. Their absence made a great void in Vivienne's life. In his, too. Whatever affected Vivienne also seemed to affect him, for some reason. Friends felt this way, he supposed.

"I know," she told him.

"I want you to know how much it pains me that I wasn't able to solve the case."

"Thank you," she said softly, not saying more.

"I assure you, I think about that situation every day. It really bothers me that I failed you."

"You did what you could, I am sure."

Her words were clipped and held great disappointment, as he heard it in her tone. He couldn't blame her. In his opinion, there was no excuse for never having found her missing family or the murderer of her parents. Damn it, it made him angry. He wanted Vivienne to have closure, but she'd never find it now. And he felt as if he were to blame.

"I promised you I'd never stop searching for answers regarding your family, and I truly mean it. Even to this very day," he continued.

"I believe you," she said. "But seven years is a long time, Sheriff. I'm not sure I'll ever find the answers to my questions." She bit at her bottom lip the way she always did when she was upset about something and trying to hold her tongue. He knew her actions better than anyone by now. There was something she wanted to say to him, but she was holding back.

"So that is what is troubling you, Lady Vivienne?" he asked her. "I should have guessed."

"You know me too well, Sheriff Fitch," she said, flashing him a quick smile.

"I am just glad you finally told me." He gave her the look he always had in the past when he'd finally been able to get her to open up to him. There was a connection between them that no one could ever tear apart.

She sighed. "I suppose I couldn't have kept it from you much longer, so I might as well tell you. I want to work with you. Not only in finding thieves, but murderers, too."

He'd kept her from doing anything during his investigation involving her parents seven years ago, even though she'd begged him to let her help. He'd objected, because she'd been so fragile and young at the time. Her life had been crumbling around her, and he couldn't bear to expose her to anything else that might hurt her. Seeing Vivienne cry, and watching the light of life disappear from her eyes had been challenging, because he remembered the true woman that he once knew and what she could actually do. Vivienne Harlowe was not the kind of lady to ever give up. Saying *no* to her only seemed to make her even more determined. Her uncle had a heavy hand in keeping her protected since that time, letting her become distracted rather than to be hounding him every day. That is why Lord Mablethorpe allowed her to learn to fight using her late father's sword. He had even turned a blind eye when Vivienne dressed like a man or climbed a tree. One day she even jumped from the battlements into the moat, just to prove she could do it. But now, she seemed so forlorn. It was as if she'd given up hope, and he didn't like that.

"I want to say *yes* to you, I really do. However, I can't let you work with me," he explained.

"Why not?" she demanded to know.

"I already told you that it's dangerous, and also not appropriate for a lady to be going places and doing things that are expected of a sheriff."

"Sheriff Fitch, I do things every day that are not appropriate for a lady, and you know it," Vivienne said with a stiff upper lip. "How in heaven's name will this be any different?"

"Under the circumstances, I'm afraid it will be too … emotional for you, Lady Vivienne. I don't want to see you get hurt. You've been through so much already. Thank you for your offer, but I prefer to work alone."

"Under the circumstances?" Vivienne's chin rose and she met his gaze with hers, not afraid to look him in the eye. "You mean you think it'll be too hard for me since my parents were murdered and that I'll break down—just admit it."

"Well, it is a possibility, and a real one at that."

Her hands went to her hips and that was never a good thing. He'd managed to irk her, when that hadn't been his intention. "If you really think of me in that way than you don't know me as well as I thought you did," spat Vivienne. "It was seven years ago when my parents were murdered. I have become much stronger as a person since that time. I am not as fragile as you might think. Not anymore."

"It's not just the murders I am referring to," he told her. "You have been through so much with the death of your husband, and the loss of your newborn baby and younger brother too."

Her eyes became glassy and it was evident that she was holding back her tears.

"Yes. Yes, I have," she responded. "And might I point out

that the disappearance of both my brother Adrian and my baby are also mysteries that you have yet to solve, as well."

Now he really felt bad, because she was correct in what she said. He had worked day and night looking, searching, questioning, but never getting even a single trace as to what had happened. Vivienne's life was a mystery. Things happened that night that no one could ever explain. He'd committed himself to finding answers, but in time it wore away at him and it almost consumed him. He would never give up the search, but there were strange forces in play here that he would never understand. How could these things have happened and two people disappear, and no one ever know where they went?

"I'm so sorry, Lady Vivienne." He reached out for her but she stepped away, keeping her face stoic and any hint of emotion from showing. "I will find both your baby and brother someday. I promise you, it is the truth. I am sure they are still alive."

"You can't say that when you have no idea if it's even true." Tears formed in her eyes, sadness and grief replacing her anger toward him.

"I also have no facts telling me that it isn't true. Have faith. Never give up hope. It's not like you."

"I will say it again, Sheriff. I want to work alongside you to find Lord Gainsborough's murderer. Because of my ... circumstances, I have even more need than ever to help others in the same situation."

"Do you really mean that?" he asked, starting to understand her reasoning and exactly how she felt. Perhaps in a way, this would be good for Vivienne. She needed to find closure. By helping others find the murderers of their loved ones, perhaps she'd find peace within herself as well.

"I do mean that. One way or another justice will be served.

Not only for me, but also for the Gainsboroughs. And I plan to be a part of bringing that about. Not only for the late Lord Gainsborough's sake, but also for the sake of my parents. And my entire family. I do not want the death of my parents to have been in vain. Something good needs to come from my whole horrible situation, or their deaths are naught but senseless wastes of lives. So, are you going to continue to try to help me by letting me help you, or not?"

Zachariah let out a deep breath, not knowing what to do. Lady Vivienne had a valid point. By helping someone else in her similar situation, it could possibly help her heal faster. Nothing would make Zachariah happier than if this were true. With everything she'd been through in her life, she needed something to look forward to, even if it was not directly related to her personal quest. If he told her *no* now, she'd only be out looking for the murderers on her own, he was sure of it. At least if she worked alongside him, he could protect her and watch over her every step of the way. Even though she didn't seem like the type of woman who really wanted or needed a man to protect her, he'd surely like to try to be the one to do so.

He smiled at her and nodded slowly. "By all means, please join me in the investigation, Lady Vivienne. I think together, and with that mutt of yours, we'll make a good team." He held out his arm to her, hoping she wouldn't reject him. "May I escort you to the great hall?"

She looked down at his arm and then back up at him and broke a smile. "This is a murder investigation, Sheriff, not a wooing. I can walk by myself, thank you." She swept past him in a flurry of velvet and silk, her gown swishing over the floor as she left with Grunt running ahead of her. Zachariah stood there alone with his empty arm still lifted up in the air. He cleared his throat and quickly let his arm drop to his side, hoping no one was watching this blatant act of rejection.

"All right, then. Meet me in the smokehouse in ten minutes

for another inspection of the body," he called out after her, slowly following the path that Lady Vivienne had taken.

Chuckling softly, he shook his head. Aye, Lady Vivienne Harlowe was a phenomenal lady. A bit prickly, true enough, but with a mind of her own. She didn't stop until she got exactly what she wanted, no matter how long it took. Determination was one of her virtues, even if having no patience was one of her vices. He had no doubt she'd help him find this murderer, since she had something to prove to not only him but also to herself.

He felt responsible for her case being unsolved after all these years. She, on the other hand, somehow felt as if it was her fault that it all happened in the first place. This was the start of something that could in time lead to answering her personal quest involving her family. He felt in his heart that this was the truth. He knew a lot about Lady Vivienne Harlowe, since they'd been friends for a long time now. What he didn't know, however, was if agreeing to work with her side-by-side was going to be a pleasurable experience ... or one he would end up regretting for the rest of his life.

Chapter Four

The door to the smokehouse closed, leaving Vivienne in the room alone with the sheriff and the corpse. Her uncle had wanted to send in a guard to watch over Vivienne, but the sheriff told him it wasn't necessary. Vivienne had agreed. After all, she'd worked with the sheriff in the past and knew him well. They'd grown up together and had been friends since childhood. She also had her hound there to protect her, not that she needed protecting at all. Sheriff Zachariah Fitch only held good intentions. He was there to help them find a murderer. Or at least try. Truth be told, he'd never been successful in finding her parents' murderers and seemed to have given up trying over the years, even though he claimed he was still looking. Then again, Vivienne had become quite disheartened as well. Hope was always alive within her, but sometimes it was so hard to just hang on. Even so, she swore she would from that day on help others to find their answers in any way she could. Even if she couldn't find her own.

Glad to have another look at the body without everyone

crowding around her and peering over her shoulder, Vivienne hoped to find something ... anything ... that might lead them to who could have possibly done such a horrible deed. Finding answers now was all that mattered. She needed an explanation for Lady Gainsborough and her son. This way they could have peace of mind and not live in fear the way she'd been living for the past seven years.

"Did you notice anything odd or interesting regarding the body?" asked Vivienne curiously, glancing over to the table that held the corpse.

"He smells strongly of whisky," said the sheriff. "I do believe that he was deep in his cups when he died."

"Yes. I noticed that too. Her stomach lurched. Witnessing all that blood and the gory state of the dead man only brought back the horrors of seeing her own parents murdered and left for dead. She closed her eyes momentarily and her body swayed. Her hand shot out to cover her queasy stomach. Mayhap the sheriff was right. Perhaps she shouldn't be here, after all. Helping him track down a thief was one thing, but this was totally different. Was investigating this murder going to be too difficult a task for her, considering what she'd been through? Her head said *yes*. Her heart said *no*. She had to push past her fears and do this!

"My lady, are you all right?" Zachariah grabbed her arm to steady her. Vivienne's eyes shot open. Why did his hand on her arm seem to calm her? It almost gave her a fake sense of security, making her believe everything would be all right. "I'll take you back to the keep at once if you'd like. After all, this is really no place for a lady."

"Nay," she protested, letting out a deep breath. She forced a smile and shook her head. "I will be fine. Honest, I will. It is important to me that I stay here. Please, don't send me away."

"Fine. But if you change your mind at any time, Lady Vivienne, you are more than free to go." He slowly released her arm, and with it went the warmth and feeling of strength and security, setting her right back on edge again.

"Yes," she answered after a slight pause. "Thank you. And mayhap you should just call me Vivienne when others are not present. We've known each other since childhood, so there is no need to be so formal, is there?"

"Is that what you want?" He raised a brow. He looked at her with those eyes that seemed to be able to see right into her very soul.

"Of course, it is, Sheriff."

"If that is true, then why are you still calling me Sheriff instead of Zachariah?"

That caused her to smile. He made a good point. Then again, she hadn't called him by his Christian name since they were children. Things changed in both their lives over the years as they grew older. They were not children anymore.

"You're right. I suppose I only do it out of habit. I mean, since you are the sheriff, I want to show respect."

"And since you are a noble, I really need to use your title, no matter what we think. What I do is an example for others. You deserve that respect and I will do anything to make sure you get it."

"Yes, I suppose you're right. If anyone happened to over-hear you, we can't have everyone walking around calling me just Vivienne, can we? My uncle would not be happy about that."

"Mayhap it is best if we keep a formal relationship after all," he suggested. "I mean, perhaps it would be best for both of us. Especially if we are working together. Otherwise, the nobles and everyone might think ... undesirable thoughts about us."

Vivienne knew what he meant. The way tongues wagged around the castle, just working together was probably going to somehow end up as gossip that they are sleeping together too. That wouldn't be good for either of them. She supposed this common sense was good advice. That was one thing she liked about Zachariah. He was always thinking one step ahead.

Since she returned to Mablethorpe, he knew that she wasn't looking for a new love in her life, and especially not a husband. He didn't seem to want to marry again either, since the death of his wife a year ago. Whenever she asked about his loss, he seemed to go silent. All Vivienne knew was that his wife, Margaret, died quickly from an illness she caught. He'd been raising his daughter Starah by himself since then. Mayhap in time, she could have heartfelt talks with him, but for now she decided it was a good idea to keep their relationship professional, and their heads clear.

"You make a good point," she half-heartedly agreed. "God knows the gossipers already have their hands full whispering about me behind my back."

"You don't need any more trouble, Lady Vivienne."

"Neither do you, Sheriff. I don't want to tarnish your respected reputation."

His smiling face turned somber. "I'm not worried about my reputation, only yours," he answered softly, sadness filling his words.

Vivienne thought better of her earlier suggestion. "You're right. We'll continue to use our titles speaking to each other, even in private." She reached out and laid a hand on his shoulder in a gentle touch, then quickly dropped her hand to her side.

"All right then," he said, clearing his throat. "It's time to get back to work."

Vivienne remembered Zachariah as a child. He'd always been such a happy boy filled with curiosity. Together, when she'd visit Mablethorpe, they'd take off on adventures and worry their parents sick when they were gone all day, traipsing through the woods. Zachariah's father had been the sheriff before him, but he died right before all of Vivienne's troubles began. Zachariah had taken over the position of sheriff at the young age of only nineteen. He had been a new father with a wife and baby daughter at the time.

Before then, whenever Vivienne had visited her aunt and uncle in Mablethorpe, she'd see Zachariah at his father's side when they'd visited town. Zachariah was a few years older than she, but that never bothered either of them. Because of Vivienne's outward interest in everything, she had befriended the boy, asking him questions about his father's work. Once, when she was twelve, she even headed to town on her own to visit him. She had been staying with her aunt and uncle for a month at the time, without her parents. Her action had troubled her Aunt Ellen. Her behavior had also caused her uncle to punish her. Still, it was all worth it to her, since she had gone out on her own and felt how freeing it had been. Adventures made Vivienne feel alive. She lived to learn, and wanted to know and do everything she could before her time on this earth was over.

"You don't have to do this," he told her once again. "I don't need your help."

"I understand. But you also know that you're going to get my help, no matter if you want it or not. I feel that I need to do this," she explained. "Nay. It is something I *have* to do."

"Why?"

"I let my family down by never finding out what happened to them," she told him. "The least I can do now is to help someone else who is in the same situation."

"So you've said." He flashed a smile and nodded. "Lady Vivienne, it has been quite a few years now, and I understand your feelings. But mayhap it is time to rid yourself of your guilt and grief concerning the deaths of your parents. You have to understand that you couldn't have done anything to stop it. And also that it wasn't your fault."

She bit at her bottom lip, feeling emotion starting to course through her. "I've heard it said that time heals all wounds, but whoever made that up must have never lost people they loved before." They stared at each other for a moment, before he finally cleared his throat once again and broke the connection between them.

"Let's take a look at the body, shall we?" He headed over to the corpse.

"Yes. That would be good." She followed him over to the table and watched as he inspected first the dead man's head, then his arms. He was careful not to disturb anything, using his fingertips to gently move aside the man's hair or clothes. His perusal led him to scan Lord Gainsborough all the way down to his booted feet. Then he continued by gently patting down the lord's tunic as if he were searching for something.

"What is it you are looking for?" she asked him curiously.

"Nothing and everything," he answered. "I don't see any weapons on him except for this dagger." He pried the dead man's fingers from the hilt. After inspecting the blade he proceeded to pull it out of the body. Vivienne's breath hitched and she quickly diverted her attention elsewhere, not wanting to watch. "Do you remember seeing a sword on Lord Gainsborough before he was murdered?"

"I-I'm not sure," she said, trying to think back to when she spoke with Lord Gainsborough at the foot of the steps. "I don't think so. Actually, I don't even remember him having that dagger, but I'm sure it is his."

"You don't remember?" He looked up and squinted slightly. "That isn't like you, Lady Vivienne. You are normally very observant."

"I am when I'm not upset," she told him. "I was disturbed

at the time that Lord Gainsborough wanted to be alone with me. So you see, I wasn't really looking for weapons."

His eyes met hers and he nodded slightly. "Your emotions got in the way. That can't happen in this business, you realize. Now do you understand why I said this might be too difficult for you?"

"I'm fine, Sheriff Fitch." She crossed her arms over her chest and raised her chin in the air.

"Ah, that defiant stance again," he said with a chuckle. "I never should have stated aloud my concerns. I should have known better that you don't like to be told what to do and will purposely do the opposite just to prove you *can* do it."

"Sheriff, I feel we are wasting precious time with idle chatter. We should get back to the investigation."

"All right then," he said, with a sigh, looking back at the dead man. "It is highly unlikely that a lord would leave his sword somewhere and not keep it with him. Especially when he is not in his own castle."

"If he felt safe and confident, he might have left it in his chamber," she suggested.

"Perhaps. But then again, a sword is a man's most prized possession."

She couldn't help chuckling, and he looked up in question.

"That amuses you for some reason? Don't you agree?"

"For most men, yes, I agree. However, Lord Gainsborough's most prized possessions were how many tarts he could get to share his bed."

"Do you know this for a fact?"

"Everyone knows it."

"Do they? Or have you made your decision on listening to idle gossip?"

"Perhaps you are right," she said, realizing she was no better than the others since she'd formed her impression of

Lord Gainsborough mainly by what she'd heard from others. "My uncle might know more about this than I do."

"Then I will be sure to ask him." The sheriff proceeded to put down the murder weapon on the table and untie the pouch hanging on Gainsborough's belt. "Whoever killed Lord Gainsborough knew just where to stab him so he'd die instantly."

"In the heart," she mumbled.

"Directly in the center of the heart. A fighting man would know where that spot is and what force is needed to embed the blade deep enough."

"A fighting man like a guard or a knight?"

"Yes." He inspected the blade closer.

"Lord Gainsborough would know that, too. Do you suppose he could have taken his own life, after all?" She didn't think so, but wanted to hear the sheriff's opinion.

"Not likely."

"What makes you say that?"

The sheriff cleaned the blood off the blade with his cloth, then positioned the dagger, facing the dead man to demonstrate his point.

"If he were trying to take his own life, he'd have held his hands high in the air to get the force for the blade to enter deep enough. Like here," he said, holding the dagger at the proper angle. The stab would have come from above."

"Yes. That's true."

"However, this thrust came from below, evident by the angle of the dagger before I removed it."

"Yes, I noticed that too. What exactly does it mean?"

"Well, it could mean the killer was shorter than him."

"Or mayhap he fell against the sharp blade held by someone else?"

"It is possible, I suppose. But force would be needed, so only if he were pushed from behind."

"I noticed the flour on his shoes," she told him.

"Aye, I saw that too."

"He was in the kitchens earlier that night. Did you see the wine stains on his fingers and clothes?"

"My, you are observant, after all," he said, seeming impressed.

"Thank you."

"He could have been drinking wine or just spilled it."

"Hmmm," said Vivienne. "Something makes me think there is a different explanation, but I don't know what it is yet."

"By the size of the bump on his head, and the bruise on his jaw, I'd say he was in a confrontation."

"Those marks on his neck look to me like mayhap scratches from someone's fingers."

"I agree." Zachariah dumped out the contents of the dead man's pouch. It was filled with coins. "Well, it wasn't a robbery, since they didn't take his money."

"He is still wearing his rings as well," she pointed out.

"No thief would leave the scene of the crime without first taking the man's wealth."

"Could it have been a robber who didn't have time to take his belongings because Grunt started barking and alerted others?"

"I highly doubt it. Usually robbers take what they want first and only kill afterwards if it's necessary."

"Yes," she said, thinking back on her own experience. Her hand covered the ring hanging from a chain around her neck that stayed hidden by her clothing. She'd never told the sheriff about it, and wondered if she should have. It didn't seem to matter since it most likely had nothing to do with the murder. As far as she knew, no one knew about the ring at the time except for her mother and father.

"When you say they only kill if necessary, what exactly do

you mean?" Vivienne couldn't help but think of that awful night once more. Her parents had seemed to be killed even though it hadn't been necessary. The attackers didn't take her father's sword or any of their belongings. They might have felt threatened by her father, but her mother didn't even have a weapon to fight back. Surely she was no threat at all.

"I'm talking about self-defense," he explained. "Or perhaps because there was a chance they'd be exposed."

"Or possibly the victim knew something he shouldn't have known, and someone didn't want that secret getting out?" She couldn't help thinking how Lord Gainsborough knew she was a bastard to the king, yet her uncle swore he'd never told him.

This was all hitting too close to her heart. She shook her head, not wanting to think about her own woe at a time like this. Not now. Right now, she wanted to focus solely on doing anything she possibly could to help find Lord Gainsborough's murderer. Vivienne swore to herself she wouldn't stop until she did.

"What about those footprints in the blood under the stairs?" she asked.

"What about them?"

"Could they be from whoever killed Lord Gainsborough?"

"They might have been, but now we'll never know. Your uncle had his men move the body. Those footprints could be from any of the men who carried him out."

"Yes, you're right," she said, wishing now she had insisted that everyone stay away from Lord Gainsborough until the sheriff arrived, instead of going up to her chamber to calm down.

"I need to start questioning people," he told her, wiping his hands and throwing down the cloth. "I don't think we're going to find anything on this corpse that will give us more information than we have now."

"I agree. I think something is escaping our attention. That must be the reason for Lord Gainsborough's death in the first place."

"The questioning might shed some light on that. I'll tell your uncle the body can be burned or buried on the morrow. I'm sure Lady Gainsborough will want to collect her husband's jewelry and coins first. However, no one is to leave the castle until they've been cleared by me."

"I'm not sure Lady Gainsborough will want her husband left here at Mablethorpe instead of being brought back to her home."

"It's her choice," he said, heading for the door. "However, I don't know how long the questioning will last, and this corpse is going to start rotting soon. That is something that no one is going to want to smell."

"I will call for Martin to start bringing the guests to the solar for questioning. I will have the steward help as well."

"We'll start with those who are the least likely to have done this. I'll leave you in charge of that." He opened the door to leave. Grunt shot out the door, seeing a squirrel and taking off after it.

"The least likely would be those who were helping put out the fire when the murder was committed," she told him.

"Aye," he answered, stepping outside and looking across the courtyard. "That kennel really burned to the ground," he said, shaking his head. "You might be right that it was done intentionally as a distraction. How much time went by between the start of the fire and the time you found the body?"

"Enough time for someone to get back to the castle and murder a man, I suppose."

"Was everyone helping to put out the fire?"

"There were many, but it is really hard to tell. The fire was strong and it was very smoky. I was lucky to get the rest of the dogs out of the kennel after Adam saved the first ones."

"Adam?"

"The kennel groom," she explained.

"Ah, yes, that's right. Usually my constable is with me to write down names and the facts. Without him, I sometimes feel lost."

"That's why I'm here," she said with a smile.

"Yes, I suppose so." He didn't smile back and she wondered why not. "So, the kennel groom is most likely in the clear since you were witness to him being at the fire."

"Well, not exactly," she said, feeling bad for what she was about to say. After all, Adam was her friend. "I saw Adam at first, but I couldn't find him again after he rescued the first batch of dogs."

"Then he's a suspect," said Zachariah. "I'll question him either way."

"I hardly believe that Adam did it," she said, blowing a small puff of air from her mouth. "After all, he cares about those dogs. More than he cares for himself. He would never set the kennel on fire and endanger the lives of the hunting animals."

"Mayhap not. But we won't know for sure until we question him. Come, there is much work to be done."

Chapter Five

By the end of the day, they had talked with most of the guests at Mablethorpe Castle and they were cleared and allowed to leave.

"Thank you. That is all," said the sheriff to a couple of guests he'd just finished questioning. Mablethorpe's guard, Richard, stood just outside the room at the door. A second guard, Herman from Gainsborough, joined them, to escort those guests from the castle.

"Richard, they are free to go." Vivienne said, after opening the door and thanking the man and woman for their time.

"Yes, my lady," said Richard with a bow.

"Shall I have the page boy bring more people for questioning?" This came from Herman, the guard who was assisting.

"Nay, I believe that is enough for tonight," Zachariah answered from the other side of the room. Vivienne saw him yawn and knew how tired he must be. He had come here directly from town, after attending to another problem. She was sure he hadn't slept at all last night.

"My lady." Vivienne's handmaid approached the door. Herman quickly stepped to the side to let her pass. "My lady, your aunt and uncle have the cooks keeping food hot for you and the sheriff," said Rosina. "They wonder when you will be down. The meal has ended hours ago and most of the castles' occupants have already headed off to bed."

"Thank you, Rosina," she told the girl. "Sheriff, will you join me for something to eat?" Vivienne called across the room.

"I'm too tired to eat, but I suppose it is in order. Yes, I believe I will," Zachariah answered, walking over to join her.

Together with the sheriff, Rosina, and the guard from Gainsborough escorting them, the group headed to the great hall to meet up with Lord and Lady Mablethorpe.

ZACHARIAH WALKED into the great hall with the others, famished and tired as all hell. Today's questioning was disheartening, having brought about no results in the least that would help him to solve this case. Everyone had claimed to know nothing, and to have been somewhere else at the time of the murder. They all had others to vouch for them as well. At least he'd been able to clear out some of the people from the great hall so he could focus on those who might truly be suspects.

"Sheriff, did you discover anything today about Lord Gainsborough's death?" Lord Mablethorpe saw him and came rushing over. His wife, as well as the widow Gainsborough and her son Wilfred were with him.

"Yes, please tell me you found out who killed my husband," said Lady Gainsborough, clutching a piece of cloth that she was using to dry her eyes. It seemed as if the woman never stopped crying.

"I'm sorry, but all information is confidential at this point," he told the little crowd, hoping to quell all the questions and just be able to relax with a tankard of ale and enough food to fill his belly.

"I am his *wife!*" sniffed the widow. "Surely, you can tell me."

"Yes, we are related to the deceased," Wilfred spoke up. "Surely you won't keep secrets from me and my mother."

"I'm not keeping secrets, just doing my job."

"The sheriff is tired and hungry," Vivienne interjected. "We heard there was food being held for us?"

"Aye. It's in the kitchens," said Lady Mablethorpe. "I'll have a server bring it at once."

"Nay." Vivienne held up her hand. "We can eat it in the kitchens, it's not a problem. Right, Sheriff Fitch?"

Vivienne motioned something to him with her eyes, but he wasn't sure what she was trying to silently tell him. Still, it seemed as if she wanted to leave this room and he couldn't be happier. Right now, all he wanted to do was eat and sleep. He'd had his fill of everyone for the day.

"Yes, there's no need to call for a server," he said with a yawn. "I'd prefer to eat in the kitchens, so that is fine."

"But my lady, the nobles eat out here. At the dais," Rosina gently reminded Vivienne.

"That's right," agreed Vivienne's aunt. "However, if my niece and the sheriff would rather eat in the kitchens, then we won't stop them."

"Ellen, what are you saying?" complained Gilbert. "It is not proper for a noble to eat in the kitchens. What will people think?"

"My lord, if I must remind you, I am not a noble," Zachariah pointed out. "I'm sure Lady Vivienne is only thinking of me."

"Yes. That's right, Sheriff. Right this way." Vivienne led the way to the kitchens and he didn't loiter.

"Good night, my lords and ladies." Zachariah half-bowed. "I will be retiring for the evening right after my meal, but will resume working at sunup."

"Thank you, Sheriff," called out Lady Mablethorpe, as Zachariah turned on his heel, anxious to get away.

"Ooomph," he ground out, knocking into someone he didn't even realize was standing there. "I'm sorry," he said, seeing a musician holding a lute. One of the strings was sticking straight out. "Oh, did I break that?" he asked. "I didn't mean to."

"Nay, it wasn't you," said the young man. "Lord Gainsborough broke it yesterday, and because of it I can't play music." His brows dipped in frustration.

"Really." Zachariah found interest in this. "Did Lord Gainsborough offer to replace the string for you? Or at least compensate you with coin to pay for it?" He thought about the amount of coins the man had been carrying on him when he was killed. Surely he had the means to take measures for his clumsy mistake.

"Of course not!" spat the boy. "Lord Gainsborough was rude and uncaring. I'm glad he's dead."

"Now, that's not a good thing to say," Zachariah warned him, wondering why he was being so vocal at a time like this.

"I mean it," said the musician. "I heard he took his own life. I'm sure no one is even going to care."

"You need to speak with respect about the nobles. What is your name?" asked Zachariah.

Now the boy looked frightened. He swallowed forcefully, clutching his broken lute. "I am Leif. Who are you?"

"I am the sheriff who is investigating the possible murder of Lord Gainsborough."

"Murder?" The boy's eyes opened wide.

Damn, he hadn't meant to say that aloud. He'd made a stupid mistake since he was so tired. "Do you live here at the castle, Leif?" He quickly changed the subject.

"Nay, of course not. I'm a traveling jongleur. I only stayed because of the insistence of Lady Mablethorpe, but I'll be leaving on the morrow. I have no working instrument anymore, so there is no need to stay."

"Nay, you won't be leaving," he warned the boy. "No one goes anywhere before I say so. I want to question you first thing in the morning regarding the man's death."

"Me? Why?"

"You do realize that because of what you said to me about the deceased, you are now a suspect in Lord Gainsborough's death."

"What?" spat Leif. "I didn't kill him. The man was a horrible person and everyone says so, not just me. It could have been anyone."

"That's right," said Zachariah. "And it is exactly what I aim to find out. Leif, I will see you at my chamber door first thing in the morning." He left the boy and continued to the kitchens. When he walked in, he saw Vivienne looking for him.

"There you are." She walked over to join him. "I thought you got lost," she said with a giggle.

"Nay. Just distracted by an irate jongleur, that's all."

"Oh, you must mean Leif."

"Do you know him?"

"Yes. Well, nay, not really. Why?"

"He made no secret of his ill feelings toward Lord Gainsborough."

"Oh, that's because of the broken string on his lute, I guess. I promised I'd replace it. I'll see about that tomorrow."

"You? Shouldn't Lord Gainsborough have been the one to offer to replace it?"

That made her laugh, as well as any of the servers standing around who had overheard their conversation.

"The man had tight purse strings," she told him. "He wouldn't pay for anything even if he should have. I swear, the only reason he agreed to have his son marry me was probably because of the dowry my uncle offered."

"Interesting," he mumbled, scratching the back of his neck.

"Sit down, Sheriff. Cook has kept food warm for us." She took his arm and escorted him over to a long wooden table that had a bench on each side. He helped her to sit and then settled himself next to her. When he looked up, he saw every single server, page, cook, and even the scullery maids all looking over and listening. He'd left the curious eyes and ears in the great hall, only managing to trade them for even more in here.

"Shall I have Cook bring the food now, my lady?" asked Vivienne's handmaid.

"Yes, thank you, Rosina," she answered.

Zachariah watched the handmaid head over to a big, bald man standing by the hearth. They spoke in hushed voices. The cook looked over at them and then back to the girl. His hands motioned in the air and it was obvious that he wasn't happy about having had to keep the food warm. Then the handmaid said something else to him and he calmed down.

Zachariah suddenly jerked when he felt something wet on his hand. He looked down and saw Vivienne's hound, and chuckled. "You took me by surprise, Grunt. Don't do that."

"Keep that up, Grunt and he'll be questioning you next," Vivienne said, reaching down to pet her dog.

"Mayhap that's not a bad idea," he said, as Rosina and another kitchen maid laid wooden plates of food down in front of them. "After all, Grunt here might just know who the killer is, since he's the one who led you to the body."

The servant with Rosina looked up in surprise. "Really,

Sheriff? Do you think the dog will be able to identify the murderer?"

"Anything's possible, Maria," said Vivienne, picking up her spoon. "After all, I'm sure if Grunt gets a scent, he can track anyone down. He has helped do so in the past when I assisted the sheriff with a robbery in town. Sheriff, mayhap we should let Grunt sniff the body again before the corpse is buried or burned. There could be the killer's scent on Lord Gainsborough's clothes."

"That's a thought, but I am done talking about the investigation for the night." He picked up a piece of bread and took a big bite.

"I'll get ale," offered Rosina.

"Never mind, I have it." Cook put down two tankards of ale in front of them. "Now, if you'll not be needing anything else, Lord Mablethorpe is waiting for me to bring him some wine."

"Yes, I am," said Vivienne's uncle from behind them. Wilfred was with him. "Did I hear you say something about letting my niece's dog sniff the clothes of the deceased?"

"Yes, I did," admitted Zachariah, knowing that everyone in the kitchens also heard him just by the way they were watching from the corner of their eyes. He really needed to be more careful. Being so tired was making him careless with what he said aloud to Vivienne.

"Perhaps we can have our wine in here and converse with the sheriff about my father," suggested Wilfred.

The kitchen wench named Maria came over and put two fruit tarts in front of them. "Will there be anything else?" asked the girl.

"Perhaps you can get Lord Mablethorpe some wine, Maria," Vivienne told her.

"Nay. We're going to drink our wine in the great hall in a

minute," announced Lord Mablethorpe. "Where nobles belong."

Hearing him say this made Zacharia wonder why he and Wilfred were even in the kitchens at all.

"Thank you, Maria," said Vivienne. "Please bring a decanter of wine and some goblets to the great hall for my uncle and Lord Gainsborough, at once."

"Yes, my lady," said the girl with a quick curtsy. She was a busty wench, and wore her gown too tight, showing off too much cleavage. Zachariah thought the girl was just asking for trouble.

"Is my father's body still in the smokehouse?" Wilfred asked him.

"Yes. You and your mother are free to take his jewelry and his pouch of coins on the morrow. Leave the dagger for now," he told them. "Oh, that reminds me, I'll need to switch out the guard posted at the smokehouse door since he's been there so long."

"I'll have my guard, Herman, take his place for now," offered Wilfred.

"That would be fine, thank you," Vivienne told him.

"When can we bring Father home?" asked Lord Wilfred.

"Not yet," Zachariah told him as he chewed his bread. "I'll let you know when I am finished."

"Thank you," said Lord Mablethorpe, turning to leave.

"One more thing." Zachariah held his finger in the air. "Do either of you know if Lord Gainsborough had any other weapons on him besides the dagger?"

"Nay, he didn't," said Lord Mablethorpe. "He was attending a celebration and we were about to eat, followed by dancing. I am sure he left his sword in his chamber."

"And the dagger. Was it his?"

Lord Mablethorpe looked over to the dead man's son. "Was, it, Wilfred?"

Wilfred seemed to become suddenly uneasy, shifting his weight and running a hand over his hair. "Of course, I didn't see it clearly, but I believe so. I mean, he always carried his dagger on him."

"Can you describe it?"

"Really, Sheriff, can't this wait until the morrow?" grumbled Lord Mablethorpe. "Everyone is tired of all this questioning and we just want to relax."

"Of course," he answered. "Until the morrow, then."

They started to walk away, but Wilfred turned back. "His dagger had our family crest on the hilt. A rampant wolf outlined by ivy. Was that the dagger that was embedded in his chest?"

Zachariah put down his bread, taking a drink of ale before answering. "Yes. That is the one. Thank you, Lord Wilfred."

"Glad I could be of help."

Once Wilfred left, Zachariah turned to Vivienne, speaking softly so everyone couldn't hear. "How well do you know Lord Wilfred?"

"Not that well since he is always so quiet. Why do you ask?"

"He seemed to be acting odd, didn't he?"

"He did seem nervous, but he is always like that. Or at least ever since I've known him."

"What about the servants?"

"What about them?" she asked, taking a bite of food.

"In your opinion, are any of them capable of murder?"

"I can't really answer that, but I don't believe so."

"What about Cook? Or that busty maid servant, Maria?"

"Sheriff?" Vivienne looked at him oddly and blinked several times in succession.

"How long has Rosina been your handmaid? What do you know about her?"

Vivienne frowned. "I thought you said you didn't want to talk about this anymore tonight. You said you wanted to relax. I think all the questioning can wait until morning, don't you? Especially since everyone is on edge and most of them can still hear every word we say. Not to mention you are accusing each one of them right now. Do you really think that is wise?"

"I'm sorry. You're right." He picked up his tankard and downed the rest of his ale.

"You seem so desperate to solve this case that everyone is a suspect to you. Next, you'll be accusing Grunt of killing the man."

Zachariah looked down to see Grunt's chin on his leg. The dog whined softly and looked up at him with sad eyes.

"Grunt, stop begging," scolded Vivienne. "I'm sorry, Sheriff. He is still sore at Cook for not giving him a soup bone. I did promise him one for finding the body, but Cook isn't in a good mood so I won't ask him about it until morning."

"No harm done," said Zachariah, taking a big bite of the venison and then putting his plate with the rest of his food on the bench. "Grunt can have my food as a reward. I think I'm done here. I'm going to retire now. Good night."

Grunt eagerly gobbled down the food. Cook looked over at the dog and started cursing.

"I think I am finished too," said Vivienne, jumping to her feet. "Come on, Grunt. If we stay here any longer, Cook might be coming after you with his cleaver again."

"Again?" Zachariah looked back at her, but then raised his hand in the air and shook his head. "Never mind. It can wait until the morning. Good night, Lady Vivienne."

"I'm sure things will go better with the search on the morrow," she told him, following him with Grunt on her heels.

"Aye," he said with a nod. "I'd like to take a close look at the kennels tomorrow, as well as to question the kennel groom, the cook, the kitchen servants, and even your handmaid."

"My handmaid?" asked Vivienne, not seeming too happy with the suggestion. "Surely, you can't suspect her of murder. She is as harmless as a mouse."

"Everyone is a suspect until proven otherwise," he answered.

"Even me?" Vivienne asked, giving him a look that could kill.

"Nay, my dear. Not you," he said quietly, knowing by rights he should consider her a suspect since she was the one who found the body. No one was with her at the time except for her hound. Still, he knew her better than that. Vivienne would never harm anyone. Even now, she went out of her way to help others when she didn't have to do so. Plus, her family's own murders terrified her so much that he was surprised she didn't faint every time she even saw blood. "Vivienne, I mean, Lady Vivienne, there is something else I'd like to say."

She approached and looked up at him with her curious blue eyes that reminded him of a bird. "Me too," she said. "I wanted to thank you for letting me assist you with this murder investigation. It really helps me feel better about things. I mean, since I wasn't able to find my own parents' murderers, this helps me to feel like I am doing something good."

"Of course," he said, feeling so choked right now.

"What was it you wanted to say to me, Sheriff?"

How could he tell her now that he wasn't sure she should be helping? It seemed to make her feel good about herself. Her assistance with his case brought back the life in her eyes again. He'd never felt like such a failure as when he couldn't help the one person who had always been there for him throughout his life. Yes, Lady Vivienne Harlowe was a true friend. Vivienne had never given up hope when his wife was sick and dying. She would tell him that he needed to have faith that Margaret would pull through. He didn't, and she hadn't. Still, Vivienne stuck by him and his daughter, Starah, acting more like a parent to the little girl at the time than he. He didn't really want her helping him with this investigation, because he was afraid something might happen to her and he didn't want her to get hurt. But he couldn't tell her this now. Not after what she'd just said to him.

"Sheriff?" she asked again, pushing a long strand of blonde hair behind her ear. "Was there something you wanted to say to me?"

"Yes." He looked the other way, losing all nerve now. "Constable Dorson will be here assisting me tomorrow."

"Oh. I see." Her disposition changed quickly. Vivienne looked down to her dog, busying herself by scratching his ears. "So, are you trying to tell me that you won't be needing my help, after all?"

He hesitated before he answered, seeing the disappointment on her face. He felt like moat scum right now, and couldn't get his tongue to form the words. "Nay. I didn't mean that at all," he told her, forcing a smile. He reached out to touch her on the arm. He truly did like her being near him. How could he ever want to push her away? "It's just that with the three of us ..." His head said to dismiss her, but his heart said not to do it.

"Go ahead," she said, her face becoming stone-like. He reminded himself that if he said *no*, she'd take that as a challenge. He also realized that having her near him, he'd be better able to protect her and keep an eye on her. "Finish your sentence," she told him.

"I just wanted to say that with the three of us working together, it'll move things along faster, that's all."

Her head snapped up, and once again the smile returned to her eyes as well as to her entire face. "I think that would be a splendid idea to include Constable Dorson in the investigation, Sheriff Fitch. After all, seeking justice is what's important here. For that, we can use all the help we can get. Good night, then. I'll be eagerly awaiting you and your constable at the kennels in the morning."

Chapter Six

Vivienne tossed and turned all night long, unable to sleep. Or perhaps it was really that she didn't want to sleep because she knew as soon as she drifted off, she'd have that horrible nightmare once again. Sure enough, when she did finally drift off, she was back on the road as a sixteen-year-old new mother, and she couldn't make the nightmare stop.

Gripping the hilt of her father's sword with two hands, Vivienne slowly stepped around the front of the wagon, just in time to see a shadowy figure stab her mother with his sword and then throw her body to the ground. Too scared to even speak, she froze. Standing in the dark, fear consumed her, making her feel as if she were in hell.

"Someone's coming. Hurry, let's get out of here," came the voice of another shadowy form atop a horse. The man who stabbed her mother withdrew his sword and headed toward his waiting horse.

"Mother! Nay!" screamed her little brother. Vivienne's head snapped around to see Adrian standing in the hay in the back of the wagon, looking over the edge, terror on his face.

"Dammit. There's someone else," shouted the first bandit to the second.

"Kill him, too," commanded the ruffian's companion. "Leave no witnesses."

The first man rushed over, but Vivienne wasn't about to let him kill her brother too. Guilt already ate away at her that she wasn't able to save her parents. She stepped out in front of the attacker, wildly swinging her father's sword in the air. Mayhap it was her anger controlling her actions, but somehow she managed to stab the man on his right shoulder with her blade. The tip stuck into his flesh and she was sure she felt the blade meet his bone. Quickly, she pulled the blade back, seeing the blood oozing from the man's wound.

"Aaaaah!" the attacker screamed, one hand gripping at his bleeding shoulder from where Vivienne had struck him.

"Dammit, there's a girl here too," shouted the other man from his horse.

The fighting frightened the horses, causing them to rear up and paw at the air, whinnying loudly. The wagon jerked and her brother fell back in the hay with his feet in the air. Then the horses took off down the road at a run, pulling the wagon along with them. The sound of Vivienne's crying baby from the bench seat inside the basket caused her to panic and become furious all at the same time. Even in her weakened state from just having given birth, Vivienne's motherly instincts kicked in and she fought like a lion. She started swinging the sword wildly at her attacker as she lunged forward, stabbing at him over and over again. All the while she gritted her teeth. No one was going to kill any of her family and get away with it! She was so angry right now, that she wasn't even scared. She wanted both of these bandits to die.

"You bastard! I'll kill you for what you've done," she shouted, causing him to actually back away from her now. His *sword dangled from his fingers as he gripped his bleeding sword arm which she had injured. God's eyes, she wished she had severed his arm altogether.*

"Let's go," called out the man's friend from his steed. "Someone's coming."

The man she'd struck mumbled something under his breath that she couldn't decipher, but it sounded as if he said the words, 'too soon.' He then turned and ran, mounting his horse, and taking off with his friend, leaving her stranded all alone.

"Vivienne," came her mother's soft cry from the ground. Vivienne spun on her heel and ran to her mother, dropping the sword and falling to her knees at her mother's side.

"Mother!" she cried, cradling the woman's head atop her lap. "They killed Father. And the horses ran off with Adrian and my baby." Tears gushed from her eyes as she looked down at her mother bathed in the scant light of the partial moon that broke through the clouds. "Mother, please don't die too! Do not leave me, I beg you. I need you!" Vivienne said the words, but knew that all the wishing in the world wasn't going to change what happened here tonight. Blood covered her mother who clutched her abdomen and moaned in pain. There was no use denying that she was not going to live. Her mother lifted her hand, yanking at a chain around her neck until the chain released. Then she slowly held out her closed fist to Vivienne.

"Take ... this ... Daughter. For you ... and the baby."

"Mother, what are you doing? What do you mean?"

"Listen ... to ... me."

"I need to get you help. I think I hear horses coming down the road. I'll signal to the riders." She started to stand, but her mother's hand on her arm stopped her.

"Too ... late," came her mother's soft reply as her eyes started to close. "Go to ... your father. He ... will protect ... you ... and the ... babe."

"Mother, didn't you hear me? Father is dead!" she screamed. "I can't go to him for help. It's too late! I need to find Adrian and my baby."

"Wait." Her mother opened her fist and Vivienne looked down to see a gold ring with a ruby gemstone embedded in it dangling from the chain. It was something her mother had been wearing around her neck, although Vivienne had never known it. "This is ... your father's."

"Mother, what you saying?" Vivienne cried. "You are delirious from the pain. Father doesn't have a ring like this. He is only a poor foot soldier." She picked it up with two fingers, taking a better look at it in the moonlight. "This is gold. With a ruby! It must belong to a very rich noble, or mayhap even a king."

"Yes. King ... Edward. He's your ... father. Don't ... tell ... a ... soul."

"M—my father?" Vivienne thought for a moment that she had heard wrong. "Mother, what did you say? You are hurt and talking nonsense. Mother, can you hear me?"

Her mother became deathly still. When the light of the moon broke through the clouds once again, spilling over her, Vivienne saw that she stared up at her with open eyes that held no life at all within them. Just like her father. Now her mother was drained of all life too. There was no doubt in Vivienne's mind that she was dead. She had just lost both her parents in a matter of minutes. This couldn't be happening. She had to find Adrian and the baby. Bid the devil, her stomach ached and her body started shaking. She looked down to see blood on her gown and it wasn't from her parents or the man she'd stabbed. It was a result of giving birth and still not being healed. Her head dizzied. The sound of approaching hoofbeats pounding on the earth echoed in her head. Then, she felt as if she couldn't breathe and everything went black around her.

. . .

VIVIENNE'S EYES sprang open and she gasped for air. Her stomach twisted. It was almost as if she felt the pain and lack of air that her mother must have experienced at the end of her life. Not to mention she was reliving that day when she passed out on the road after all these terrible things happened. Her heart pounded like a drum. Panic as well as grief coursed through her. A slight film of perspiration dampened her brow, and her legs shook.

"My lady? Are you having that nightmare again?" Rosina hurried across the room and yanked open the shutters covering the window, letting the morning light as well as fresh air into her bedchamber. "Are you ill?" she asked from her position by the window, stretching her neck, looking out to the courtyard as she spoke.

Vivienne found herself clutching the king's ring that she'd worn on a chain around her neck for the last seven years. It was the same ring that her dying mother had given her, right after telling her that she was a bastard child of King Edward III. Opening her fingers, Vivienne stared at the ring with the ruby stone that reflected the morning light. It almost seemed to wink at her, as if it was assuring her that everything would be all right. The ring with the king's crest of three lions on it embossed into the solid gold, felt warm and somehow filled with life. She didn't understand it at all.

"What's that you're holding?" Rosina stretched her neck, looking over toward the bed.

"Nothing," Vivienne answered, quickly tucking the ring back under her nightrail to keep it from being seen.

"Let me help you dress, my lady." Rosina walked to the wardrobe.

"You know I prefer to dress myself." Vivienne couldn't take

the chance of anyone seeing the ring, so she'd always dressed herself, refusing her handmaid's assistance.

"As you wish. But you'd better hurry." Rosina gathered up Vivienne's russet gown made of taffeta from the wardrobe, heading back with it in her arms. "This might be nice to wear today."

"That's one of my best gowns, Rosina." Vivienne yawned and stretched. "You know I only wear that on special occasions."

"Today is a special occasion."

"By the rood, what now?" Vivienne threw her legs over the side of the bed, hoping to hell it wasn't a holy day. Or at least not another one of her uncle's ridiculous gatherings.

"Aren't you supposed to meet up with Sheriff Fitch this morning? I thought I heard you talking about it in the kitchens last night."

"Yes, I am." It was clear to Vivienne now that every servant in the kitchens knew her plans. Now, Vivienne was glad and she and the sheriff hadn't discussed the servants and their loyalty last night, or their possible ability to murder a man. If they had, each of her servants would probably not be speaking to her this morning.

"I just saw the sheriff out the window. He is already at the kennels looking around," reported Rosina.

"Oh no! I overslept." Vivienne shot out of bed, grabbing the gown that Rosina offered.

"I really wish you'd let me help you dress just once. After all, it is my job, my lady. I'd like to know I'm useful to you."

"Nay. I'm fine, but thank you. And you know how much I value you, Rosina. You have always cared about me more than anyone. I think of you not only as my handmaid, but someone who is starting to turn into a good friend as well."

"Thank you for saying that, my lady." The girl was so touched by this that she wiped a tear from her eye.

Vivienne dressed, making sure to keep the ring hidden, since her mother's dying words were to keep it a secret. The only people who knew about the ring were Vivienne's aunt and uncle. Her only remaining family. Ever since the night they found her lying on the road along with her dead parents, they had cared for her, making her their ward.

Vivienne trusted them, so she'd told them everything that happened that night. In her fragile state, she'd needed shoulders to cry on, and her aunt and uncle gave her just that.

"Rosina, please run down to the kennels, or should I say what is left of the kennels. Tell the sheriff that I will be with him shortly."

"Aye, my lady." Rosina curtsied and hurried out the door.

Vivienne walked over and looked out the window to see the sheriff standing with a constable outside of the burnt kennels. Adam was there talking with them as well. He looked stiff and uncomfortable. That told Vivienne that the kennel groom was most likely being bombarded with questions from the sheriff and his constable. She needed to hurry and get down there to help poor Adam. Grunt sniffed around the ground at Adam's feet. Vivienne really wanted to know what they were all talking about, and cursed herself for sleeping so late. She needed to hurry.

Just as Vivienne had finished dressing, there came a knock at her door.

"Just a moment," she called out, picking up her boar's-bristle brush, running it through her hair as she made her way to the door. The knocking continued. "I said, just a minute." She pulled the door open and her jaw dropped. There stood Lady Gainsborough all by herself. Her hair was mussed and there was dirt on the front of her gown.

"Lady Gainsborough? What are you doing here? What happened to you?"

"I need to talk to you, Lady Vivienne." Her eyes moved back and forth as she looked first in one direction down the corridor and then the opposite way. "Something awful has happened. I wasn't sure where to go or whom to tell, so I came directly to you."

Vivienne looked up and down the corridor as well, but didn't see anyone. Not even the lady's son or her guard. Odd, she thought. Lady Gainsborough never went anywhere unescorted. "Are you here all by yourself, my lady?"

"I am," said answered, looking as if she'd been crying. Her eyes were swollen and had red rings around them. Her nose was red as well. She sniffled a little.

"Come in." Vivienne opened the door wider, allowing her to enter the room. She really didn't have time for this, but Lady Gainsborough seemed distressed. It was as if she had something of importance to tell Vivienne, so she couldn't just turn her away. "Please, sit down." She pulled out a chair, offering the seat to the widow.

"I'll only stay a moment since I am sure Wilfred will be worried sick about me when he discovers I am gone." The woman fanned herself with her handcloth, using it to brush off the chair, then settled her round body atop it.

"Yes, I'm sure he will be." Vivienne put down her brush and came and sat next to her in another chair, wondering why Lady Gainsborough hadn't told her son where she was going. "Is there something I can help you with, my lady?"

"I shouldn't have gone there, but I just had to, you see."

"Gone? Where did you go?"

The woman gripped the square of cloth tightly in her hands, twisting it as she spoke. Vivienne noticed that it looked wet. And dirty. "I wanted to go by myself, because I wanted privacy."

"I'm sorry, Lady Gainsborough, but if you want my help then you are going to have to give me a bit more information."

"Oh, yes. Sorry." She let out a big sigh. "I suppose I'm not making much sense, am I?"

"No, not at all."

"I'll start from the beginning then, I guess."

"That's a good place to start." Vivienne heard Grunt barking outside. Her head turned and she tried to listen through the open window but couldn't hear conversations this far up. What she really wanted to do was to jump up and run over to look out the window. But she didn't. Not with Lady Gainsborough here and in this condition. "Continue, please."

"Lady Vivienne, I awoke early this morning before sunup. I couldn't sleep because I'd been thinking about my husband." She dabbed a corner of the cloth to one eye and then the other.

"Of course. That is understandable." Vivienne smiled and looked at her, but then her attention went back to the open window. What was happening out there? She hoped the sheriff would wait for her and that Rosina had told him that she'd be there momentarily. With the widow taking up her time, Vivienne felt like she'd never get there. She had to urge her on. "Then what happened? Please, just speak freely. Tell me everything."

"I had to see him, Lady Vivienne." The woman started to cry again, making Vivienne feel as if they'd never leave the room now. "I just had to go to his side, even though it was still dark."

"Are you saying you went out to the smokehouse to see your dead husband?" Just the thought of it sent a shiver up Vivienne's spine.

"I did."

"Lady Gainsborough, why on earth would you do such a thing? Now tell me, why did you go there by yourself? And in the dark? That is dangerous. You could have asked any of the guards or even your son to escort you."

"Nay, I couldn't," she said, looking down to her lap and twisting that damn rag again.

"Why not?"

"Because ... because I wanted to tell my poor husband how sorry I was for not trusting him around you."

"Around me?" That took Vivienne by surprise. Out of all the things she thought the woman might say, this was surely unexpected. "I'm sorry, my lady, but I really don't understand what you are trying to tell me."

"Lady Vivienne, my husband was a ... skirt-chaser." The woman whispered the last word as if she were ashamed to say it aloud, or feared that someone might hear her. Not that everyone didn't already know this, but Vivienne wasn't going to be the one to tell her so.

"So you think your husband was being unfaithful to you?" Her husband was a cur and always chasing after anyone who wore a skirt. Even without listening to gossip, Vivienne could see this for herself. Still, Vivienne had to ask questions, prompting Lady Gainsborough to spill her secrets. Mayhap something she would say could aid in helping to find her husband's killer.

Lady Gainsborough rolled her eyes and sniffed at Vivienne's question. "Don't pretend you don't know, because it insults me. Everyone knew it but me." So, it seemed the woman did know after all.

"My lady, I admit to hearing gossip about your late husband, but I'm sure not everyone believed it."

Lady Gainsborough narrowed her eyes, glaring at Vivienne now.

"I mean, not really." This was becoming an uncomfortable situation and Vivienne wanted to be anywhere right now but here. This was almost as bad as having to attend one of her uncle's gatherings. Grunt barked again, the sound echoing in the courtyard, making Vivienne wonder if her dog was trying to tell the sheriff something. If so, he'd never understand. She really needed to get down there.

"Let's speak plainly, shall we?" snapped Lady Gainsborough.

"I'd like nothing more."

"I thought my husband Dinadan wanted you, but I realize now that I was wrong."

"I see." Vivienne had thought the same thing, until she'd found out differently from her uncle that he'd only wanted to tell her about the betrothal. Lord Gainsborough had always eyed up women like he wanted to rut with them in the dirt. It was a normal expression for him, so what was she supposed to think? Then again, it no longer mattered. The man was dead now. Perhaps they should leave it alone. "It's in the past, my lady. We need not talk about it any longer."

"Lady Vivienne, I want you to know that I was not privy to the knowledge that my husband had made an alliance with your uncle. I had no idea they planned to wed you to my dear son, Wilfred."

"You aren't the only one," Vivienne commented under her breath. She truly wondered why the woman's husband hadn't told her. She also was still wondering why the woman had come to her door today in the first place.

"I felt guilty when I discovered Dinadan only wanted to walk alone with you in the garden to tell you about the betrothal, and for no other reason at all," Lady Gainsborough continued.

"You felt *guilty*?" That seemed like an odd word for her to use. Or mayhap Vivienne's head was just too wrapped up with finding the guilty person that she was starting to get like the sheriff last night, suspecting everyone. "What do you mean you felt guilty? Can you explain?" Vivienne looked at her from the corner of her eyes, half-expecting the woman to admit to having killed her husband, but she didn't.

"I felt guilty for telling Wilfred I didn't want him to marry you because you were a ... a ... whore." She quickly looked the other away, her face becoming a bright shade of red.

"What!" Vivienne jumped up, highly insulted. She would not sit there a moment longer and be called a whore to her face. It infuriated her so much that she wanted to throw the noblewoman out of her chamber and tell her to never return. "Lady Gainsborough, I don't know where you got that idea, but it is the furthest thing from the truth! I'll have you know I was married once and even had a baby. But I lost everyone I ever loved. I assure you, I do not give of myself freely to every man who passes by, especially not your husband! So please get that idea out of your head right now."

Lady Gainsborough's thin brows arched in surprise. She started to fan herself again with the handcloth. "You were married? Really? And you had a baby? This is news to me. Where are your husband and baby now?"

Vivienne groaned inwardly. In her hurry to defend her reputation, she'd been careless. Everyone knew about her parents being murdered, but the rest of Vivienne's sad personal story was not common knowledge. Neither did she ever want it to be. Now, because of her emotions, she was sure all her personal business would be on the tips of wagging tongues of everyone from alewives to the nobles to the servants on the morrow. Vivienne felt doomed. Oversleeping was causing her lots of problems this morning. First, she almost let her hand-maid see her ring, then she was missing her meeting with the sheriff, and now she had accidentally told a woman who thought she was a whore the sad story of her life, when it was none of the woman's business. If she had been just a little quicker, she wouldn't have been in her room to open the door when Lady Gainsborough came calling. Vivienne needed to work on her timing, that was for certain.

"Excuse me, my lady, but I have an appointment I need to keep. You'll have to leave now because I am already late and must go."

"Mmmph," sniffed Lady Gainsborough, wrinkling her nose and pursing her lips as she slowly pushed up off the chair and got to her feet. "Your appointment is with that meddlesome sheriff, isn't it?"

"Meddlesome?" That was another odd thing for her to say. "Yes, it is. And may I point out that Sheriff Fitch is working hard and actively looking for your husband's murderer. I'd hardly refer to that as being meddlesome. Now, I will ask you once again to please leave my chamber."

The woman's pinched face slowly softened. The tears were back in her eyes, almost as if she could cry on command. "I am sorry, Lady Vivienne. Please forgive me. I know you're right about the sheriff. He is doing what he can. I suppose I am just so rattled and filled with grief about what happened this morning, that I'm not thinking straight, that's all." The woman crossed the floor and was about to walk out the door when Vivienne stopped her.

"Wait a minute," she said, keeping her from leaving. "What exactly is it that happened this morning? You never told me."

"I've been trying to tell you, but you are not making it easy." The woman wiped her brow with her handcloth.

"I apologize to you as well, Lady Gainsborough. I suppose I am a little on edge this morning. Please, tell me. I'd really like to know." Vivienne held the door, blocking the way back into the room, not wanting her to wander inside and sit down again. If so, she'd never get out of here. She needed to end this as quickly as possible.

"When I entered the smokehouse this morning, I found my husband's body."

"Yes. That is where he was laid out. You know that."

Her eyes opened wide. "Mayhap so, but surely at the time he was not naked!"

"Naked?" asked Vivienne. "What are you talking about?"

"My husband was naked, Lady Vivienne. Surely you know what that means, unless you are a simpkin. The man was not wearing any clothes."

"Are you sure? That is not the way the sheriff and I left him last evening."

"Of course I'm sure," she snapped. "Don't you think I know what a naked man looks like? There was only a cloak covering his naked body, the poor man. Are you doubting my word?"

"That's not what I mean, Lady Gainsborough. Oh, never mind. Thank you for telling me. I will let the sheriff know about it." She tried to squeeze out the door to close it behind her, but Lady Gainsborough's large frame blocked the way.

"Wait. There is more," said the woman, holding up her hand. She glanced one way down the corridor and then the other.

"What is it now?" Vivienne was starting to wonder why Lady Gainsborough couldn't have revealed all this at once? Mayhap she was purposely trying to distract her for some reason, or perhaps keep her from her meeting with the sheriff.

Lady Gainsborough leaned her heavy body forward and whispered to Vivienne behind her hand. "When I was in the smokehouse, I heard a noise."

"A noise? What kind of noise, my lady?"

"It sounded like shuffling feet or someone walking. When I

called out to see if anyone was there, I was attacked in the dark."

"Attacked? Why didn't you tell me this right away? What happened?"

"Someone ran out of the smokehouse, knocking me to the ground."

"Did they hurt you?"

"Not really."

"Did they take anything from you?"

"Well, no."

"That doesn't sound like anyone was attacking you, Lady Gainsborough. It just sounds like you surprised someone and they knocked into you being in a hurry to get out of there and not be caught."

"Mayhap, but I doubt it."

"Why do you say that?"

"I say that, because the man was obviously there to steal something from my dead husband. Thank goodness I was able to get the rings off Dinadan's fingers and the coins from his pouch before they could take it all from me." Vivienne noticed the woman said take it from *me*, and not *him*.

So, that is why she was there. Now the truth came out.

"You went to the smokehouse to collect your husband's things?"

"Yes. The sheriff said it was permitted to do so, as long as I left his dagger."

"Why didn't you wait for your son to go with you?"

"He was sleeping and I didn't want to wake him."

"Why didn't you wait until first light then?"

"Wait?" She threw Vivienne a disgruntled look. "As you see, I was almost too late as it was, Lady Vivienne. The thief almost got my poor, dead husband's riches. I am just glad I decided to go to the smokehouse when I did."

"When you took your husband's rings and coins, his clothes were already gone then, right?" She tried to make sense out of this odd situation.

"Yes, I told you that already. Don't you listen when I talk? There was just a lady's cloak covering his naked body, but he was wearing nothing else."

It was her cloak, but she wasn't going to point out that fact to the woman. It would probably only make her think that she was a whore again somehow, so Vivienne stayed silent about it.

"I'll go now, and take no more of your time." Lady Gainsborough sighed and turned away.

Vivienne shook her head, not understanding any of this. If a thief was hiding inside the smokehouse, why hadn't he taken the jewels and coins before Lady Gainsborough got there? And why were her husband's clothes missing? No thief would want the torn and bloodied clothes off a dead man's body. Would they? Then, Vivienne remembered something. She and the sheriff were talking in the kitchens last night about having Grunt sniff the dead man's clothes to possibly track down the killer. Perhaps the killer was in the room at the time and wanted to destroy the evidence.

"Did you by chance see who your assailant was?" she asked.

"Yes, I think so." The plump woman raised her double chin in the air and looked down her nose as she answered. "It was dark and smoky in there, so it was hard to see, but I am sure the man wore a cloak with a hood covering his head. I could also tell he was big and bulky."

"Well, that could be anyone."

"Nay, not anyone. I smelled the strong scent of garlic on the robber. And when he knocked into me, his hood fell and I am sure he was bald. It was that big, bald cook from the kitchens. You know who I mean. The man who is always waving around his cleaver in the air and cursing at the top of his lungs."

"You mean Cook?" Vivienne's attention heightened at hearing this bit of information. Mayhap the woman had been of help after all. "Are you sure it was him, Lady Gainsborough? After all, this is a serious accusation."

"I said it was him, didn't I?" She sounded angrier than she ought to be. "I know what I saw so why don't you believe me?"

"I'm sorry. Yes, I believe you. What do you mean it was smoky? Cook isn't smoking any meat in there right now."

"How should I know? But it was so smoky that I had to cover my nose with my handcloth. That made it hard to collect my poor husband's things."

"Thank you, Lady Gainsborough. I promise I will look into this situation with the sheriff at once."

"Thank you, my dear." The woman patted her hair into place. "Oh, and please don't mention this incident to my son. Wilfred has a weak heart. I wouldn't want to worry him."

"Thank you, Lady Gainsborough," said Vivienne, reaching to the hook on the wall for her cloak, but her hand came up empty since her cloak was covering a dead man right now. She left the room, having another thought. "Lady Gainsborough," she called out, running down the corridor to catch up with the woman.

"What is it, my dear?" The woman no longer seemed to be crying. She almost seemed to have a slight grin on her face, but then it dissolved quickly.

"Wasn't there a guard at the door of the smokehouse when you went out there?"

"Nay. There was no guard," she said.

"But last night your son said he'd get your guard, Herman, from Gainsborough, to relieve the Mablethorpe guard posted at the door."

"Oh, Herman was there for a while." She waved a hand through the air. "I had Wilfred dismiss him late last night. After all, we didn't see a need to have him stay awake all night to protect a dead body. It just didn't make good sense." She shrugged.

"You shouldn't have done that, as is now evident. If so, the attacker wouldn't have been in the smokehouse when you entered. Besides, it was by the sheriff's order that a guard stay posted at the door. You and your son had no right to go against Sheriff Fitch's orders."

"Oh, my. I didn't realize we were doing anything wrong." Her hand went to her mouth. The woman truly looked sorry. "Herman is important to me. To all of us at Gainsborough. He needed to eat and sleep, just as well as the rest of us did. He has always been like one of the family. I just couldn't leave him out there all night long."

"If you were going to dismiss your guard, you needed to tell me. I would have ordered one of Mablethorpe's guards to take his place."

"I'm sorry. I will remember that from now on. I suppose I wasn't thinking clearly and I made a mistake. You are right. If Herman or another guard had been there, that rotten cook wouldn't have stolen my husband's clothes. Good day."

"Good day," Vivienne answered with a sigh, feeling more confused than ever. She could see now why the sheriff was acting like he suspected everyone. It was because there was so many crazy things happening, that it did make everyone look guilty. She needed to get this information to the sheriff right away and mayhap they could figure it out together.

"Good morning, Lady Vivienne," Zachariah greeted her as she walked up to the kennels. "I'd like you to meet Constable Dorson. He will be working with me today."

"Nice to meet you, Constable Dorson." Vivienne bent over to pet Grunt, noticing that the sheriff had said the constable would be working with *him*, not *them*. That told her that Zachariah Fitch still did not consider her an equal in this murder investigation. Most men wouldn't consider a woman as a partner, she supposed, so she shouldn't be surprised by his action. But they were friends. He had given her his word. She had thought he was different than most men. Perhaps he had her fooled, just like the killer had everyone fooled right now. Looking over at her kennel groom, she greeted him as well. "Good morning, Adam."

Grunt left her and ran over to Adam with his tail wagging. Adam ignored the dog.

"My lady." Adam didn't sound happy at all. He couldn't even look at her, and that disturbed her since they'd always been on good terms with each other.

"Were you able to inspect the kennels?" Vivienne asked Zachariah, trying to break the feeling of tension in the air between everyone.

"Yes," he answered. "And we believe the fire was set intentionally."

"We found the spot where it all started," said the constable. "It looks like tallow was used to ignite the flames."

"Animal fat? Really?" This made her think that someone with access to the kitchens could be involved after all, since tallow was used for cooking. It was also used to make candles, or soap that was used for bathing, scrubbing dirty pots and pans, or even washing laundry. Even healers used tallow in making balm for the skin.

"Since it was animal fat, which I don't use with the hounds, why aren't you in the kitchens questioning the cooks instead of bothering me?" grunted Adam. "The evidence is right there. I think the answer is obvious."

"Adam? Are you all right?" asked Vivienne, noticing his rigid body and the way he snapped at everyone this morning.

"Nay, not really, my lady." He crossed his arms over his chest. Grunt nuzzled Adam's leg with his nose. "It seems the sheriff here tells me that he heard from you that I wasn't present at the fire the entire time. Because of you, I am now a suspect in the murder of Lord Gainsborough."

"Because of me?" Vivienne didn't like being accused of pointing a finger at Adam, even if she supposed it *was* her fault that the sheriff suspected him now. Still, it was a true fact. If Adam was innocent, then why was he acting so odd?

"Adam, you never did tell me where you were at that time," said Zachariah.

"I was with my hounds. In the barn," Adam answered through gritted teeth.

"You were there, yet I believe there were still two dogs trapped in the burning building unless I'm mistaken. Is it normal that you'd turn your back on any of the kennel dogs in distress?"

"Nay, never!" the kennel groom answered.

"Then why did you?" asked the constable.

"Adam, I have to admit that it is odd that you didn't return to the kennels that night during the fire," said Vivienne. "You have to realize that sounds suspicious."

"Lady Vivienne, it wounds me that you could ever think I'd do anything to endanger the lives of the hounds. You told me straight away that you'd save the last two dogs, and that I should go. Besides, the ones I had already saved were wounded and needed my attention." Adam looked directly at Vivienne this time. "I believed you when you said that! Why wouldn't I?"

The constable chuckled. "You thought a woman could save hounds from a burning building? You expect us to believe that? Really?"

"Constable, that's enough," said Zachariah under his breath, causing the man to be silenced.

"Yes, Constable Dorson, I could save the hounds and for your information, I did," Vivienne told him. "And now that Adam brought it to my attention, I remember telling him just that during the fire. He is not lying."

"Can anyone confirm you were in the barn at that time like you said, kennel groom?" asked the constable.

Adam shrugged. "Mayhap. I don't know for certain." He stared at the ground when he spoke. "I was tending to my hounds that were injured. I was trying to calm them down since they were so upset. I wasn't looking around to see who was watching me, if that's what you mean."

"Thank you, Adam. That'll be all for now," said Zachariah. "We'll let you know if we have any more questions." He nodded at Adam and the man grunted once more before leaving in a huff. Grunt whined and ran back over to Vivienne, sitting at her feet. "What do you think, Constable?" asked the sheriff.

Constable Dorson shook his head. "He's much too upset about all this. He seems guilty to me."

"I know." Zachariah looked over to Vivienne next. "In your opinion, is that man to be trusted?"

"I've never known Adam to lie to me or to anyone for that matter. However, I have to admit that he was a little sullen this morning. Then again, that might only have to do with me. Actually, I believe everyone is not themselves today, and coming across as possible suspects right now." She pondered her conversation with Lady Gainsborough earlier.

"Lady Vivienne, if you'd be kind enough to call for your

pageboy, I have a list of names of the people that the constable and I will be questioning today. I'd like the boy to give it to the steward so we can get started. We have a lot to do." Zachariah handed her the list.

"Yes, that's right," said Constable Dorson. "The sheriff and I have a lot of work to do and we can't keep getting delayed and distracted."

"Of course I will, but what about me?" she asked, not liking the feeling of not being included.

"I'm sure you have other responsibilities around the castle," said Zachariah. "We wouldn't want to distract you. You can join us later if you'd like. Come, Constable Dorson. We will be talking to people in my chamber and need to prepare our questions." They started to walk away, and then the sheriff turned back. "If you'd be kind enough, my lady?" He nodded at the paper in her hand that had the names upon it of whom they'd talk to next. He had the nerve to smile at her while he was ordering her around instead of including her in this investigation. What happened to *the three of us*? What was all that talk last night about the investigation going quicker with her involved? Something was so wrong here, and she wasn't sure how to handle it.

"Of course, Sheriff, I'll call for Martin at once." She held the list in the air. "I wouldn't want to slow the two of you down at all."

"Thank you, my lady." He nodded and headed away talking with his constable.

Vivienne watched them go, knowing full well that she hadn't told them about what happened this morning in the smokehouse regarding Lady Gainsborough. Then again, if they weren't going to include her in their doings and share what information they had, then why should she tell them what she knew? Nay, she decided. She would keep to herself what she knew. At least for now.

"My lady, there you are." Her handmaid came running over. "I gave the sheriff your message and went back to the bedchamber, but you weren't there. One of the chambermaids told me she saw you heading this way with Lady Gainsborough."

"Yes, Rosina, that's right." She still held the list of names, watching the sheriff and constable leaving her behind. It was hard to believe this was really happening. Mayhap Zachariah wasn't as good of a friend as she had thought, after all.

"What is that, my lady?" asked Rosina, nodding to the paper she held. Grunt walked over and sniffed the handmaid. Rosina quickly stepped aside. She had always been wary about Grunt, saying she felt anxious around big dogs or any dogs for that matter. That is why Vivienne usually didn't have Grunt sleep in the bedchamber with her, and when he did, Vivienne usually kept the dog on the bed with her. Rosina slept on the pallet at the foot of her bed. Her handmaid wasn't very brave, and Vivienne didn't want to do anything to frighten her further.

"It's a list of names that the sheriff wants me to give to Martin so he can fetch these people for questioning today."

"Oh, my lady, I know my name is on there and it makes me nervous."

"Really? Why?" asked Vivienne.

"You know that I get upset easily. If it weren't for you calming me down over these past few months every time something upset me, I think I'd be in my grave by now from nerves. My lady, please don't let me face them alone. I want you by my side when they question me."

"Don't worry," she told her handmaid, laying her hand on the girl's shoulder. "I promise to be at your side during your questioning. It seems a lot of people are having a difficult time with this." She thought of Adam and how he had instantly turned against her. Vivienne knew these people and they weren't murderers. They were her servants, and also her friends.

"Oh, thank you, my lady. That makes me feel so much better already. I just hope they won't make me look at Lord Gainsborough's dead body again. I think I would swoon if they made me do that." The girl twisted her hands, showing her nervous state.

"Don't worry, they won't. Or at least not when they discover that someone has stolen the clothes right off the corpse."

"They did what?" Rosina's eyes opened wide.

"That's right," she told her. "I heard from Lady Gainsborough just after you left that someone stole her husband's clothes, probably sometime during the night."

"Do you think the murderer came back to take them for some reason?" she asked.

"Anything is possible. However, I can see them stealing the valuables, but not the clothes right off a dead man, leaving the jewels and coins there untouched. I can't say that makes any sense at all."

"I suppose not, my lady. Could they be taking the clothes because of your comment about having Grunt sniff them yesterday? Mayhap the murderer is afraid his scent will be on them and the dog will sniff him out?"

"I think you're right, Rosina. I thought the same thing. You are good at figuring things out. Mayhap I don't need to work with the sheriff, after all. I can do this by myself."

"Mayhap I can help you, my lady," said the girl excitedly. "I will be your assistant in any way I can, if you'll allow me."

"Thank you, Rosina. That is a thought." Vivienne realized

it would be nice to have another woman to talk to and to work with her. Just like the sheriff had Constable Dorson. Mayhap this was something to consider since the sheriff no longer seemed to want her help. "I was going to work in my herb garden today to try to relax." Vivienne knew how much Rosina liked plants. This might be the perfect time to bond with her handmaid. After all, Vivienne could really use a friend right now. "Would you like to assist me in the garden?"

"Oh, yes. Of course. I'd love to, my lady. Thank you for asking." Just that simple act of kindness seemed to make Rosina's nerves calm down. Vivienne knew it always helped her to relax when she was in her garden, and what better place for two women to discuss important things?

"I will meet you there after I give Martin this list and stop by the smokehouse."

"The smokehouse? Where the body is being stored?" asked Rosina.

"Yes. I need to assign a guard to the door as well. I would ask you to join me, but you made your feelings clear about not wanting to see the corpse again."

"Oh, nay, I don't want to go there!" Rosina shuddered. "I will meet you in the herb garden, my lady. Mayhap I can pick some calming herbs to infuse in hot water for us to drink."

"That would be nice, thank you. Come on, Grunt. It's just you and me, I guess," she told her dog, heading toward the smokehouse. "Mayhap you can work with me, too, since the sheriff and constable don't seem to need or want my help." Grunt barked happily, as if he knew what she was saying to him and he agreed.

Chapter Seven

Vivienne was halfway to the smokehouse when she spied Martin talking to the steward. "Martin, John," she called out, waving her hand in the air.

"My lady?" John hurried over to her with the pageboy at his side.

"I have a list of people that the sheriff wants to question today." She handed it to John. "Will you and Martin please contact these people and bring them one at a time up to the sheriff's chamber?"

"I'll do it, I'll do it," said Martin, jumping up and down, always more than eager to help Vivienne. She had taught the boy to read, so Martin was very capable of carrying out this task, as well as most any task that she handed him.

"Of course, my lady." John looked at the list and frowned. "I see my name is on here as well as Martin's and many of the servants from the kitchens."

"Yes. Don't be alarmed. The sheriff just wants to speak to everyone, hoping someone saw something the night of the murder."

"I thought you were working with the sheriff," he said, folding up the paper and sticking it into his pouch.

"I was. However, Constable Dorson is helping Sheriff Fitch today. I'm headed to the smokehouse to check on something else."

"The dead body is in the smokehouse," said Martin, looking concerned. "Why do you want to go there?"

"Yes, that is not a good place to go by yourself, my lady," agreed the steward. "Let me call on a guard to assist you."

"I'll be just fine," she said with a smile, reaching out to ruffle Martin's hair. "After all, the man is dead. How much danger could I be in?"

"There were two ghosts there this morning," said Martin, looking scared. "I saw them when I went to the well to fetch some water for Cook."

"Two ghosts? Really?" This interested Vivienne. "Was one of them Lady Gainsborough by any chance?"

"Nay. They seemed to be ghosts wearing flowing robes," Martin insisted. "I think one of them looked like Lord Gainsborough."

"Now, that's just bein' silly," John interrupted. "Boy, you know there are no such thing as ghosts. Lord Gainsborough is dead. He isn't haunting the smokehouse."

Martin started to say something, but John pulled him away. "Come on, boy, we have work to do for Lady Vivienne and the sheriff. We don't want to let them down." The steward pulled Martin away with him.

Grunt ran up with his tongue hanging out, and sat down at Vivienne's feet.

"Come on, Grunt. We have a job to do, even if Sheriff Fitch no longer wants our assistance."

"BRING THEM IN, Richard. One at a time, please," Zachariah told the guard standing watch outside his open chamber door. "We are ready to start the questioning now." Zachariah took his copy of the list of names and laid it on the table. "The first one is Rosina, the handmaid of Lady Vivienne," he told his constable.

He heard voices at the door and looked up to see the steward and the young page boy talking to Herman, the guard from Gainsborough, who stood outside the door as well.

"You can't go in yet," Herman protested. "The first name on the list is Rosina. Where is the wench?"

"She's not here, I tell you," John replied.

"Herman, let the steward and the pageboy in, please," Zachariah called out.

"Aye, Sheriff," said Herman, finally letting them pass and enter the room.

"Step up. Don't be shy," ordered the constable. "We haven't got all day."

"So sorry," said John, slowly walking into the room. Martin stayed right near him, reaching out to hold John's hand.

"You don't need to be frightened, Martin," said Zachariah. "We're not going to hurt you."

Still, the boy clung to the steward, hiding half his face against the man's sleeve.

"Come on, come on," complained Dorson, becoming impatient.

"Constable, there is no need to make these people feel ill at ease," Zachariah told him. "Let me handle this." He got up and walked over to them. "Have a seat." He motioned with his hand to the empty chair, as well as the chair he'd just vacated.

"Mmmph," grunted John, finally sitting. Martin stood next to him rather than to take Zachariah's chair. "I don't know what you want us to say. We don't know nothin.'"

"We are just trying to get to the bottom of a man's murder," he explained.

"Well, I didn't do it! And I sure as hell don't think the boy did," John said, remaining guarded.

"Where were you during the fire, John?" Zachariah paced as he spoke.

"I was helping put out the fire with buckets of water. Just like Lady Vivienne ordered all of us to do. I was running the water line until Lord Mablethorpe showed up and took over."

"So others saw you there? The entire time?" asked the constable.

"Of course, they did. You can ask anybody."

"What about the boy? Weren't you the one to discover the kennels on fire?" asked Constable Dorson. "Did you see anyone run out of the kennels just before it happened?"

"No," said Martin, so quiet his response was barely heard. He sidled up even closer to John.

"Speak up, boy! We can't hear you," snapped the constable.

"He said *no*," John relayed, looking down at Martin, putting his arm around the child to comfort him. "You'll have to excuse the boy's behavior. He's pretty shaken up this morning. He swears he saw the ghost of Lord Gainsborough earlier by the smokehouse and he is still a little frightened."

"I did see ghosts! Two of them," the boy responded with wide blue eyes.

"There is no such thing as a ghost, boy." John scowled at him. "How many times do I have to tell you? Now, stop making up stories. Pages aren't supposed to lie."

"I'm not lying."

"Ghosts, really." Constable Dorson chuckled and looked down at the list. "Why didn't you bring in this handmaid, Rosina? She was first on the list. You are not following our orders."

"I tried but she wouldn't come with us," said John. "She said she was joining Lady Vivienne in the herb garden and was going to be her assistant."

"Assistant?" asked Zachariah. "She's her handmaid. Was Lady Vivienne there too?"

"Nay," said Martin in a soft voice. "She went to the smokehouse to see the ghosts, I think. Rosina didn't go with her cuz she was scared."

"Scared? Of ghosts, I suppose?" Constable Dorson looked over at Zachariah and rolled his eyes.

"Rosina also said Lady Vivienne promised to be with her when you questioned her and she wouldn't come without her," John relayed the information.

"Ah. So, she's scared of us, and rightly so, I suppose." Zachariah looked over at his constable, thinking that the man did come across as frightening and that he couldn't blame the girl. The constable even had a child and a steward scared at the moment. He needed to be less harsh with these people and he'd have to have a talk with him.

"Yes. I think so," said John. "I have to say that the servants are all frightened to talk to you. I, myself, felt hesitant about coming here this morning."

Zachariah continued to pace, his hand on his chin. "So Lady Vivienne went to the smokehouse by herself?" He sincerely wondered what she was up to.

"Grunt went with her to see the dead man," Martin spoke up.

"I see." He stopped pacing, suddenly feeling bad about leaving Vivienne behind. He had promised her that she could work with them, but the constable convinced him that she would only serve as a distraction. Now, he realized that he should have stuck to his word. Vivienne Harlowe was a good friend. She also wasn't a woman to take rejection easily. Especially from him. By sending her away, he might have just pushed her right into the path of trouble. "Martin, when did you see these ... ghosts at the smokehouse?"

"It was early this morning before it got light. I was hungry and went to the kitchens to find some food. I was told to go to the well to get water, since Cook didn't do it."

"Is that Cook's job?"

"It is." Martin nodded, his shaggy blond bangs hanging across his eyes.

"Where was Cook that he couldn't do it himself?"

"I don't know." Martin shrugged. "Probably sleeping."

"All right, that's enough for now. Thank you," said Zachariah, walking over and pulling open the door. "Constable, continue with the questioning. I'll be back soon."

"Where are you going, Sheriff?" the constable called out after him.

"Let's just say, I'm going on a ghost hunt." He left the room, eager to find Vivienne and apologize to her, hoping it wasn't already too late.

VIVIENNE PUSHED OPEN the door to the smokehouse, flinching as the stench of rotting flesh mixed with acrid smoke wafted through the air, assaulting her senses. Standing on the threshold, she looked back, having forgotten to ask John to send one of the castle guards to watch the door. He and Martin had already disappeared so she'd have to ask him later.

"Oh well, it'll have to wait," she said aloud, not wanting to take the time to find a guard on her own right now. She wanted to investigate the smokehouse before the sheriff came looking for her. "Grunt, if we're lucky, we can find something in here to shed light on the murder. Then the sheriff will see how valuable we really are and why he shouldn't have dismissed us, breaking his promise."

Grunt barked in agreement, pushing past her, entering the hut, sniffing the floor as he walked in circles inside the room.

The smokehouse was made of stone and had no windows, just the one door. The roof was gabled, allowing the smoke to vent from the pit in the middle of the floor where hard wood was burned. A long wooden table was on one side of the room. Meat to be cured was hung from hooks and also the rafters to protect it from thieves or vermin, but only after it had been packed in barrels of salt for about six weeks first to remove the moisture from the flesh. Usually, the smoking process took about two weeks. Most of the smoking was done in the winter. Pigs were usually smoked in December to last throughout the cold weather. It was only June now, and not much smoking happened during the summer months.

Vivienne left the door open, coughing a little from the smell of smoke, just like Lady Gainsborough had mentioned. She looked over and saw something smoldering in the center of the pit on the earthen floor. "That's odd," she said to herself, not remembering embers in the pit when she was here with the sheriff yesterday. However, Cook just did get finished smoking some leftover meat from the last hunt about a week ago. Perhaps the coals smoldered longer than she'd thought.

She walked over to the center of the room, looking down into the embers to see a slight glow. There had been a fire in here quite recently, and she didn't think it had reignited from an entire week ago. Bending down, she held her hand over her nose, noticing a speck of bright red in the center of the pit. She hurriedly ran over to pick up an iron poker attached to the wall. Returning, she poked at the ashes, and carefully pulled out a piece of red cloth, holding it up with the iron rod to observe it. "Lord Gainsborough's clothes," she said aloud, slowly standing.

It seemed as if whoever had stolen the dead man's clothes, ended up burning them in the fire, and she thought she knew why.

"Lady Vivienne?" came a voice from the open door.

She spun around to see the sheriff peering into the semi-darkened room. A stream of sunlight filtered in through the open door, making a hazy stream from the smoke inside the room.

"Sheriff Fitch. I'm over here." She carefully took the piece of burned cloth and replaced the iron poker on the wall. Grunt ran over with his tail wagging to greet the sheriff.

"Why are you in here? And why are you alone?" He entered the smokehouse leaving the door wide open.

"I'm not alone. Grunt is with me."

"You know what I mean."

"Well then, if you must know I am here searching for answers. And I'm alone because you so blatantly dismissed me after you promised I could work with you."

"I know," he said, coughing a little from the smoldering embers. "I came to apologize for that. It was the constable's idea, not mine." He walked to the center of the room, making his way toward her, but she went to the table holding the corpse instead of meeting up with him.

"Perhaps you should dismiss the constable instead, and work with me," she said snidely, not caring how rude she was being right now. "You know we make a good team. Or perhaps you forgot?"

Grunt saw a mouse nosing around the threshold and took off at a run after it, his nails scratching the dirt floor as he tried to get traction. In a moment, he'd disappeared.

"It seems I'm not the only one who abandoned you," he told her, staring out the door at the path the dog had taken.

"Did you want something?" she asked him, approaching

the corpse, feeling her heart already beating faster. It was a mixture of anxiety from getting close to a dead man as well as being alone with the sheriff once again.

"I wanted to make sure you were all right, my lady."

"Hrmmph," she said with a sniff. "How did you even know I was here?" She slowly reached out and touched the edge of her cloak that was covering the naked body of the Lord Gainsborough.

"Martin told me." He walked across the room, stopping right behind her, looking over her shoulder.

Vivienne stared down at the dead body covered by her cloak, feeling her stomach lurch. She knew there was so much dried blood on the corpse that it would make her feel weak and lightheaded to look at it again.

"Sweetheart, you don't need to do this." His hand covered hers and her eyes flashed over to his. Caring brown orbs drank her in, making her feel his concern.

"I told you, I *do* need to do this. If I can't find my parents' murderers, then at least mayhap I can help Lady Gainsborough and Lord Wilfred instead. No one should have to live through losing a loved one to murder and never knowing who did it."

"Nay, they shouldn't," he agreed.

"Questions will be answered this time. I will make sure of it." Her gaze traveled down to his hand covering hers. He slowly dragged his thumb over the top of her hand in an endearing nature as he spoke.

"Come back to the castle with me and we'll solve this mystery together."

She almost agreed to go with him, but realized it was the touch of his hand against hers that was making her heady and not able to think straight. She wouldn't be fooled by him again.

"Nay!" She pulled her hand away from his, yanking the

cloak down more to expose the man's entire chest. "I want to have another look at the body."

"He's ... naked," said Zachariah, creasing his brow when he looked at the corpse. "How did that happen?"

"Wouldn't you like to know?" She leaned in, noticing something that she hadn't seen before.

"Yes, Vivienne, I would! If you know something, you shouldn't be keeping the information from me."

Her head snapped around to face him. "So, you're calling me Vivienne now? I thought we had an agreement to use our titles."

"*Lady* Vivienne," he ground out, the look of frustration contorting his face. "I said I was sorry, so can we just move on with the investigation?"

"I'm not sure I believe you." She walked around him, looking through a bucket of tools, finding a tallow candle in a jar. She brought it over to the smoldering ashes, finding some kindling that wasn't burnt and using it to get enough fire to light the wick of the candle.

"What can I do to prove to you that I am sorry about breaking my word?"

"Well, now that you mention it, there is something you can do." She walked back over to the bucket, digging inside and pulling out a small metal cup and a rag.

"Just name it."

"Go to the well and get me a cup of water, please." She shoved the cup into his hand.

"What?" He made a face, almost causing her to laugh.

"I need water to clean away some of the dried blood. I think I saw something."

"There is a rain barrel right outside the door with water in it." He tried to hand the cup back to her.

"Good," she said with a smile, turning back to inspect the

body. "Then you won't have far to go, will you?"

"You are incorrigible, do you know that?" he grumbled, heading across the room to the door.

"As if you didn't already know that." She smiled as she held up the lit candle over the body of the corpse, trying to breathe through her mouth so she wouldn't retch.

"Here is your water," he said, returning momentarily and handing the cup to her.

"Spill some of it over the wound, please," she said, moving her face closer to Lord Gainsborough's chest. "And use the rag to wipe away the remnants."

"What are you doing, Lady Vivienne? We've already inspected the body."

"Well, I think there is something we missed. Now, please stop fighting me and just do what I ask."

"If you were anyone else," he said under his breath, doing what she wanted.

As soon as the dried blood was washed away, Vivienne could see clearly a piece of evidence that they'd missed. "Ah hah!" she said with a nod.

"What? Do you see something?" Zachariah moved his face lower to look as well.

"See that?" She held the candle closer for light, pointing to the wound.

"The stab mark. Yes. What about it?"

"Look again. There is a second stab wound right next to the first."

"What?" He surveyed the wound and stood up, shaking his head. "You're right. I cannot believe I missed that. I wonder what it means."

"It means, this poor man was stabbed not once, but a second time as well."

"So, mayhap he wasn't dead the first time." Zachariah

nodded as he thought it over. "The killer wanted to make sure he died, and stabbed him yet again."

"Mayhap," she said, throwing the edge of her cloak back over the body, knowing that she'd never wear this cloak again. "However, I have another thought."

"Which is what?" He raised a brow.

"I think what you said could be true. But what if ... no, it's silly."

"What? Tell me, Lady Vivienne. Please. It could be important."

She let out a sigh, realizing this would sound ridiculous, but wanting him to know her thoughts.

"What if he was really stabbed with a different dagger?" She pulled back the cloak again and nodded at the dagger lying at the dead man's side. "Then it was removed and replaced by his own dagger."

"Yes," said the sheriff with an approving nod of his head. "The murderer wanted this to look like Lord Gainsborough killed himself."

"So they removed their blade to get rid of the evidence," she said. "Then they stabbed Lord Gainsborough with his own dagger, hoping no one would notice that he'd been stabbed twice."

"I'm impressed by how you think," he complimented her, making her heart swell with pride.

"It's the way the murderer thinks, not me," she corrected him.

"Who's in here?" came a gruff voice from the door.

Vivienne turned to see Cook's body outlined by the sunshine as he stood in the doorway with his hands on his hips.

"Cook," she said. "Come in, please. You are just the person I want to see."

"Lady Vivienne?" Cook squinted, looking into the semi-darkened room. "Sheriff? Is that you, too?"

"It is," said Zachariah. "What are you doing here, Cook?"

"I saw the door to the smokehouse open and wondered if someone was in here again like they were this morning."

"This morning?"

"Yes," answered the cook, stepping inside, slowly walking toward them.

"Mayhap it was when they stole Lord Gainsborough's clothes and burned them in the embers," Vivienne spoke up.

"Is that what happened?" asked Cook. "I noticed he was naked. I thought you took his clothes as part of the investigation."

"Cook, did you see someone in here earlier?" asked the sheriff.

"I saw the door open when I got up this morning before sunup, like I usually do. I didn't want anyone to steal the last of the smoked meat, so I came to look," said Cook.

"What did you find?" asked Vivienne.

"Nothing. There was no one here. So, I gathered up the rest of the meat I had left here, and that's when I thought I saw someone over by the dead body."

"Who?" asked the sheriff.

"Well, I'm not sure I should say." Cook looked down to the ground, kicking at the dust.

"Go ahead," said Vivienne, trying to sound kind so the man wouldn't be frightened. "It is important that you tell us everything."

"Yes," answered the sheriff. "If you know something about the murder and keep it from us, you are no better than the murderer and can be tried as an accomplice to a crime."

"What?" Cook looked up so quickly, that she wasn't sure he didn't jam his neck. "I didn't know that."

"It's true," said Vivienne. "Now tell us. Was it Lady Gainsborough you saw in here?"

"Aye," he answered slowly. "She was doing something over by the body."

"She was?" The sheriff looked over at Vivienne. "How did you know this?"

"Lady Gainsborough came to my chamber earlier and told me about it," stated Vivienne, smugly. It felt damned good to know something that he didn't.

"She did?" Now Zachariah scowled at her. "Why didn't you tell me this before?"

"If you would have asked if I knew anything, I would have told you. But you and the constable didn't seem to want or need my help."

He groaned at hearing her comment.

"Lady Gainsborough startled me, and I was afraid she'd try to make me look guilty, so I ran," Cook told them. "I accidentally knocked into her and she fell."

"You knocked into a noblewoman and didn't stop to help her up?" Zachariah scowled at Cook next.

"Like I said, I was afraid she'd accuse me of something."

"Like murdering her husband?" asked Vivienne.

"Yes. I mean, I did have a confrontation with him. But I swear I never touched him. I am not a murderer, my lady."

"I understand," said Vivienne.

"I have food cooking and need to get back to the kitchens before it burns," said Cook.

"You are free to go for now," the sheriff told him.

"Thank you. If you'll just excuse me, there is something I need to get." He walked over to the far end of the smokehouse and reached up, taking down a small piece of smoked meat that Vivienne hadn't even noticed was hanging there. He tucked it under his arm and headed for the door.

"One more thing, Cook."

"Yes, Sheriff?" The big bald man turned around.

"Was this pit of ashes smoldering when you were in here earlier?"

"Nay. I can't say it was."

"Thank you. You may go."

Cook turned and hurried out the door.

"Do you think he's telling the truth?" Zachariah asked her.

"Partially," said Vivienne. "Or at least he wasn't lying when he said he came to get some smoked meat that was still hanging here. He proved that, didn't he?"

"Yes, but I feel he's hiding something."

"I think so too," said Vivienne, holding up the scrap of clothing that hadn't been burned in the fire. "Lord Gainsborough's clothes had to be smoldering when he was in here. Cook would have noticed. After all, he is in charge of the smokehouse. If something was burning when it shouldn't be, I highly doubt he'd just walk away. Even if Lady Gainsborough was in here."

"Did she say anything was smoldering when she was here?"

"Yes. Well, she said it was very dark and she only had a small candle but mentioned it was smoky and hard to breathe. She couldn't see her assailant clearly because everything seemed to be hazy."

"Assailant? So are you saying she was attacked?"

"Nay, not really. Knocked down only, as Cook rushed out," Vivienne told him. "The woman said she thought it was Cook, and it looks like she was right."

"Where was the guard that was supposed to be posted at the door?" asked Zachariah.

"That was my question too," she told him, blowing out the candle and placing it back in the wooden bucket. "It seems that Lady Gainsborough and her son decided Herman shouldn't have to stay watch all night long, and so they dismissed him."

"I see." The sheriff scratched his head in thought. "Have you spoken to Lord Wilfred about this at all?"

"Not yet," said Vivienne.

"I think Wilfred and his mother are the next ones we need to question."

"We?" Vivienne's heart jumped. "Are you asking me to work with you once again, Sheriff?"

"Yes. I think you were right in saying we make a good team. I'd like to give it another try, if you don't mind." He put his hand at the small of her back and escorted her to the door.

"Well, what about Constable Dorson?" she asked.

"I'll find something for him to do. After all, we do need a guard at the door to this smokehouse until we can prove our theory that Lord Gainsborough was stabbed twice." He chuckled lowly.

Vivienne walked out into the sunshine and turned and smiled at Zachariah as he closed the door behind them.

"Yes, Sheriff, you are right. I suppose *we* do need to find the constable another job for now."

Chapter Eight

Vivienne spent most of the day in the chamber with Zachariah, questioning people about the murder. Constable Dorson wasn't happy to have to guard the smoke-house, but when the sheriff told him everything that they'd learned, he agreed it was important to keep anyone away from the corpse. Of course, the man wouldn't be guarding the smoke-house during the night, but Vivienne's uncle appointed another guard he considered trustworthy to do the job.

Questioning so many had taken longer than they expected. It was tiring, and also important they write down the facts they'd learned. Therefore, the questioning was stopped for the day and would restart again in the morning. For now, they'd get something to eat. She walked together with the sheriff to the great hall, their conversation light since they didn't want to discuss the murder in front of others.

"My lady, I have been looking for you," came Vivienne's handmaid's voice from behind her. She stopped and turned around.

"Hello, Rosina. I have been with the sheriff all day questioning people. I'm sorry. I should have sent word to you so you knew where I was."

Rosina stopped in her tracks. "Hello, Sheriff."

He nodded. "Lady Vivienne, I'll talk to you later," said Zachariah. "I have sent a replacement for Constable Dorson and I want to talk with him over our meal."

"Aye," she answered with a nod.

Once he left, Rosina seemed to calm down. "Is there anything I can help you with, my lady?"

"Yes. You can tell me why you seem so nervous around the sheriff." They walked together to the great hall.

"I'm not sure," she responded, wringing her hands. "But I have to admit that everyone in the kitchens and all of the handmaids feel as if he is always watching them, like a wolf waiting to pounce on a lamb for its meal."

That made Vivienne laugh. "Oh, Rosina, you are too funny. Sheriff Fitch isn't like that at all. He's actually a very nice man once you get to know him. He just takes his work very seriously.."

"You like him, don't you?"

"Of course, I do. Why do you even ask?"

"I mean, in a romantic way."

Vivienne gave her handmaid a scolding glance. "Now, Rosina, it's not like that and you know it. The sheriff and I are old friends and that is the extent of it. Please don't be saying things to insinuate it is more than a business relationship or I will be at the center of tomorrow's gossip. And believe me, I don't fancy that at all!"

"Oh, I didn't mean anything by it, my lady. I just wanted to know how it felt to be in love.'"

"In love?" Vivienne was about to scold her handmaid again,

when she realized where this might be going. "Rosina, is there a man in the castle who you have your eye on?"

"Mayhap." Rosina smiled slyly. "All right, yes, there is. However, I don't really know if he feels the same way about me that I do about him. I mean, I thought he liked me, but now I'm not sure."

"Why don't you just come out and ask him?"

"Oh, no. I could never do that."

"Why not? Does he have his eye on another girl? Perhaps Maria?" Vivienne referred to the busty kitchen maid that she was sure every man there had his eye on. The girl was cute and very friendly. Not that Rosina wasn't. But Maria seemed to befriend everyone she met. Rosina, on the other hand, wasn't as outgoing. She had a habit of staying in the shadows and letting others have all the attention.

"Maria? Oh, I hope not. Do you really think so, my lady?"

"I don't know. Why don't you tell me who the man is and I will let you know my opinion then?"

"Nay, I wouldn't want to bother you with something so unimportant, my lady. Excuse me, but I need to go to the kitchens."

"All right. I will see you later." Vivienne smiled, watching Rosina dash off for the kitchens. Vivienne lingered, being nosy and wanting to know whom the girl had eyes for. To her surprise, she saw Rosina wander inside the kitchens and walk right up and start talking to Cook. Maria was nearby watching the two of them. "It's Cook," she said aloud, with a giggle.

"What about the cook, my dear?" Her aunt walked into the great hall holding on to the arm of Vivienne's uncle.

"Oh, nothing," Vivienne answered, not wanting them to know the personal life of her maid servant. If she told them, she'd be no better than Rosina gossiping about each other.

"Vivienne, how is the investigation of Lord Gainsborough's murder going?" asked her uncle.

"We've discovered a few things," she said with a satisfied nod. "However, it is going slower than I had anticipated. Since there were so many people here for my ... betrothal, it has really slowed us down."

"Speaking of your betrothal," said her uncle, clearing his throat.

"Gilbert, not now," scolded her aunt, squeezing his arm.

"What betrothal?" asked Vivienne, as they approached the dais. She noticed that Lady Gainsborough was already seated, and her son Wilfred had been placed right next to where Vivienne usually sat. "Please don't tell me that you still plan to marry me off to Lord Wilfred. I thought that plan was extinguished, now that Lord Gainsborough is dead."

"It doesn't have to be," said her uncle.

"Oh, yes it does," she responded, becoming upset that he was even mentioning this right now. "I told you before and I will tell you again, I am never marrying anyone. Especially not Lord Wilfred."

"I've been talking to his mother, and she still seems to think that the marriage would be a good alliance, just as I do," said her uncle. "After all, now that her husband is dead, her son will inherit everything. It is important that he has heirs as soon as possible."

"Heirs? You've got to be jesting," she spat, feeling disgusted by the idea of possibly marrying such a man, let alone coupling with him and having his babies!

"Gilbert, please," begged her aunt. "At least wait until after the investigation before bringing this up again."

"Never bring it up again," she warned him, turning and heading to the kitchens, not wanting to sit with the nobles at the dais, after all.

"Vivienne, where are you going?" her aunt called out to her.

"I haven't seen Grunt for a while, and I need to make sure he's not bothering Cook." She hurried into the kitchens, feeling more comfortable among the servants than when she was sitting with the nobles. "Grunt," she called out, looking around the room for her dog. She spied him at the opposite end of the kitchens. Martin's back was toward her, but the boy was on the floor playing with the dog. "Grunt, are you causing trouble again?"

She looked down to see her dog licking something from the boy's fingers.

"Hello, Lady Vivienne," said Martin. "I was just giving Grunt a treat for being a good dog."

"What is that?" She hunkered down and stretched her neck to see what he had in the jar. "Is that tallow?"

"Yes," he said. "Cook doesn't use it all. And since he won't give Grunt a soup bone, I thought he would like a treat."

"Well, I suppose, it's all right, but just not too much. I don't want him getting fat."

"Yes, my lady." Martin reached out and threw his arms around Grunt's neck, giving him a big hug.

"You sure do like dogs, don't you?"

"I want to have my own dog someday when I'm a knight."

"A knight?" That made her laugh. "It'll be a long time before that happens. And if you don't prove to Lord Mablethorpe that you're any good at being a page, he might send you back home and tell your father. Martin, you'd better get up and get out to the great hall right now."

"Tell my father?" The boy jumped to his feet, seeming terrified. "Don't let them send me home, Lady Vivienne. I like it at Mablethorpe. I like living with you and Grunt and everyone. Please, I want to stay here." He wiped the animal fat off his fingers and onto his breeches. Grunt sniffed the boy's leg and began to lick it.

"Stop that, Grunt," Vivienne said. "Or do I have to put you out in the kennels all by yourself?"

"Nay, you can't do that," cried Martin. "The kennels are burned down. They have to fix them first or the dogs will escape. That's why Adam is keeping the dogs in the barn for now."

It seemed like everyone was on edge today, even the young boy. She supposed this murder made everyone nervous. It did to her, that was for sure. She only hoped that she and the sheriff could solve it soon so things could calm down and get back to normal.

"Martin, you let me worry about the dogs." She took his shoulders and turned him around. "For now, I want you to go out to the great hall and have something to eat with the other pages. The steward or possibly my aunt or uncle might need a page, so you need to be there to do your duty. Do you understand me?"

"I do! I'll do my job and do it good, my lady. I promise." He held his hand over his heart. Then Martin took off at a dash for the great hall, eager to prove his worth just so he wouldn't be sent away.

"What's Martin's big hurry?" asked Maria, picking up a large tray of food and balancing it on her shoulder, preparing to carry it out to the great hall.

"He doesn't want to be sent home, and is eager to prove he's a good page, that's all."

"I like the little boy," said Maria. "He's so sweet and also cute. I hope you don't plan on getting rid of him any time soon."

"Nay, it's not my intention to do that at all," she told the kitchen maid. "Martin reminds me of someone I once knew. I like having him around. I will make certain that he is never sent away, I assure you."

"I like it here too, my lady. I hope you don't plan on getting rid of me." Maria looked to Vivienne for confirmation of her position at the castle.

"No, of course not, Maria. Why would I send you away? You've been living here at Mablethorpe Castle since you were old enough to pick up a tray of food. Why would you say such a thing?"

"I don't know." Her eyes roamed over to the other side of the kitchen where Rosina was still talking to Cook. They both smiled at each other and Cook actually laughed. It was odd to see the man in such a good mood. Perhaps he liked Rosina just as much as she liked him.

"You think I like Rosina more than you, don't you?" Vivienne asked Maria.

"Well, don't you? I mean, she's only been at the castle for less than a year and you already made her your handmaid. I've been here, like you said, for most of my life."

Vivienne's heart went out to the girl. She had no idea that Maria had ever been interested in being her handmaid. The girl was loyal and a good worker. Mayhap she would have been a good handmaid after all.

"Maria, that food is getting cold, and I won't have Lord Mablethorpe complaining to me because you are so slow," called out Cook from the other side of the room.

"I'm going," she mumbled, throwing him a daggered glare and heading out to the great hall with her tray loaded down with food.

Rosina noticed Vivienne in the kitchens and came running right over. "My lady, is there something I can do for you?"

"Nay, not now," she answered, deciding that mayhap she'd better go back out to the dais to eat her meal, after all. "I'm just going to get something to eat. I'm tired and will be turning in early tonight."

"Then I'll go up to the chamber to wait for you, my lady."

"Nay. Stay here and get some food." She looked up at Cook and then back to Rosina. "Actually, I won't need you at all tonight. You can sleep in the great hall with the other servants."

"You don't need me?" The girl seemed put out.

"Rosina, I just thought you'd like more time to visit with … people." She smiled and looked back at Cook who was actually humming as he stirred the pottage. "Or anyone who might have caught your eye. You have to fight for what you want sometimes, my dear. Please don't let anyone tell you otherwise."

"You sound like you're talking about a man."

"Mayhap I am."

"Who?"

"Oh, for heaven's sake, Rosina, I am not blind. I am talking about you and Cook."

"You are?" Rosina glanced over at Cook and flashed him a smile. He noticed Vivienne watching him and turned quickly, pretending not to see them.

"I know you two like each other, so take the night and get to know him better."

"Ooooh," she said with a shy smile. "I suppose I see your point now."

"Keep an eye on Maria while you're at it," said Vivienne with a giggle. "She was watching you and Cook earlier and I could tell how upset it made her."

"Do you really think so?"

"Put it this way," said Vivienne, as she started to walk back to the great hall. "If looks could kill, you'd be dead."

Rosina gasped and ran out the back door.

"Mayhap I shouldn't have used those exact words," Vivienne said to herself, as she headed to the great hall, knowing how sensitive the girl was and how she might have just scared Rosina more than she already was about everything that had happened at the castle lately. Vivienne wished this murder was already solved so everyone could stop being so nervous about every little thing. All she wanted was for life at Mablethorpe Castle to be like it was before the murder.

Chapter Nine

Vivienne pulled on a pair of men's breeches and shoved her feet into boots. She'd actually had a good night's sleep for once without that damned nightmare haunting her. Today she felt alive and as if she could take on the world. Pulling an oversized tunic out of a trunk, she pulled it over her head and belted it around her. Then she proceeded to fasten her weapon belt around her waist.

Needing a break from the murder investigation, she decided this morning she would head to the practice yard and spar with the men. Mayhap that would clear her muddled mind. She had no idea hunting down a murderer would be such a difficult and energy-draining task. When she'd convinced Sheriff Fitch to let her assist him, she had truly believed she could find some answers and be of help to him. Now she was starting to wonder if she took on more than she was capable of doing. It made her feel even more respect for Zachariah and what he did. Especially when he was trying to raise his young daughter by himself.

Even with all the questioning, she and the sheriff were still no closer to narrowing down who could have murdered Lord Gainsborough. Mayhap taking time away from the investigation would help somehow. One thing Vivienne knew from her own experience was that thinking too much about anything would only drive one mad in the end.

There came a soft knock at her door.

"Rosina, will you please answer that?" Vivienne walked over and picked up her father's sword, sliding it out of the scabbard and holding it reverently in two hands. This sword had probably killed many men in her father's lifetime. He'd used it to protect the king and those he loved. He was a good soldier, and it saddened her that he lost his own life trying to protect his family. Grief filled her heart, making her want to cry, remembering the look on her father's face that night when he'd been killed. A shiver coursed through her. It never should have happened. Her father and mother did not deserve to die. If only she could have fought off the murderers and helped to save her family's life. The knocking on her door dragged her from her thoughts.

"Rosina, why aren't you—oh," she said, suddenly remembering that she had given her handmaid the night off so she could spend time with the man she loved. Vivienne smiled as she slid the blade back into the scabbard, placing it reverently on the bedside table. She would have to talk to Rosina later to find out how her evening progressed. The girl seemed to fancy Cook, as big and burly and brash as the man was. She supposed Rosina could refine him if given the chance. After all, people changed all the time when they were in love. Or so she'd been told. She might have been married at one time, but Vivienne didn't believe she was ever in love.

The knocking continued.

"I'm coming," she called out, hurrying over and pulling open the door. At first, she saw no one. Then she looked lower and saw little Martin standing there with a long-stemmed red rose in one hand.

"Martin?" She giggled, thinking how cute he looked standing there with a flower as if he were a suitor. It made her wonder what the boy would be like when he grew up. Would he truly be a knight, wooing ladies by bringing them roses? She truly hoped so. But what in the world was he doing, bringing her a flower right now?

"What is it, Martin?" she asked in a gentle voice.

"This is from the sheriff." He pushed the rose into her hand. When he did, one of the thorns pricked her finger, causing it to bleed.

"Ow!" she exclaimed, pulling back her hand, putting her finger to her mouth.

The little boy's eyes opened wide. "Did I hurt you? I'm so sorry, my lady."

"Nay, you didn't hurt me, Martin. Not really." She smiled kindly at the child, not wanting him to feel afraid. He was still scared so much from the kennels burning down that he wouldn't even go near them now, although he used to spend a good amount of time there petting her uncle's hunting dogs. The boy loved animals of every kind. Especially strays. There wasn't a week that passed when Martin didn't bring back to the castle a stray cat, a hurt rabbit, or a baby bird that fell from a nest. He truly had a good heart. She liked to see that in people, especially him, since he was so young. Vivienne only hoped it would continue when he turned into a full-grown man. Most men had no thoughts at all for animals, or even women for that matter. No thoughts unless it was what a women could do for them. Especially in bed. "Thank you, Martin," she told him, gingerly reaching out with two fingers to take the offered rose. "But why is the sheriff sending me a flower?"

"I don't know," he said with a shrug. "He just asked me to bring it to you and I did."

"Well, I thank you kindly."

He started to turn to leave when Vivienne stopped him. "Martin, I was headed to the practice yard to spar with the men. Would you care to come with me to watch?"

"Would I!" His bright blue eyes lit up in excitement. "Since I'm going to be a knight someday, I should start sparring too, don't you think?"

The boy amused her with his zest for life. Why couldn't everyone be just like him?

"Let me just get my sword and we'll go." She headed back into the room, sniffing the rose and placing it down on the table before picking up her sword, which was still in its sheath. When she turned around, she almost tripped over Martin, since he was right behind her and she hadn't even heard him enter the room.

"Can I hold your sword?" Want showed in Martin's eyes.

"Oh, I'm not sure, sweetheart. It's very heavy."

"I'm strong! See?" He raised his skinny arms up in the air and pretended to flex invisible muscles. He made a grunting sound, his eyes staying fastened to the blade all the while.

He was so cute and curious that Vivienne didn't have the heart to say *no*. "I'll tell you what. I'll hold the sword with you," she said, not wanting to give her father's weapon to the boy, since he was young and the blade was sharp. She removed the sword from the scabbard once again, lowering it to his level, but keeping her fingers grasped around the hilt. "Go ahead," she said with a nod.

Martin eagerly grabbed for it, and she pulled it away just as his hand was about to be cut.

"Slowly," she warned him. "If you are not careful, you will be cut by the blade."

"Like you were hurt by the thorn from the rose?"

"Similar, but different." She lowered it again, and with his gaze fastened to the sword, he slowly wrapped his fingers around it.

"I'm holding a sword," he said excitedly. Pride showed on his face.

"Yes, you are, sweetie." She giggled at his enthusiasm. "Didn't your father ever let you try holding his sword before you came to Mablethorpe to be fostered?"

The boy's hands slid off the hilt and his smile disappeared. He lowered his head when he answered. "Nay. My father doesn't like me. That's why he sent me away to begin with."

"Martin! Don't say such things. I'm sure that's not true." She didn't know much about his family and decided she would ask her father about them once she had the chance. "Hold it again, but this time I am going to let go so you can feel the weight of it all on your own."

"All right." That seemed to make him smile again and forget all about his father.

"Steady now," she told him.

"I've got it. Don't worry, Lady Vivienne."

Vivienne slowly released the sword. Because of the weight and the boy not having the strength to hold it properly, the tip of it fell, hitting the floor with a clunk. She quickly grabbed it again.

"You see how heavy it is? You are too young yet and should start out with a wooden sword. I will talk to my uncle and make sure you get one."

"Really? I would like that. So when will I be able to kill a man, the way the murderer did when he stabbed his blade into Lord Gainsborough?"

"Martin!" she shouted, standing up with her hand around the hilt of the blade. "How can you even say such a thing?"

"Is it bad to kill, Lady Vivienne?"

"What do you think?" She was shocked that she even had to have this conversation with the boy.

"I hear the knights talking about killing men on the battlefield all the time. They sound happy about it."

"That is different. They are happy about defeating the enemy to keep our people and their king safe. They are trained soldiers, and I assure you they are not happy to end someone's life for no reason at all." She would have to tell the knights to be careful what they said to each other when they were around him. She didn't like to think that Martin was being influenced this way. From now on, she would have to keep a closer eye on him.

"Did you ever kill anyone with your sword?" His eyes were back on the weapon again.

"Nay! Of course not. And it is not really my sword. It was my father's. He was a foot soldier."

"If it's not yours, then why do you practice fighting with it? Are planning on killing someone?" The boy was full of questions today. He had an eagerness to learn, reminding her of herself while growing up.

Vivienne hesitated before she answered. Killing had been her reason for learning to use the weapon. Vivienne promised herself she'd find out who murdered her parents and then she'd take their lives in return. Revenge filled her heart and it was getting so strong through the years that no matter what she did or thought, she couldn't seem to push it away.

"I just want to be able to defend myself if I need to," she explained. "And of course, to protect those I love, that's all."

"Did you ever have to actually use that sword in a battle? To defend yourself?" The child's questions never seemed to end. As much as she wanted to tell him the truth, she saw that no good could come from it. Still, she didn't want to lie to the boy either. Mayhap she could tell him just enough to satisfy his curiosity and leave it at that.

"As a matter of fact, I did have to use it once."

"So you stabbed someone?" Martin climbed atop her bed, crossing his legs in front of him. "What did it feel like?"

She'd managed to avoid thinking of her horrid past, not having had the nightmare last night. But with Martin's questions, her memories of that terrifying night were pushing to the surface once again. She didn't like it in the least.

"I think I'd better get out to the practice field." She strapped the sword on to her weapon belt.

"Where did you get that sword?" Martin continued to fire questions at her, and her stomach was starting to twist in a knot.

"I told you, it was my father's sword. Now, let's go." She grabbed his hand and he hopped down from the bed.

"Where is your father now?"

Vivienne stopped, her hand slowly releasing his and moving upward to cover the king's ring she wore hidden on a chain under her clothes.

"He's ... he's dead," she said, hurrying to the door. Martin ran after her.

"How did he die, Lady Vivienne? Was he stabbed to death the same way the murderer killed Lord Gainsborough?"

She got to the door and yanked it open. The boy's question caused an image of her dead father with his throat slit to fill her mind. Vivienne's eyes closed and she swayed, holding on to the door so she wouldn't fall. But her legs seemed too weak to hold her, and she stumbled forward, only to be caught by someone who had been walking down the corridor.

"Lady Vivienne, are you not well?"

Her eyes sprang open to find Zachariah's arms fastened around her waist.

"Sheriff!" She pushed away and took a step back. "What are you doing here?"

"I wanted to make certain that Martin delivered the rose I asked him to give to you."

"I did, Sheriff. It's right there." Martin pointed into the room.

"Yes, he did. Thank you," she said, finding it hard to breathe right now. She supposed it was just from the gripping memory of her dead father that made her feel this way.

"Didn't you like it?" Zachariah stretched his neck, looking into the room.

"Of course, I did. Even if I don't know what it's for."

"Do you always throw things you like on the floor?"

"What?" She turned to realize that the rose must have fallen off the table when she was letting Martin hold the sword. "Oh, no," she said. "Martin, please go and get the flower and place it in my wash basin with the water so it can have a drink."

"Yes, my lady." He ran to do as told.

"Sheriff Fitch, you still didn't tell me why you sent me a rose." She looked back at the sheriff and he seemed to suddenly become uncomfortable. He averted his gaze from her. Then he busied himself by removing the tie holding back his shoulder-length hair, and refastening it behind his neck once again.

"It was just something I wanted to do. For yesterday." He still didn't look directly at her.

"Oh, I see." She realized he'd felt guilty for breaking his promise after all. She liked seeing him squirm. It made her feel as if he cared what she thought about him. "So, you are trying to say you are sorry for not keeping your word to me?"

He pressed his lips together and nodded, still not looking at her.

"And that you made a mistake by listening to your constable and that in the future you'll listen to me instead?"

That made him look up, just like she knew it would.

"Are you purposely trying to rile me? Because if so, it is working."

"Then my job here is done," she answered with a giggle, looking back into the room. "Come, Martin. We can stop at the kennels and see how the new construction is coming along before we go to the practice yard."

The boy ran out of the room and Vivienne closed the door.

"I just remembered, Lord Mablethorpe wanted me to do something," said Martin, fidgeting with his belt and looking at the floor.

"Really? What?" she asked, knowing the boy was lying.

Before Martin could answer, Grunt ran down the hall to join them. Tail wagging, the dog went right over to Martin instead of to her. The hound licked the boy's face, making him giggle. Martin hugged the dog around the neck and kissed him on the nose.

"Grunt is telling me he's hungry," said Martin. "Would it be all right if I took him to the kitchens to get him something to eat instead of watching you spar today, my lady?"

"It would be fine, Martin. Go on."

"Come on, Grunt, I'll race you," said the little boy, taking off at a run down the corridor with the barking dog leading the way.

"Just be sure to keep Grunt out from under Cook's feet," she shouted after the boy.

"I will, my lady," called out Martin, as he and the dog headed down the stairs and disappeared.

"You really seem to like that page boy," commented Zachariah with a smile.

"I do," she admitted. "He's a sweet child."

"Any special reason?"

"Not really. He's just cute and he makes me feel happy when he's near. That's all."

ZACHARIAH KNEW EXACTLY why Vivienne liked the boy so much, even if she wouldn't admit it.

"The son you lost would be the same age as Martin right now, wouldn't he?"

She remained quiet as they walked. Finally, she answered.

"I'd rather not talk about that, please."

"I can see it on your face, Lady Vivienne. You miss being a mother, and rightly so."

"I miss a lot of things," she told him. "It doesn't make me want to be something that I am not." She would like to think of herself as a mother, but the harsh truth was that she no longer could call herself that. She wasn't a wife anymore either. Nay, sadly, she was nothing at all.

"Sometimes it is the small things in life that bring us the most happiness," he told her. "We shouldn't ignore them, my lady. Instead, we should embrace them and be happy for what we have."

"I appreciate the rose, if that is what you're hinting at."

"It wasn't," he said, grinning. "But I will admit that it is nice to hear you say that."

She stopped and faced him. "Sheriff, you've been through some hard times as well."

"Yes, I have."

"Well, tell me, how do you cope with losing one you love?"

"My lady?"

"You must miss your wife. Your daughter must miss her too."

"Yes. Very much so."

"Does the hurt ever go away?"

"Margaret has only been gone for a year, but I won't lie—yes, it still hurts. However, I imagine it gets easier over time."

"Nay. You're wrong. It doesn't."

"Vivienne ... Lady Vivienne, please don't think that way. It's not healthy. You need to let go."

"I can't help it. I still have nightmares about that horrible night, and I am constantly thinking about the family I lost. My mother, my father, my brother, and my son. Not to mention my husband too."

He rested his hand on her shoulder. "You have been through so much over the past seven years that I cannot even imagine how you feel.

"It makes me angry as well as sad."

"It's understandable. The hurt doesn't go away overnight."

"Nay, it doesn't." She raised her chin up, releasing a deep breath. "That is why I need to spar right now on the practice field. To release some of my worries and pent-up emotions."

"Does that really help?" They continued to walk to the stairs.

"It does for me."

"Then by all means, I think you should do it. Take an hour or two, and we'll get back to the questioning later."

"Would you like to join me?"

"Join you?" Did she really think he was going to spar with knights using a sword? He chuckled. "Nay, I think not. I'm afraid you'd outshine me, my lady. It would not be healthy for my self-importance to be at such a disadvantage to such a talented female as you."

She giggled. He liked to see her smile, even if she was really laughing at him, which he didn't even mind.

"I didn't mean to spar with me. I meant to watch me, nothing more."

"I'd like to, but unfortunately I have some work to do before we continue with the questioning."

"Work? What kind of work?" She blinked too much. That told him she was irritated by what he'd said.

"I have to go into town to take care of some things. I am the sheriff and have other responsibilities as well, you realize. This murder case is not my only concern."

"Oh. Of course not." Her face relaxed. "I will meet you back at your chamber in an hour then?"

"Nay. Make it two."

"Of course."

"We will finish up the questioning today and then you and I will discuss what we've learned. We will put our heads together and try to bring closure to this investigation. Lady Gainsborough cornered me this morning in the great hall and insisted that I allow her and her son to leave. They are in a hurry to get back to Gainsborough and I cannot say that I blame them."

"Will you let them go home so soon?"

"If we feel they had nothing to do with the murder, then yes, I think so."

"I suppose it would be best if they left and took the body of Lord Gainsborough with them. That corpse in the smokehouse only seems to be scaring everyone. The sooner it is gone, the better."

"I agree. Besides, Cook is claiming he needs to smoke a ham and can't do it with a dead body present."

"He wants to smoke a ham?" This seemed to surprise her.

"That's what he said. Isn't it his job to do such things?"

"Yes, it is. However, he just smoked some meat two weeks ago. And the ham will need to be cured first, soaked in vats of salt. That will take at least a few weeks' time."

"Mayhap your uncle is planning another feast or celebration soon," he told her. "He seems to like showing off to the other nobles."

She sighed. "That sounds like him. I just hope he's not planning on springing any more surprises on me."

"Surprises?" he asked.

"Betrothals," she said, making a face.

"Oh, I understand. We wouldn't want that now, would we?"

"Nay," she said, her eyes interlocking with his, neither of them able to look away. "Nay, we wouldn't want that, Sheriff."

Chapter Ten

"My lady, have you had something to eat?" Rosina called out, after spotting Vivienne as she passed by the washwomen congregating by the well.

"Nay, Rosina, I didn't. But I'm not hungry," Vivienne called back, continuing on her way to the practice yard. Rosina ran over to join her.

"Wait for me, my lady," said the girl. "I feel as if I am not doing my job. What can I do for you?"

"Well, for starters, you can tell me what happened last night with Cook." She looked at her handmaid from the corner of her eye.

"I'm sorry, but I don't understand what you mean."

"I gave you the evening off so you and he could spend time together. I hope you didn't squander away your precious free time."

"Oh, that! Things went quite well, I must say." Rosina held up her skirts, trudging over the wet dirt.

"How well? Did he tell you his feelings about you by any chance?"

"Yes, I suppose he did."

"And did you tell him how you felt about him as well?"

"I don't think there was a need for that, my lady." She blushed. "Cook already knows."

"What about Maria? Did your interaction with Cook upset her?"

"It did, but I don't care."

"Well, good for you. Don't let her get in your way, Rosina. If you want a man, then go after him."

"My lady, is that proper advice to be giving me?"

"Probably not." She giggled. "However I'm not a proper lady, as you know. If I were, I wouldn't be dressed in a tunic and breeches, with a sword at my side, and headed to spar with men in the practice yard right now."

They both got a good laugh out of that. Until they approached the practice yard and saw who was there.

"Oh!" gasped Rosina.

Vivienne spied her uncle strutting around like a caged lion, waiting to spar with whoever would agree to take him on. Wilfred was sparring with his guard, Herman. Ladies Gainsborough and Mablethorpe sat in the lists, talking and visiting while they watched the show. The jongleur, Leif, sat with the ladies, plucking on his lute, minus the one broken string. It sounded discordant and out of tune.

"Mayhap we should return to the keep, my lady," suggested Rosina. "I am not sure I should be here. The nobles won't like it."

"Nonsense! Don't be afraid of my uncle or the others. Even if Lord Mablethorpe yells at me, which he is sure to do, I promise it will not reflect badly on you, Rosina. I will not allow it."

"Thank you, my lady," said Rosina with a curtsy. "Still, I think it is best if I leave for now. If you'd allow me to go back and tidy up your bedchamber, I feel my talents would be used more wisely there than watching you spar like a man."

"Mayhap that would be best," she agreed, not wanting Rosina blamed for her behavior. "I will meet you back in my chamber after I practice."

"Thank you, my lady." Rosina curtsied again and ran off toward the keep.

"Vivienne, what do you think you are doing?" growled her uncle as soon as she walked up.

"I am going to spar, Uncle. Isn't it obvious?"

"More than obvious." His angered perusal caused his face to redden. "I don't want you here. The practice field is no place for a lady."

"I know that. But you also know that I won't leave."

"God's eyes, Vivienne, start acting like a lady around our guests," he said under his breath. "You are embarrassing me. Especially dressed like that!"

"Guests?" she asked, letting her gaze follow his. He was looking at Wilfred.

"Oh, you're afraid Lord Wilfred won't want to marry me once he finds out I sometimes dress like a man and wield a sword as well as most men?"

"I'm sure he already knows that," mumbled Lord Mablethorpe. "However, seeing you do it might prove to be quite unsettling."

"Good," she said, climbing through the slats of the wooden fence that portioned off the section where the men fought. "I want him to be so unsettled that he will not agree to the betrothal, even though you and his mother are most likely forcing him to do it."

"Vivienne, get back here," called out her uncle, but she just kept right on going.

Wilfred and Herman saw her approach and lowered their swords.

"Good morning, Lord Wilfred. Herman," she said with a nod. She reached over and pulled her father's sword from the scabbard. "Which of you would like to spar with me first?"

"My lady, that is not proper," said Herman. "I couldn't."

"How about you, Lord Wilfred?" she challenged the milksop. "Or are you afraid your mother might object?" She purposely goaded the man, hoping to anger him enough that he'd take her up on her offer.

"Lady Vivienne, my mother does not control my actions. However, I will not spar with you either."

"Oh, then it's because of Lord Mablethorpe? Are you afraid he'll object to this?"

"I am sure he will. I will not go against him. Besides, you are a girl. I do not fight girls." Wilfred looked as if he were about to sheathe his sword. Herman hurried away, apparently not wanting to be near when trouble started.

"My uncle is afraid you won't want to marry me if you see me sparring with the men."

"What?" His head snapped up. "What do you mean?"

"I am going to speak bluntly, my lord."

"Please do," said Wilfred.

"I don't want to marry you any more than you want to marry me."

"What do you mean by that?"

"Just what I said! I thought it was crystal clear."

"I'm sorry, my lady. You make no sense."

She let out an exasperated breath of air from her mouth. "Bid the devil, Lord Wilfred. If you don't start acting like a man, no woman will ever want you as her husband."

"I am a man!" His brows dipped and his jaw clenched. "I will marry whomever I choose, not whom I am told to marry."

"Well, now that your father is dead, I'd say you are the man of your castle, so that would be a good move."

"Did your uncle really say he still plans on betrothing you to me?"

"Aye," she answered. "Does that bother you that he and your mother are planning our future?"

"Yes, it does."

"Me too. So why don't you do something about it."

"I'm not sure what you want me to do."

"God's eyes, Wilfred, do you want to end up with me for your wife?"

The look of horror on his face was so amusing that she almost laughed aloud.

"I ... I'd rather not marry you if I didn't have to," he admitted in his meek tone.

"You don't have to. If you stand up to your mother and my father like a real man, no one can make us get married, or for that matter do anything that we don't want to do."

"How do you suggest I stand up to them?" he asked, seeming desperate but not knowing how to stop this from happening. His attention shot over to the stands where his mother sat, and then back over to her uncle who was talking with his squire.

"Spar with me," Vivienne challenged him, having an idea.

"What? Nay. Why?"

"Spar with me, and then tell my uncle that you can't marry a woman who can beat you in a swordfight." She was trying to anger him so he'd be caught off guard when she questioned him about the murder. Sure enough, it worked.

"Beat me? You can't beat me, I'm a man, a soldier, and a knight. No woman can beat me in a swordfight!" he spat, raising his sword high in the air.

"Are you sure about that?" she asked with a grin, making figure eights with her father's sword.

"Do your best, Lady Vivienne," he spat. "But I assure you, you'll not belittle me today."

She raised her sword just in the nick of time to stop his blade from hitting her.

"My, that was aggressive," she said, not sure he wouldn't have taken off her entire arm if she hadn't blocked him in time. This was a side of Lord Wilfred that she had yet to see.

"Vivienne, get off that field right now!" commanded her uncle.

"Wilfred, what are you doing?" screamed his mother from the stands.

"Go, Lady Vivienne," shouted Leif, waving his lute in the air. "You can beat him!"

"Sit down, boy, and stop urging her on," came her aunt's warning to the jongleur.

"Where were you when your father got killed?" asked Vivienne, her sword clashing against his. "I didn't see you helping to put out the fire."

"I was trying to talk my father out of having to marry you," he said, lunging forward. She quickly stepped to the side.

"Oh, so then you were with your father just before he was murdered?"

"I don't like what you're insinuating, Lady Vivienne."

"And what might that be?" They continued to spar.

"I didn't kill him if that's what you're thinking. God's eyes, he was my father!"

"I didn't say you did, Lord Wilfred. I only asked where you were. So tell me, how did your father react to you not wanting to marry me?"

"He wasn't happy about it."

"So, did things become violent between the two of you?"

"Nay." He swiped at her, and she jumped aside and swiped back. "He was too busy eyeing up that kitchen wench to be bothered with me. He brushed me off like he usually did."

"Kitchen wench? Which one?" Vivienne slowly lowered the tip of her blade.

"That busty one. The one he pinched on the ass in the kitchen," spat Wilfred, lowering his blade as well.

"Lord Wilfred, what did you do after talking with your father?"

"I left him near the stairway and went back to the great hall, looking for my mother."

"Can anyone verify that? Did you speak to anyone when you returned?"

"Let me think," he said, rubbing his chin. "Oh, yes. I saw your handmaid. She brought me a goblet of wine and we sat down by the fire to chat."

"You did?" Vivienne didn't understand this. "While a fire was blazing outside, you saw fit to sit down with a drink and talk with a girl?"

"My mother didn't want me to fight the fire," he told her. "She insisted I stay inside."

"And where was your mother during all of this?"

"I'm not sure. I saw her in the great hall with your aunt at first, but then things got chaotic. I was upset about my conversation with my father, and Rosina was kind enough to give me wine to calm me down."

"Yes, I'm sure she was," said Vivienne, wondering why Rosina hadn't been helping to fight the fire either. "Did you happen to see Cook that night?"

"The big bald man with the cleaver?" he asked.

"That's the one."

"Yes. He was watching me and your handmaid from the

door of the kitchen. He didn't seem at all happy about the fact that we were together."

"Who else did you notice inside the keep while the kennels were on fire?"

"A lot of the servants, and some of the noblewomen. However, after a little while they all started heading outside to watch. Even most of the musicians left."

"Most of them? What do you mean?"

"Well, there was one musician sitting in the corner with his lute. He was quiet and stayed in the shadows."

"Can you identify him?"

"Mayhap."

"Look over to the lists right now. Where my aunt and your mother are sitting."

He turned to look. "What am I looking for?"

"Is that the musician you saw inside the keep the night of the murder?"

Wilfred stretched his neck to see. He slowly nodded. "Yes, I think so."

"Think so? I need you to be sure."

"I can't quite remember. But I do know he was playing music that sounded awful."

"How so?"

"It was almost like he was missing quite a few notes."

"Or missing a string, mayhap?"

"Aye, I suppose that could be why it sounded so bad."

"Uh oh, here comes my uncle," she said, seeing him from the corner of her eye storming across the field. "If you are going to act like a man, this is the time to do it."

"I am not looking forward to telling him I don't want to marry you."

"If you don't, you're going to end up with me for your wife. For the rest of your life. And I swear, if that happens, I will be much worse of a nightmare to you than your own mother."

That did the trick. His blade came down hard and she blocked him once again. He fought like a madman. Vivienne honestly fought for her life. There was a man hidden inside of Wilfred, and right now he was showing it. The scared boy was pushed aside, and he came at her as if he were fighting a knight on the battlefield.

"That's enough, Wilfred," she said, but he didn't stop. He continued to fight her like he had a raging anger inside and was finally letting it out after all these years.

Vivienne was tiring fast, not used to keeping up this pace. And just when his blade came down at her again and she was sure he'd hit her, her uncle's sword swept in, stopping the attack.

"What the hell is the matter with you?" shouted her uncle, taking Wilfred by the front of his tunic and shaking him hard. "You could have hurt her!"

"Sorry, my lord. I'm not sure what came over me." The scared boy had returned. Wilfred lowered his sword and held up a hand. "Please don't hurt me, Lord Mablethorpe. I promise it'll never happen again."

"You are damned right it won't."

"Wilfred, are you all right?" Lady Gainsborough ran across the practice field, coming to her son's aid.

"Vivienne, what is going on?" shouted her aunt.

"Lady Gainsborough, I think it is best if you and your son left Mablethorpe at once." Her uncle released Wilfred, but kept his sword in hand.

"I agree. What about the betrothal?" asked Lady Gainsborough.

"I don't think I want my niece marrying your son after all."

"But we had an agreement," protested Wilfred's mother.

"The agreement was with Lord Wilfred's father, not him, not you," Vivienne pointed out.

"Mother, I don't want to marry Lady Vivienne," Wilfred finally spoke up.

"We'll talk about this later, Wilfred," his mother told him in a soft voice. "Let's get back to our chamber at once."

"You can start packing your things," said Lord Mablethorpe.

"Uncle, they can't leave yet," Vivienne told him. "The sheriff has yet to question them, and he's not going to be here until this afternoon."

"They'll leave if I say so."

"Gilbert, calm down," warned Vivienne's Aunt Ellen. "We cannot go against the word of the law. Until the sheriff says they are free to go, they must stay. Vivienne is right."

"This is a murder investigation, Uncle. Don't you want the murderer of your good friend caught and punished?" asked Vivienne.

"Of course, I do." Her uncle calmed down, running a hand over his face. "I just want this all to be over. It is making everyone so uncomfortable."

"We all do, dear." His wife took him by the arm. "Let's go get you a drink of whisky so you can relax."

Vivienne turned to leave, seeing the jongleur watching them from the stands and listening to their every word. She was about to call out to him but he picked up his lute and ran from the stands, headed back toward the keep.

Chapter Eleven

Zachariah made his way back to his home in town, eager to see his daughter, Starah. She'd been staying with the constable's wife and children during this investigation. While he worked, he paid the woman to watch over his daughter, not wanting to leave her alone since she was only seven years old. He decided to stop by his own house in town and freshen up before going to visit his daughter. He missed her dearly. Ever since the death of his wife, he felt a void in his life that couldn't be filled. Whenever he was around Starah, that emptiness seemed just a little less hard to cope with. He thought she felt the same way as well.

Pushing open the door to his home, he found Starah huddled in a dark corner, hugging her knees to her chest. The room was dark and cold. There was no fire on the hearth.

"Starah? What are you doing here, sweetheart?"

The little girl looked up, tears streaming down her cheeks. "Father!" she cried, jumping up and running to him. She threw herself at him, hugging him so hard that she almost knocked him over. "I'm so glad you're finally home."

He picked her up, holding her cold little body to his, trying to calm down her shaking.

"Starah, you were supposed to be at the constable's home with his wife watching over you. Why are you even here?"

"I'm tired of living with others who ignore me," she said, still sobbing.

"Ignore you? Constable Dorson has three children for you to play with, darling. I thought you'd be happy there while I was at work."

"I'm not happy there," she told him. "I miss you and I miss Mother."

"I know. So do I." He brushed back her oaken hair from her eyes, kissing her atop her head.

"Are you home to stay now?" she asked him, looking up at him with big brown eyes that looked so much like the eyes of his late wife that it made him want to cry as well. This past year without seeing Margaret's happy face to greet him after a hard day's work had been difficult. Starah used to be such a happy child and so filled with life that she never wanted to sleep. Now, all she seemed to do was cry. His heart broke, knowing how this change in their lives had been affecting his little girl. He didn't like to see her so unhappy.

"Nay, I'm not home to stay yet, but I'll return soon."

"Father, you've been gone so long."

"I know, baby," he said, kissing her on the cheek. "Just a little longer. I have been staying at the castle because there are a lot of people to question about a murder that happened there."

"Then you'll be there for a while yet?"

"I'm afraid so," he told her, wishing he could wash away her pain and sadness. He wanted nothing more than to rid himself of those same feelings as well.

"Then take me with you." The child sniffled, wiped her

nose with her sleeve. She looked up at him with all the hope in the world shining in her wet eyes.

"I wish I could, but you know I can't. I explained to you that when I am working, it is very dangerous and I want to keep you safe."

"Why can't I stay at the castle with you?" She had a valid question. If he was going to keep up a life like this, he was going to have to do something different. Being away from his daughter for such lengths of time was doing neither of them any good.

"It's hard to explain, but it won't work. There might be a murderer at the castle. It is too dangerous to have you there. I don't want you to get hurt."

"Aren't there other children there at the castle, Father?" She pouted, looking him right in the eye.

"Well, yes."

"Then I can play with them."

"I don't think so." How could he explain to her that he was doing this for her own good? He'd be so distracted with her there at his side. Plus, it wouldn't be proper to take his young daughter with him to work.

"You'll be better off staying with Mrs. Dorson and her children."

"Nay, I'm afraid to stay in town without you. The rats are taking over the streets and that rat catcher man is sooooo scary. All my friends say that he is the devil and that he's here to steal children's souls. Is that true?"

"What?" he asked in surprise. He realized there was a problem in town, but he didn't think it was this bad. He also didn't know that the other children were filling his daughter's head with stories that weren't true and that were scaring her even more than she already was. "Nay, Starah. No one is the devil, and no one is going to steal any children's souls, I promise. Especially not yours."

"Starah, are you here?" The constable's wife burst into the cottage, holding her baby in one arm and the hand of her five-year-old daughter with the other. Her ten-year-old son was barefoot and right behind her. "Oh, Sheriff, you're here," she gasped in surprise.

"Mrs. Dorson, I pay you well to watch over my daughter and protect her while I'm gone. Yet, I return to find her here in the dark, cold house, crying and scared and all alone."

"I'm sorry about that. She must have sneaked out while I was tending to the other children."

"Well, no harm done, I suppose," he said, putting his daughter down. "However, it seems your children have been scaring her with stories about the Pied Piper."

"Who's the Pied Piper, Mama?" asked the woman's daughter.

"Anabel, hush," scolded Mrs. Dorson.

"He's talking about that devil man who catches the rats on Rotten Row," her son blurted out, only managing to scare Starah even more. His daughter shrieked and clutched his leg tightly.

"I said hush!" Mrs. Dorson reprimanded her son.

"It's all right, Agatha," said Zachariah. "I am sure Archibald didn't mean anything by it."

"We're scared," cried out little Anabel, clutching to her mother's skirts. The baby in Agatha's arms started crying.

"Sheriff, I need my husband at home right now," said the woman. "I have my hands full with our own children and it is proving to be too much for me to watch over your daughter as well. This Pied Piper has everyone scared out of their minds, not to mention the rats are terrifying. Especially when nightfall comes. I swear I don't ever sleep anymore."

"I will look into the situation soon," he promised. "I assure you there is nothing to fear. It is a good thing to have a rat catcher in town. Without the rats, everyone should feel so much safer." He pulled his daughter closer in a side hug.

"I suppose you're right," said Mrs. Dorson, looking as if she were about to collapse. There was no way he could leave his daughter with her now. He needed to do something to make all of them more at ease.

"I'll settle the matter then," he said. "I have someone else working with me at the castle trying to solve the murder so I will send your husband home."

"Oh, will you?" The woman's face lit up.

"He'll still have to work, but Constable Dorson will stay here in town to look after things until I return. That way, he can be near whenever you need him."

"Then you'll really send my Emery back to us?" she asked with hope in her voice.

"I will for now. So, you see that you and your children won't be alone at night or have a need to be frightened anymore."

"Oh, thank you, Sheriff Fitch. You don't know how much that means to me." She bounced her baby, trying to calm him. "Come along, Starah." The woman held out her hand. "I need to get home to start preparing supper."

"Father, I don't want to go." Starah looked up to him with those sad eyes eating into his heart. He didn't have it in him to leave her at a time like this. The poor child was still so upset over losing her mother. He needed to be there for her, just as Constable Dorson needed to be with his family. He wanted to protect Starah and comfort her. Aye, he wanted to be a good father. "Can't I pleeeeease stay with you?" she begged.

He might regret what he was about to do, but he felt as if he needed to do it. "Mrs. Dorson, Starah will be coming with me to the castle, but I thank you kindly for offering to watch her. However, right now, I think my daughter needs her father."

VIVIENNE CHANGED into a gown after her sparring session, still trying to calm her heart from the scare she'd had, fighting Lord Wilfred. Part of her thought she was lucky to be alive.

"You look much better now," Rosina told her, unpinning her hair and using a boar's-bristle brush to comb out the tangles.

"I have to admit I feel better, too," she told her handmaid. "I am still a little shaken about what happened on the practice field."

The girl's brushing slowed. "What happened, my lady?"

"You should have stayed to see it," Vivienne told her. "Lord Wilfred fought me like a madman. To be honest, his fury scared me a little."

"Really? Lord Wilfred did that?"

"Yes. It is highly unbelievable, but for the first time since I've known him he acted like a man and not a milksop."

"Milksop? My lady, you sound like the alewives when you call him that."

"You're right. I'm sorry. All I'm saying is that he truly surprised me. I cannot believe he actually stood up to my uncle and his mother both."

"He did? What happened?" Rosina stopped brushing and looked at Vivienne in question.

"He told them he didn't want to marry me. Isn't that wonderful?" Vivienne smiled, feeling so relieved.

"And your uncle agreed with that?" asked the handmaid.

"Well, yes. Actually, he was the one to say it first, and then

Wilfred said so afterwards. Now that I think of it, mayhap he wasn't acting quite as manly as I thought."

"Oh, no, my lady, I agree with you." She started brushing Vivienne's hair again. "Lord Wilfred seems to have a hidden side to him that no one sees."

"Have you heard more about him acting this way?" Vivienne looked at the girl without turning her head.

"Nay. I just mean that he spoke up for himself, like you said. And he fought you like a lion."

"*Madman* is what I said, but I suppose you could compare his actions to a lion. How well do you know him?" she asked.

"Me?" The handmaid put the brush down on the table. "Not well. Why?"

"I just wondered if you thought that perhaps Lord Wilfred could have gotten angry enough with his father that he acted like a madman with him, too."

"My lady! Are you suggesting that Lord Wilfred murdered his own father? How could you?"

"I didn't mean anything by it," she said, standing up and stretching. "I am just looking at the murder from all angles. With trying to find the murderer, I mean."

"Oh, of course. I understand. Have you and the sheriff found any clues yet?"

"Well ... I'm not supposed to say."

"You know I won't tell anyone."

Vivienne looked at the girl, wondering if she really thought Vivienne would believe that. Rosina was one of the biggest gossips Vivienne knew. To think she'd keep quiet about this was silly.

"What have you heard, Rosina?" she asked instead, trying to draw out what she might know. "Have the alewives or servants or anyone been saying anything about who they think murdered Lord Gainsborough?"

"Oh, my lady, it is not for me to say."

"I am not asking you who *you* think did it. I am only wondering what everyone else is saying, that's all."

"Well, if you insist. I heard something last night in the great hall."

"What did you hear?"

"Some of the musicians are talking about that traveling jongleur."

"Leif," she said with a nod. "What about him?"

"It seems he is spouting off about how Lord Gainsborough deserved to die. Doesn't that sound a little suspicious to you?"

"I hardly think a man voicing his opinion makes him a suspect."

Rosina shook her head in disbelief. "But he said he was glad Lord Gainsborough died and that he deserved it. He also seems to have good reason to kill the man, since he is so upset about Lord Gainsborough breaking his lute string. I mean, that's a clue, nay? Isn't that what the sheriff looks for?"

"Yes, I suppose so. However, I highly doubt a musician would actually kill a noble over a broken lute string. It seems petty, and it is so risky since Leif is a commoner. Killing a nobleman could very well mean his death."

"I suppose you're right." Rosina picked up some ribbons and ties and walked back over to her. "Allow me to pin up your hair, my lady. After all, you'll want to look pretty for the sheriff when he returns."

"Rosina!" She was shocked the girl would say such a thing.

"Don't you like him, my lady? All the kitchen servants are saying you and he were sitting together in the kitchen eating and neither of you could keep your eyes off each other."

"You know that is naught but gossip. Besides, you were there too. I wasn't looking at him in any flirtatious manner, was I?"

"I'm not sure, my lady. I wasn't looking at you. I was too shocked watching Lord Gainsborough yelling at Cook, kicking your dog, and pinching that lightskirt, Maria."

"Lightskirt? Why do you call her that?"

"No reason, my lady. Let me fix your hair please."

"Nay. I'll wear it long and down today, thank you." Vivienne didn't want to be accused of trying to attract the sheriff. Especially when it was just gossip and not even true.

"Whatever you say." Rosina walked back to the dressing table and put the ribbons and things back down.

"Did you call Maria that name because she has her eye on your man?" asked Vivienne.

"I suppose so. I'm sorry. It's just that the girl shouldn't expose so much cleavage. She attracts the eyes of every man, tempting them in ways she shouldn't. Then, when they touch her, she acts surprised."

"They touch her? Is something going on with Maria in the kitchens that I don't know about?"

"Not anything that isn't usually happening, I guess. I'm sorry, I suppose I got carried away."

"A little," said Vivienne, thinking how jealous Rosina sounded right now. Then again, Maria was quite a tart, that part was true. Vivienne supposed she should tell Maria to cover up more. She hadn't done so before because Vivienne, unlike most women, thought it wise for all females to make choices on their own. However, this choice could get the girl in trouble if she weren't careful. "We'd better get going," said Vivienne, heading to the door. "The sheriff will be awaiting us."

"Us? Oh, my lady, do I really have to go for questioning? That man makes me so nervous."

"Why?" she asked her. "Do you have something to hide that you think he's going to discover?"

"Nay. Should I?"

"Not that I know of. Now, come. I told you that I'd be there with you to support you, and so I shall."

They were halfway out the door when Rosina stopped. "My lady, I would really like to someday work with you to solve murders and mysteries, the way you are doing with Sheriff Fitch."

Vivienne smiled, liking the enthusiasm her handmaid was showing. "You are really interested in such a thing, aren't you?"

"Oh, I am. I want to be like you. You are such a strong woman, and I am inspired by your actions."

"Thank you. I think." Thoughts ran rampant through Vivienne's head of what her uncle would say if all the women in the castle started admiring Vivienne's ways and acting like her. She chuckled inwardly, thinking it would drive him mad, even if Vivienne loved it.

"What would I have to do to work with you and the sheriff?" asked her handmaid.

"Slow down, Rosina. I never said it was going to happen. Honestly, I am not even sure that Sheriff Fitch really wants *me* working with him right now."

"I understand." Rosina's smile disappeared and she looked down. Vivienne didn't want to dash anyone's dreams. Especially not those of a young woman.

"However, if you want to get on the sheriff's good side, bring him information," she explained.

"What kind of information?"

"You know. Like, if you hear or see something that seems suspicious, tell him about it."

"I'm not sure I feel comfortable enough around him to do that."

"Then just tell me and I'll let him know."

"You mean you want to know the gossip I hear about anything that pertains to the murder?"

"Yes, I suppose so."

"But gossip isn't true all the time. Is it?"

"Nay, not usually. However, there is a grain of truth in everything. Even in a lie."

"Is there? I didn't know that."

"Yes, Rosina. One just needs to know how to look through the lies to find that grain of truth. And once it is found, all questions will be answered."

Chapter Twelve

Zachariah paced the chamber, looking out the window for the third time in the past five minutes. Vivienne was late. Again. The woman couldn't seem to get anywhere on time. She knew they had a lot of work to do today, and yet she dawdled. He never should have agreed to let her help him because all she was doing was slowing down this investigation.

"Father, why do you keep walking back and forth like that?" asked his daughter Starah from his bed. He'd had no choice but to bring her along with him, but was already starting to regret it. As much as he wanted to protect her and spend time with her, the child was only going to prove to be a distraction.

"I'm anxiously awaiting Lady Vivienne, who can't seem to be on time if her life depended on it."

Someone cleared their throat and he spun around to see Vivienne and her handmaid standing inside the door to his chamber. Richard, the guard, was holding the door open.

"Lady Vivienne here to see you, Sheriff," announced the guard.

"Yes. I see that. Come in," he said with a nod.

"I brought Rosina along for her questioning session," Vivienne told him, strolling across the room to join him. "Shall we start?" She sat on a chair, resting her hands atop the table. Rosina followed Vivienne, but stood there stiff as a board.

"Nay. Not quite yet." He motioned to his daughter on the bed.

"What?" Vivienne turned to look. "Oh, Starah is here! Why didn't you tell me?" She jumped to her feet and ran over to the bed excitedly, giving his daughter a big hug. "How are you, sweetheart? It is so nice to see you once again. It has been much too long."

"Hello, Lady Vivienne," said the girl, looking upset.

"What's the matter, sweetheart?" Vivienne spoke in a soft and caring voice. "You seem upset about something."

"I am," said Starah. "I'm scared of the Pie-eating man."

"The what?" Vivienne's laughter filled the room, bringing a warm feeling to Zachariah's heart. Damn, it had been so long since he'd heard a woman's laughter. He hadn't thought he'd missed it much until now.

"It's Pied Piper," he corrected his daughter. "Not pie-eating man, sweetheart."

"Oh, thank you for explaining ... my dear." Vivienne grinned. "But I really think you should use my title as we've agreed."

His heart jumped and a heat washed through him. "I was talking to my daughter, not you! My lady," he added as an afterthought."

Her face broke out into a full-blown smile. "I know. I just like to see you squirm, Sheriff."

He groaned under his breath.

Vivienne's attention returned to the girl. "Why are you here, Starah?"

"She'll be staying with me for the duration of this investigation," Zachariah answered before his daughter could say a word.

"Oh, how nice." Vivienne sat down on the bed and put her arm around the little girl's shoulders. "Then we'll have plenty of time to spend together, Starah. Perhaps I'll even show you the battlements and the practice yard later."

"Oh, I'd like that!" cried Starah, jumping up and down atop the bed now.

"Starah, stop that!" he shouted, then looked over at Vivienne next. "My daughter doesn't need a tour of the castle, thank you."

"Well, why not?" asked Vivienne, standing back up and grabbing Starah, having her sit down on the bed. "I think she would really like it. I'll hold her hand the entire time so it won't be dangerous at all."

Zachariah was starting to lose his patience. He was here to work, and this was nonsense. Why had he thought it was a good idea to even bring his daughter here in the first place? "Lady Vivienne, Starah will not be staying in here during the questioning. It wouldn't be proper. Actually, I wanted to ask your advice about where she should wait for me while I'm working."

"Excuse me, my lady and Sheriff Fitch, but the steward and the page boy have brought the rest of the people to be questioned," said Richard, sticking his head back into the room.

"Tell everyone to just calm down and wait their turn. They'll be called in one at a time," he instructed the guard.

"Aye, of course." Richard was about to close the door, when Vivienne stopped him.

"Richard, can you send in the steward and the page, please? I'd like to speak with them now."

"Yes, my lady. Right away." He looked down the corridor and motioned with his head for them to enter.

Martin walked in with John trailing right behind him.

"Hello, Lady Vivienne," said Martin.

"My lady. Sheriff," the steward greeted them with a quick nod.

"John, I'd like you and Martin to take the sheriff's daughter, Starah, to the courtyard to meet and play with the other children today."

"Yes, my lady," said John with a bow.

"Do you mean I get to play with the other children too?" asked Martin, looking excited about the idea.

"Yes. That is exactly what I mean." Vivienne went back to her chair. "Starah, come here and meet Martin."

The girl jumped off the bed and hurried over. "Hello," she said.

"Hello. I'm Martin," the boy told her. "I'm a page but going to be a knight someday."

"I'm the sheriff's daughter. How old are you?"

"Seven. How old are you?"

"Seven, too."

"Do you like dogs?" asked Martin.

"Yes," she answered. "Why?"

"Because I found a ball in the garden and I'm going to throw it around for Grunt to chase." Martin reached inside his tunic and pulled out a small raggedy ball made from an animal bladder stuffed with rags and sewed together to create the toy.

"What is a Grunt?" asked the little girl, wrinkling her nose. It caused Vivienne to laugh once again.

"Grunt is my dog," Vivienne told her. "And I think he would appreciate the two of you throwing a ball for him. It is his favorite thing to do."

"Besides to sniff out robbers and murderers," said Martin. "Grunt helps to solve crime."

"He does?" The little girl seemed fascinated. "I'd like to meet him. Can I, Father?"

"Yes, of course," Zachariah answered, shuffling through some papers, nodding his thanks to Vivienne.

"Meet us in the great hall later for the meal," Vivienne called out as the children left the room together.

"I'll make sure they get there safely," John promised, following them out of the room.

"Stay with Martin and don't go outside the castle walls, Starah," Zachariah called out to his daughter.

After they'd gone and the door was once again closed, Zachariah finally sat down next to Vivienne to start the questioning. "All right, then. Shall we proceed?"

"Yes," said Vivienne. "My handmaid, Rosina, is one of the last people we need to question."

"Then let's get started. Have a seat please." He held out his hand, motioning to the chair. The girl stood there shaking and wringing her hands together. She looked over at Vivienne and waited until she nodded before she actually took a seat.

"There is no need to be nervous," he told the girl. "We just have a few questions. It's routine."

Rosina nodded but didn't say a word.

"How long have you been Lady Vivienne's handmaid?" he asked the girl.

Vivienne leaned over and whispered. "Sheriff, what does this have to do with the murder?"

"I'm just trying to make small talk to get her to relax," he whispered back.

"I see. All right, go ahead, Rosina," Vivienne told the girl.

"I don't know. Not that long. Mayhap ... five months?"

"It's been six, actually," Vivienne corrected her. "She took over for my last handmaid, Justina. Justina got married and moved to town to be with her husband and start a family. It was my recommendation she do so. Justina was the one to point out that she thought Rosina would be a good handmaid to take her place."

"Lady Vivienne, I am questioning your handmaid, not you," Zachariah reminded her.

"Oh. Of course. I'm sorry. Go ahead."

"Rosina, can you tell me where you worked before you were Lady Vivienne's handmaid?" he asked.

"Where did I work?" Her gaze shot over to Vivienne.

"He means, what did you do?" said Vivienne. Then, once again, Vivienne took control by answering for the girl. "Rosina was a kitchen maid right here at Mablethorpe Castle, before she got the position of my handmaid. She makes the best pies you've ever tasted."

Zachariah let out a deep sigh. "Lady Vivienne, may I have a word with you in private, please?" He shot up to his feet and walked over to the window. Vivienne followed.

"What are you doing?" she asked, joining him at the window. "I thought we were questioning people about the murder? Are we pausing already?"

"We *are* questioning people," he said in a low voice. "Or should I say that is what I am trying to do, but you don't seem to understand the process."

"The process?" She looked at him and blinked. "I didn't know there was a certain process to this."

"Egads, don't you understand?" He could tell by the blank look on her face that she didn't know what he meant. "You need to stop answering for the girl. It is getting annoying."

"But she's sensitive and scared. I am only trying to help."

"Well, stop it! I need to hear *her* answer the questions, not *you*. Otherwise, how am I ever going to find the answers I seek?"

"Oh." Her chin raised up as if she felt insulted. "Sorry. I didn't know it was that important. I won't interfere again."

"Good. Thank you," he said. "I know you are new at this, but you need to learn how I work."

"Of course. I understand. Can we continue?"

"By all means."

As soon as they sat back down and he was about to continue the questioning, Vivienne spoke up, asking a question of her own instead. It left him sitting there with his mouth hanging open.

"Tell us, Rosina, where were you the night that Lord Gainsborough was murdered?"

"I was looking for you, my lady. Don't you remember, we got separated in the crowd?"

"Yes, I remember."

"I was going to help put out the fire, but you said you'd save the dogs and that I should go to the kitchen and tell everyone to help fill buckets of water to douse the flames."

"Yes, I did say that. You're correct."

"Lady Vivienne, what are you doing?" Zachariah said through gritted teeth.

"I'm questioning the girl instead of answering the questions for her. Just like you suggested."

"It sounds more like she's the one questioning you. Now please, just let me do this."

Vivienne threw her hands up in the air and leaned back on the chair, crossing her arms over her chest. "Be my guest, Sheriff. I wouldn't want to ruin your investigation."

"You need to remember that I've been doing this a lot longer than you," he told her. "Just ... let me continue in my own way."

"Hrmmph," she scoffed, turning her head to stare out the open window rather than to watch him work.

"Rosina, what did you do after you told the servants to help put out the fire?" he asked. "Did you go to the kennels to help as well?"

"I started to go, but then I saw Lord Wilfred coming from the corridor. He looked upset about something."

"Really? Did you ask him what had him so upset?" Zachariah leaned forward. Now they were getting somewhere.

"I did. He said he'd had a spat with his father. He also said he needed a drink so I went back to the kitchens and returned with a goblet of wine."

"Then what?" asked Zachariah, taking notes on a piece of paper. He dipped his quill in the ink and held it up, ready to write.

"Then we talked until everyone returned."

"What did you talk about?"

"I don't know. Nothing in particular." Rosina's gaze flashed over to Vivienne, but Vivienne thankfully didn't say a word. "I told him about the food we'd planned to serve that night and he told me that I was easy to talk to, unlike most people."

"What about the spat with his father? What was that all about?" Zachariah felt like they were finally getting somewhere now.

"I—I'm not sure. He didn't say another word about it, and neither did I ask."

"What?" Zachariah pounded his hands down on the table in frustration and jumped to his feet. He must have frightened the girl because she cried out and ran over to stand behind Vivienne.

"You are scaring the poor girl, now stop it," spat Vivienne with a stiff upper lip.

"We need to know more about that confrontation between Lord Wilfred and his father. Guard, bring in Lord Wilfred next," he shouted.

The door opened and Richard stuck his head inside. "Lord Wilfred?" He scanned the crowd. "I'm sorry but I don't see him here, Sheriff."

"Then find him," instructed Zachariah.

"Don't bother." Vivienne waved her hand through the air. "I already questioned Lord Wilfred this morning as we sparred on the practice field."

"You did what?" He couldn't believe what he was hearing. "You had no right to do that. It was not part of the plan. In this room is the only place we're supposed to be questioning others."

"You never stated that directly, so I didn't know." Vivienne reached out and took Rosina's hand, patting it to calm her down. "Now, do you want to hear what the argument between them was about or not?"

Zachariah sighed and slowly sat back down. "Go ahead."

Vivienne continued "Lord Wilfred was upset with the betrothal and told his father so. He said he didn't want to marry me, but his father didn't take it well."

"That's right." Rosina lifted her finger in the air. "I do remember him saying something about that to me. But it wasn't until after he was relaxed from the wine."

"Did a fight break out between them?" he asked.

"According to Lord Wilfred, no," Vivienne answered. "He said his father was too busy paying attention to Maria to even bother with what he had to say."

"I see." Zachariah scribbled on his paper. "And who exactly is this Maria?" he asked.

"She's the kitchen wench with all the cleavage," answered Rosina, seeming to find her courage at Vivienne's side.

"Have we questioned her yet?" He leaned forward and started to flip through the notes he'd made, trying to find out.

"Nay, she is out in the corridor waiting to be questioned right now. I saw her as we came in," Vivienne explained.

"All right, you may go then, Rosina." He dismissed the handmaid. "Tell the guard to send Maria in next."

"I will. Thank you, Sheriff," Rosina answered, running for the door.

"Oh, wait! One more thing," he said, causing her to stop.

"Yes?" She slowly turned around.

"What kind of wine did you serve Lord Wilfred?"

"I am not sure what it was called, I'm sorry."

"Nay, I mean, was it white or red wine?"

"Oh. It was red wine, Sheriff."

"Thank you, that'll be all."

As soon as Rosina left the room, Vivienne leaned over to talk to the sheriff. "Why did you ask her about the color of the wine?"

"I'll tell you later. Next, please," he called out to the guard.

Vivienne thought back and realized the answer on her own. "It's because we found red wine stains on the deceased's fingers and tunic, right?"

"You're starting to figure out how this works."

"What does that mean? About the wine, I mean?"

"I'm not sure yet. But I have some ideas we're going to need to discuss."

"I'd like that," she told him, appreciating that the sheriff was now including her in his plans.

"I am Maria," said the kitchen maid, entering the room and taking a seat across from them.

Vivienne noticed the sheriff looking at the girl's cleavage. For some reason, that really bothered her. Could it be because she wished he would look at her that way? Nay, she decided. It was only because of how distracting it was proving to be. Rosina's accusation of Maria being naught but a whore still rang in her ears. Vivienne remembered Lady Gainsborough accusing her of the same thing. It hadn't felt good. No one should have to put up with being called that! Especially since Vivienne believed Maria was naught but a sweet and innocent girl who only liked to flirt with the men.

"Maria, please pull up your bodice," she instructed.

"My lady?" Maria seemed confused. "Did I do something wrong?"

"You are showing too much cleavage. It isn't appropriate to be working in the kitchens like that."

Maria looked down to her breasts. "No one has ever complained about it before."

"I understand," Vivienne answered. "However, it would be in your best interest right now to try to stay more covered up. So, either lace up the bodice tighter, or I'll have you wear a full apron that covers your chest all the way down to your feet."

"I'm sorry, my lady." She started to untie the lacing to make it tighter, but all it did was expose her breasts even more.

"Never mind. Do it later," said Vivienne, seeing the distraction becoming greater. Zachariah was a man like any other. Vivienne wanted him to keep his mind on the murder and not on a lusty wench's bosom. "The sheriff has some questions he wants you to answer."

"Of course, my lady. I will do the best I can."

After talking to Maria and Cook, they both acknowledged the whereabouts of each other the night of the murder. It seemed that they had stayed in the kitchen to keep the food from burning and to make sure the meal was ready when everyone returned from putting out the fire. Lady Gainsborough and even Vivienne's aunt and uncle were also questioned, which was more than uncomfortable for Vivienne. Still, everyone seemed to be in the clear. And when the castle healer said she'd seen Adam with the hounds in the barn during the fire, suspicion of the kennel groom diminished as well. The list of suspects was dwindling quickly and they still didn't have any answers.

"There are only two more people to question and then we're done," said Richard, sticking his head into the room once more.

"Who are they?" asked Vivienne.

"Herman, the guard from Gainsborough, and that jongleur boy, my lady."

"And you too, Richard," added the sheriff.

"Sheriff?" The guard seemed surprised to hear this.

"Yes, that's right. Everyone needs to be questioned," Vivienne explained to her guard.

"Of course, my lady." Richard suddenly seemed nervous now, just like everyone else who had been questioned over the past few days. Everyone was on edge, and it did nothing to help read their true reactions.

Thunder boomed outside, the low rumbling still sounding a distance away. Glancing out the open window, Vivienne realized the sky had become quite dark. It was not only because nightfall was moving in, but because of the angry clouds filling the sky. It was shaping up out there, looking to be a bad storm.

"Damn," she heard the sheriff mumble, his attention out the window instead of on the investigation.

"Is something wrong?" she asked him.

"Nay, not really." He looked down to his notes and picked up his quill, dipping it in the ink and scribbling something on the piece of paper. "It's just that Starah is really afraid of storms. Let's get this completed quickly. I need to go to her. She is going to be looking for me."

"I can question the last few by myself," Vivienne told him.

"Nay. I'd prefer to be here too," the sheriff answered, never even stopping for a minute to consider she was more than capable of doing the job. "Richard, please come in and bring the others with you," he called out.

It was a little frustrating for Vivienne that Zachariah didn't trust her enough to let her continue the investigation without him. Then again, she supposed since it was his job he had the right to do things his way. Or mayhap it was just because he was a man and more than stubborn and set in his ways than if he were a woman.

The two guards stood behind the jongleur, Leif, who sat in the chair. The sheriff went through the normal questioning routine. It was revealed that Richard had helped on the water line. Vivienne agreed that she'd seen him there since he'd assisted her to her feet when she'd exited the burning kennels and had been knocked to the ground. Herman, on the other hand, said he'd gone to Lady Gainsborough's chamber as requested to fetch her cloak. It seemed that she had been afraid of the flying ashes hitting her good gown since she was headed out to the fire with Lady Mablethorpe.

"Did anyone see you go to the bedchamber?" asked the sheriff.

"I don't know," said Herman. "I didn't speak to anyone, if that's what you mean. I was focused on my task, hurrying so I could join the others in putting out the fire."

"Did you ever give Lady Gainsborough her cloak that night?" asked Vivienne, having seen the woman outside and not remembering her wearing a cloak at all.

"Yes," answered the guard. "However, it did take me a while to find her. By the time I did, everyone was frantic because it seems that pageboy was saying someone had been killed inside the keep."

"What about you?" Vivienne asked Leif. "Where were you when all this was happening?"

"I'm a musician, my lady. I was up in the gallery for most of the night."

"You mean to have us believe you were playing music with a broken string?" asked the sheriff.

"Lord Wilfred said he saw you sitting in the shadows with your lute," added Vivienne.

"I was trying to fix my instrument." Leif looked from Vivienne to the sheriff and then back again. "Can I ask a question now?"

"Sure," said the sheriff. "What is it?"

"Where did Lord Wilfred say he saw me? And where was he at the time?"

"That is confidential and none of your concern," growled the sheriff.

"I think we should tell him," said Vivienne, doing so without waiting for him to give her his opinion. "Lord Wilfred was by the fire sipping wine and talking to my handmaid at the time," Vivienne explained. "He said you were in the shadows, but didn't specify exactly where. Why do you ask?"

"I'd like to speak privately," said Leif.

"Guards, you may go," the sheriff dismissed them. "Close the door behind you, please."

Rain started to pelt down hard outside, and once again, the sheriff's attention was out the window instead of on the investigation.

"Go ahead, Leif," said Vivienne. "What did you want to say?"

"I think someone is lying." Leif crossed his arms over his chest.

"Mayhap it is you?" asked the sheriff.

"Nay, I'm not. I don't have anyone to vouch for me, I agree," said the boy. "But I was up in the gallery with my lute and very angry."

"Angry with Lord Gainsborough," said the sheriff. "Angry enough to want to kill the man?"

"Yes," he answered, surprising both Vivienne and Zachariah.

"Did you? Kill him?" asked Vivienne, her heart beating rapidly, not knowing what they would do if he confessed to the murder right now.

"If I did kill him, do you think I'd be sitting here telling you about it?" Leif answered snidely.

"Watch your attitude, young man," the sheriff warned him.

"What is it exactly that you are trying to say?" Vivienne took over the questioning since the sheriff seemed so distracted by the weather that his mind didn't seem to be focused on the questioning anymore.

"I am just saying that I was in the gallery the entire time and I never saw Lord Wilfred and that handmaid sitting by the fire drinking wine and talking."

"Are you sure?" asked the sheriff.

"Aye. However, I did see them go into the kitchen in a big hurry. They were with that big cook and that busty serving wench."

"All right, thank you, that'll be all," said the sheriff, getting to his feet and heading to the door.

"Am I free to leave the castle now?" asked the boy.

"Nay, Leif. Not yet," Zachariah answered. "I will have to look into what you just told me and I might have more questions for you. Also, since no one saw you, you are still a suspect."

"But Lord Wilfred did see him in the great hall and he told me so," protested Vivienne.

"And this boy says Lord Wilfred was lying, so that puts suspicion on both of them." The sheriff held the door open.

"Leif said he didn't see them by the fire but in the kitchen instead," Vivienne corrected him. "So mayhap when Lord Wilfred said he saw Leif, it was true."

"Someone is not telling the truth, and until I get to the bottom of it, everyone will stay put," answered the sheriff with conviction.

Vivienne realized the sheriff was too worried about his daughter and the storm right now to care about anything else at the moment. Any more questioning would have to wait. "Leif, I'd like to purchase a new string for your lute like I promised."

"That would be appreciated, my lady."

"Will you travel with me to town in the morning? I believe there is a fair taking place there tomorrow, and I am sure we can find a musician selling strings."

"Thank you, my lady. That would be fine." The boy got up and bowed.

"Meet me by the main gate just after the morning meal to break the fast."

Leif bowed once again and sidestepped the sheriff as he left the room and bounded down the corridor.

"What was that all about?" asked Zachariah, as they left the room, heading to the great hall together.

"Whatever do you mean?"

"You seem like you are trying to protect everyone, Lady Vivienne."

"You are making these people nervous and I am just trying to calm them back down, Sheriff. I don't see anything wrong with it."

"You cannot be siding with the suspects, my lady. It's not right."

"I am not siding with anyone. I am just going to buy a string for Leif's lute like I promised. I, unlike some people, do not break my word."

He scowled at her and it was evident he knew she had meant him. Still, he didn't answer. They walked at a good clip toward the great hall as thunder echoed off the castle walls.

"We are no closer to solving this case than we were several days ago," he told her. "We need to discuss what we've learned and find the information that seems to be alluding us."

"And so we shall," she told him. "That is exactly what we'll do when we go to town with Leif."

"We?" His eyes flashed over to her as they continued to walk. "I'm not going to town with you."

"I think you should."

"Whatever for?"

"I believe it would be nice to take Starah along with her new friend Martin with us. We could make a day of it. The children would enjoy the fair and it would be nice to get away from here for a while. Don't you agree?"

"Nay, I don't agree. We don't have time for senseless outings! We have a murder to solve, unless you're forgotten."

"I didn't forget," she assured him. "However, sometimes we need to pay attention to the little things in life. Little things like those we often take for granted. You are thinking too much about the murder and you need to relax. You must open your tight fist and let loose what you're holding on to before you can grasp anything new."

"What in God's name are you rambling on about?" His dark eyes scrutinized her.

"Sheriff, if I may be blunt, please."

"Why not? You always are. Go right ahead."

"I think you need to spend some time with your daughter. She is young and scared and all alone without a mother. It is important to her right now to know she hasn't been abandoned."

"Perhaps you're right," he said, running a hand through his hair. "I do feel as if I've been ignoring Starah, since all I do is work. She really does need me right now."

"Exactly. That is why we're taking her with us tomorrow to the fair."

"What about the case? I need to work."

"We will both be working, but the others won't even know it," she told him.

"What does that mean?"

"It means, I am starting to see things in a different light," she told him, feeling sure of herself right now.

"If you know something about the murder, Lady Vivienne, you need to tell me."

"What I know is that we need to invite some people to join us on our outing in the morning."

"Who?"

"You'll find out tomorrow. I'll take care of everything, so don't worry about a thing. Now, tonight all I want you to think about is spending time with your daughter. Make her feel safe from the storm."

"I hope you know what you're doing, Lady Vivienne."

"Me?" She shrugged. "Not really. You see, I never know what I'm doing until I actually do it."

He groaned. "That's what I'm afraid of."

They approached the great hall just as another big boom of thunder rattled the shutters. This time it was so loud that it seemed to echo through the entire castle.

"Father!" Starah ran to Zachariah and he scooped her up, holding her tightly to his chest. "I'm scared of the storm. I'm so happy you are here." She hid her face against his chest.

"Yes, I'm here now, sweetheart. There is nothing to worry

about. Everything is going to be all right." Zachariah walked off holding his daughter.

Vivienne had never seen anything so sweet in all her life. Her heart ached with longing for her own baby, whom she had never had the opportunity to cuddle and comfort in this way. She could still see her son's sweet face and those bright blue eyes staring up at her that night, as she held her baby for the first and last time ever. She should have been able to protect him the way the sheriff was protecting his daughter right now. Vivienne failed her son and she would never forgive herself for not doing more to keep him safe. If only she had been able to find him after the attack, mayhap things would be different in her life right now. She prayed to God that her baby's death had been quick and that the little boy had not suffered at all. Then again, prayers weren't the answer to her problems she realized by now. After all, God had punished her by taking her child away and she didn't know if she could ever forgive Him for not only that loss, but the loss of her entire family.

Grunt's wet nose against her hand gained her attention. He looked up to her with his tongue hanging out as he panted heavily. She swore the damned dog was smiling!

"What are you so happy about?" she asked her hound, her heart softening, since Grunt was like her baby now. She hunkered down and scratched behind his ears, following it up with a kiss to the hound's head.

"Grunt has been chasing a ball around the courtyard all afternoon." Her aunt approached, bending over to pet the hound as well. "Martin didn't stop playing and neither did the sheriff's daughter. It does my heart good to see children play. Somehow, I think of all the children at the castle as my own, since I have none." Vivienne's aunt and uncle had been blessed with three sons over the years. But sadly, none of the babies lived to be more than a year old. Yes, her aunt and uncle were no strangers to emptiness, sadness, and loss, just as she was now.

"I know what you mean," said Vivienne, standing back up. "A woman's heart needs to feel that love. I miss it too. In a way, just like you, I think of all the children at Mablethorpe as mine somehow.

"They will be so tired tonight. I'm sure they'll fall asleep as soon as their heads hit the pillows."

Vivienne looked over to the trestle table to see the pageboy, Martin, with his head down on the table, resting on his crossed arms. He sat with the other children of the castle who were normally lively, but seemed tired now just like her aunt had said. The food had just started to be served and instead of chattering like they always did, the children were eating in silence.

"Tomorrow will be a special day for some of them," she told her aunt.

"Really? How so?"

"You see, the sheriff and I are taking his daughter to the town fair. Since Martin and Starah seem to get along so nicely, I'll be taking the page with us as well."

"You and the sheriff are going? Together? Really?" Her aunt looked at her in that knowing way and grinned.

"It's not what you think, Aunt Ellen. The sheriff has been so consumed with his work lately that he's been ignoring his daughter. I don't like to see children suffer, so I suggested he take the day to have some fun with Starah. That is all there is to it."

"I think that is a grand idea, Vivienne. I am happy that you will be going along as well."

"I am going with them to buy Leif a string for his lute like I promised."

"Leif?" asked her aunt in question.

"Yes. The jongleur. It was Lord Gainsborough's fault that

the musician's string broke. I feel it is the least I can do for the boy, since he uses his lute to make a living."

"Is that a wise idea, my dear? I mean, word around the castle is that the jongleur is the one who killed Lord Gainsborough."

"Well, he certainly does seem to have a motive, I suppose. But I am sure the boy didn't do it."

"How can you be sure?"

"I'm not, actually. I suppose since I like the boy, I am just hoping it wasn't he who committed murder."

"I'm not sure your uncle will like this idea at all. It could be dangerous, Vivienne."

"Since the sheriff and I don't have enough evidence to decide upon the killer, I suppose everyone is in danger until the murderer is exposed."

"I, for one, will be happy when this is all behind us. Did you know that Lady Gainsborough and her son are planning on leaving in the morning and taking her husband's body back to Gainsborough to be buried?"

"Nay. They can't leave yet. We still haven't solved the murder."

"They are impatient and eager to return to their home. You can't blame them. Her husband needs to be put to rest."

"They'll need a coffin to transport the body," she told her aunt.

"Yes, they will. Your uncle is going to have some of his men construct one tomorrow."

"I have a better idea."

"What is that, my dear?"

Vivienne had to think quickly. She didn't want this murder going unsolved just like what happened to her own parents. She had just a short time before the Gainsboroughs left for good. With them gone and with the body taken with them, there is a good chance the investigation would fall by the wayside. The last thing she wanted was for the killer to somehow escape without being punished for the heinous crime.

"The Gainsboroughs were always good friends with you and Uncle Gilbert, weren't they?" she asked her aunt.

"Yes. However, this investigation has seemed to put a strain on our friendship. And after that argument between Lord Wilfred and your uncle on the practice field, I'm afraid we might not be allies after all."

"Then we need to do something to fix that, don't we?"

"We?"

"The way I see it, men are stubborn and too self-absorbed to admit when they are wrong. They also don't like to apologize. Making amends is just like having an alliance, if you ask me. Even without a betrothal. Don't you agree?"

"I do see your point, Vivienne. Lord knows Gilbert is as stubborn as they come. But what are you planning to do?"

"Listen closely, Aunt Ellen because I need your help."

"My help? How can I help you?"

"This is what I need you to do."

Chapter Thirteen

Zachariah stood in the courtyard the next morning, looking at the two wagons filled with people that were now joining them at the fair today. This wasn't at all what he'd expected when Lady Vivienne suggested they take the day off from working and instead take the children to the fair. He had envisioned it as a private outing, not dragging half the castle with them.

"I don't understand," he said to Vivienne, who was standing next to him. His daughter was in one wagon being driven by Richard. Vivienne's aunt and uncle were on the bench seat next to the guard. In the back of the wagon sat Starah and Martin, along with the jongleur Leif, and Vivienne's handmaid Rosina. Martin held on to Vivienne's dog. The second wagon was being driven by Gainsborough's guard, Herman. Next to him sat Lady Gainsborough and her son Wilfred. In the back of this wagon were the kennel groom Adam, Cook, and the busty kitchen maid, Maria. "Why in God's name are all these people coming with us to the fair?"

"I asked them all to be here," she told him. "Well, actually, my aunt helped with getting them all to agree, I must say. She convinced my uncle to come, as well as urging Lady Gainsborough and Lord Wilfred to join us. I mean, after that spat between my uncle and Wilfred, this was a monumental accomplishment. Wouldn't you say?"

"I'd say I hope you have a damned good reason for bringing so many people along with us today."

"I do. And I'll explain it to you, but not now. I'll do it as we are riding. Now mount your horse. The wagons are heading out and we don't want them to leave us too far behind."

"We don't?" Zachariah walked over to help Vivienne atop her horse, but she didn't need his help and he was sure neither did she want it. She hoisted herself atop her steed, throwing one leg over the saddle and riding astride, even though she wore a gown. He had never seen anything like this. Except from her.

"Move quickly, Sheriff," she instructed, smiling down at him, turning her horse in a full circle. The wagons creaked and groaned as they moved forward, heading out the gate and over the drawbridge. "Did you need assistance mounting your horse?" She raised her brows and looked at him mockingly.

"Stop it, Lady Vivienne. You don't want to anger me before we're even through the gate." He jumped into the saddle and got in front of her, riding over the drawbridge after the wagons, with Vivienne right behind. Once they were on the road, he slowed down and waited for her to catch up to him. "All right, then. Tell me what is this all about."

"Slow down a little," she instructed, waiting until the wagons were far enough away from them so the others couldn't overhear their conversation.

"Is that better?" he asked, nodding to his daughter who waved at him from the wagon. Grunt had his front legs up on the sidewall, and his nose sniffed at the air as they traveled.

"This is going to be a great day," she said. The crisp

morning air made her cheeks rosy. Her long blonde hair was braided today, trailing down her back all the way to her waist. The wind picked up the edges of her cloak as they rode, making her look mysterious and regal all at the same time.

"Why would you say it's going to be a great day?"

"Because, I think this will be an exciting adventure."

"I am not looking for excitement, my lady. I thought this was supposed to be a relaxing time spent with my daughter. How is that ever going to happen with all these people tagging along?"

"Did you notice anything about the people who are accompanying us? Besides the children, I mean."

"Yes. Besides all of them being more or less irritating in one way or another, they are also the prime suspects in the murder case we are working on."

"Exactly," she answered proudly, her back straightening as she sat a little taller in the saddle. Still, Zachariah wasn't sure what she was up to and almost dreaded to ask.

"Lady Vivienne? Did you want to expound upon that answer?'"

"Certainly," she told him, looking at him slyly from the side of her eye. "I gave this some thought and realized that our questioning everyone separately might not have been the best idea."

"How so? That is what I always do with suspects I am interrogating."

"True. But mayhap it is time to start thinking more like a woman and less like a man."

He threw his hands in the air as he rode. "Like that makes any sense at all?"

"It does," she told him. "You see, I realized that we are having a hard time finding clues and getting answers."

"Go on."

"The Gainsboroughs are leaving soon and taking the dead body with them."

"I can't keep them here any longer," he admitted. "And the body is starting to decay. They need to get the corpse buried."

"True. That is why I suggested the Gainsboroughs come to town with us, and purchase an already-made coffin from the undertaker instead of using one crafted by my father's men. I played up their sense of importance, telling them that Lord Gainsborough deserved better. Plus, since this coffin will already be constructed, they won't have to wait for my father's men to make one."

"All right," he said, still not understanding this female way of thinking.

"I also got Aunt Ellen to convince my uncle as well as the Gainsboroughs to make up after that spat. Since the betrothal is off now, it is best they stay on good terms for the future. Don't you agree?"

"I suppose it makes sense. But did they have to come to the fair with us in order to do that?"

"Nay, not at all. However, I wanted to see how all these people interact when they are together."

"I still don't see why it is important."

"Let me explain. Or actually, let me ask you who you think murdered Lord Gainsborough."

"Well," he said clearing his throat. "If we are looking at who had the most to gain by the man's death, I'd say it would have to be his son, Wilfred. After all, he is the one to inherit everything now that his father has perished."

"True. But he would have eventually inherited it all anyway. Therefore, I see that as a moot point."

"Perhaps he was in a hurry, I don't know." The sheriff shrugged his shoulders.

"Mayhap. But if he's the murderer, why would he even tell

us that he had a spat with his father because he didn't want to marry me? It would make him sound more than suspicious."

"True. And I highly doubt he would have told your hand-maid about the spat if he was the murderer."

"You see? He's known to everyone as a milksop, staying by his mother's side for protection."

"Yes. So what's your point?"

"I'm not quite sure, actually. But I want to point out that when I was sparring with Wilfred in the practice yard, he became irate with me. It was so odd that he'd act that way."

"I agree. Getting irate doesn't sound like Wilfred at all. He'd never act that way on his own."

"All right, I admit that I provoked him. That is what happened."

"Now that sounds exactly like you," he said with a nod.

"I only did it to try to catch him off guard. I had hoped that if he was keeping something from me, he'd accidentally spill his secret."

"And he did."

"Well, not exactly. He said he didn't kill his father, not admit to being a murderer."

"Lady Vivienne, this is going in circles. If there is some-thing you are trying to prove, I suggest you do so quickly."

"I am just saying that something odd happened on that practice field. He got so upset about the betrothal that all his anger came out at once and he nearly struck me down right there."

"Vivienne," he said, not using her title. "Why didn't you tell me this before? Were you hurt?"

"Nay. Thankfully, my uncle intervened. That was when the argument between him and Lord Wilfred happened, and he decided the betrothal was off and the Gainsboroughs were going to leave and go back home."

"None of that sounds extremely suspicious."

"Nothing except for the fact that Lord Wilfred is damned good with a sword and has anger bottled up inside him that he finally let out."

"I see your point. So, he could have had an argument with his father that night and killed him. However, his father was a fighting man too. I hardly think Wilfred would be able to overpower him."

"Not normally. However, Lord Gainsborough was well in his cups and not himself that night. We noticed he was drunk by the smell of the whisky on him, not to mention the red wine on his fingers and that was spilled on his tunic."

"If he was drinking whisky, he wouldn't be drinking wine as well. So whoever killed him might have had a goblet of wine on them at the time, and it spilled in the tussle between them."

"Now, you're starting to think like a woman," she said, more or less cheering him on by the fist she shook above her head.

"I'm not sure that is a compliment," he grumbled.

"I think there could be more than one person involved in Lord Gainsborough's death," she told him.

"I agree. Hence, the two stab wounds to the man's chest. I believe one was from the weapon of the killer."

"And the second was when the murderer removed their weapon so as not to get caught," she added.

"It was actually ingenious of them to use Gainsborough's own dagger and to wrap his fingers around it to make it look like a suicide."

"Something that bothers me is that everyone seems to have a defense as to where they were during the fire and murder. I mean, Cook vouches for Maria and she for him."

"Yes," he agreed. "Lord Wilfred and Rosina claim each other was innocent as well."

"Leif says differently about that."

"Leif is also one of the only ones who has no proof he didn't do it. And Herman of course."

"I don't know about Herman, but I really don't think the minstrel boy is guilty."

"He did seem very angry with Lord Gainsborough for breaking his lute string. He had motive to kill the man."

"He did. However, I am thinking that mayhap our murderer didn't have a clear motive."

"Lady Vivienne, that makes no sense. Every crime has motivation of killing behind it."

"Let me clarify. Mayhap there was reason, but it is something we are not privy to knowing. After all, it is not as if the murderer is going to tell us his innermost secrets."

They approached the fair and the roads became crowded as they rode into town.

"Keep your thoughts to yourself for now. There are too many people around to be talking about this in the open."

"I agree. We need to keep our eyes and ears open today because I believe the truth is about to come out, and we don't want to miss it."

"I hope you're right," he told her. "If not, this will be another unsolved murder and I really don't want that on my record, I assure you."

"Hrmmph," she said with a roll of her eyes. "Spoken just like a man."

VIVIENNE PAID the coin to the vendor and took the lute string, handing it over to Leif. "As promised, here is your string," she said, happy to have helped the boy.

"Thank you, my lady." He stuck the string in his pouch. "I will use it on my lute as soon as we return."

"I'm not sure what you are doing buying that boy anything," scoffed Lady Gainsborough, approaching them on the street with her son and guard on each side of her. "He is a murderer, I tell you," she said, sticking her nose in the air.

"Lady Gainsborough, please don't say such things." The sheriff had been holding his daughter up to look into the window of the bakery shop. He put her down next to Martin, hurrying over to join them. "Talk like that can cause a lot of trouble."

Rosina was with the children, and glanced over to see if trouble was starting.

"Sheriff, if you can't see that this boy is a killer, then you don't deserve to be sheriff of this town." Lady Gainsborough just wouldn't shut up.

It was Vivienne's aunt and uncle who interceded this time.

"Lady Gainsborough, please don't say such things," said Aunt Ellen. "The sheriff as well as my niece are doing all they can to find justice for your husband's death."

"That's right," agreed Uncle Gilbert. "You shouldn't be dabbling in things you don't understand."

"What is there to understand?" asked Wilfred. "The jongleur has no proof he didn't kill my father."

"Neither does your guard," Vivienne pointed out, seeing Herman look up sharply and then squirm.

"Lady Gainsborough, for all we know, you or your son could have killed Lord Gainsborough and are trying to blame it on someone else," said her uncle, spewing accusations, being no better than her.

Vivienne could see Wilfred's face getting redder. She didn't want episode with him like the one she encountered on the practice field, and had to do something to stop this quickly.

"Do you still think your plan is working?" whispered

Zachariah. "You'd better do something fast or we might just have a bloodbath on our hands."

"Lord and Lady Gainsborough, the woodworker's shop where the undertaker makes coffins is just up ahead," Vivienne spoke up. "Perhaps my aunt and uncle would be kind enough to escort you inside where you can pick out a proper coffin for your husband."

"What are you doing?" the sheriff whispered, looking more than nervous. "Purposely sending them there together? Did you miss the part that they're arguing?"

"Shhh. Trust me," she whispered back.

"If it'll get the Gainsboroughs to leave my castle faster, I'll personally carry them to the undertaker's shop on my back," growled her uncle, stepping around them, leading the way.

"Gilbert, please," begged her aunt, hurriedly running after him. "We need to all get along."

Rosina hurried over. "My lady, will we be going with them to the undertaker's shop? I am not fond of picking out coffins, and would rather not step foot inside the store."

"Nay, I don't believe we need to be there. Actually, I was hoping that you and Adam would take Martin and Starah to get a hand pie from one of the street vendors. Martin has been begging me for one since we got here." She dipped her hand into her pouch and gave the girl a few coins. "Buy something for yourself and Adam as well."

"But I was going to take my daughter for a hand pie," objected Zachariah.

"We will meet up with them in a short while," she told the sheriff. "I have need of your help with an errand first."

"I don't see why I'm even here," complained Adam, the kennel groom. "I need to get back to the kennels to inspect the new construction as well as to check on the state of my hounds."

"I was hoping you could keep Grunt under control while we're here, Adam," she told the man.

"Grunt doesn't need lookin' after." Adam seemed to be very unaccommodating today.

Just then, a rat ran across the street and Grunt took off after it, barking like crazy. He knocked into an apple vendor, sending the apples rolling down the street. Some of the children attending the fair saw it happen and squealed, running after the apples to collect them before they rolled down the hill.

"Mayhap you can have Richard help pick up the apples as you're fetching the dog," Vivienne told Adam.

"I see what you mean. I will, my lady." Adam ran toward the wagons and their horses where Richard sat guarding them.

"I'll just walk back to the castle now," Leif told her. "I'm in a hurry to get my lute strung and be on my way. I've stayed in Mablethorpe much longer than I've intended."

"Leif, I really wish you'd stay here with the rest of us," Vivienne told him. "It is dangerous on the road alone."

Leif chuckled. "I'm a traveling minstrel, my lady. I am always on the road alone. I can take care of myself. Thank you for the string. I'll be on my way now." He left, heading down the street in the opposite direction.

"Wait," Vivienne called out, but was stopped by Zachariah's hand on her arm.

"Let him go," he said in a low voice.

"Is that wise?" she asked him.

"You said you didn't think he was the killer."

"But we haven't proven it yet. And as you said, he is one of two people who cannot really be accounted for during the time of the murder."

"Then let's cut this trip short and head back, picking him up along the way."

"Sheriff, we promised the children a fun day. We wouldn't want to disappoint them."

"We're not even with them, my lady," he answered, running his hand through his hair and looking down the street at the chaos. "I feel as if I should be with my daughter and yet I am not."

"She will be fine."

"She might be with murderers."

"Then let's do my errand quickly and get back to her as soon as possible."

"What is this errand you keep talking about?" Zachariah asked, following her down the street.

"I heard talk lately. There is an old friend of mine who works in the butcher's shop, and I need to stop by and visit with her." She opened the door to the butcher's and headed inside. The little bells above the door announced their presence and a very pregnant woman waddled out from a back room to wait on them.

"Lady Vivienne?" The woman's eyes lit up when she saw her.

"It is you! Oh, it's so good to see you again." Vivienne hurried over and gave the girl a hug.

"You know her?" asked Zachariah.

"Yes. This is Justina, my past handmaid. You remember her, don't you?"

"Well, yes, now that you mention it," he said nodding to the girl. "It's just that it's been a long time and I don't remember you looking like ... that."

Justina giggled, rubbing her belly. "Sheriff, I am eight months pregnant now with my first child."

"We're raising a family and have just procured jobs with

my uncle here at his shop. He is a butcher," said a man emerging from the back room.

"Charles, so good to see you." Vivienne wasn't shy about giving the man a hug too.

"Hello, I'm Sheriff Fitch," said Zachariah, walking over to shake the man's hand.

"Yes, I know who you are, Sheriff. Everyone in town does," said Charles.

Suddenly, Zachariah felt horrible that he wasn't familiar with everyone who lived in town the way they were with him. He'd have to make it his business to get to know all of the townsfolk on a more personal level.

"We are all very concerned about that madman who comes out at night," mentioned Justina. Her smile disappeared.

"Yes. The Pied Piper, they call him," explained Charles. "All the children are afraid of him, and we hope he'll be gone before our baby is born. We don't want our baby to grow up around people like him."

"He's a rat catcher," Zachariah said aloud. "I assure you there is nothing to fear. As soon as his job is finished, he'll leave town. You'll see."

"I hope he stays down on Rotten Row and doesn't venture up to the high part of town then," said Justina with a shudder.

"Justina, I am sure he'll go wherever there are rats," Vivienne pointed out.

"That means everywhere then." Justina gave a concerned look to her husband.

Zachariah cleared his throat. "Lady Vivienne, I'd like to get going if you don't mind."

"Yes, in a moment," she said. "First, I'd like to purchase a soup bone for my dog." She pulled a coin out of her pouch and handed it to Charles.

"Of course. I'll get one from the back. I have a nice big one from a cow I just butchered this morning." Charles took the coin and put it in his pouch and headed to the back room to get the bone.

"How is good old Grunt?" asked Justina, settling herself atop a stool behind the counter. "I do miss that dog."

"He's causing just as much trouble as always, but still in good spirits," said Vivienne, walking over and leaning her elbows on the counter. "Justina, I wanted to ask you about Rosina."

"Your new handmaid?" Justina's eyes flashed upwards. "Isn't she working out for you? I thought she'd be good taking over my position when I left."

"Are you friends with her?" Zachariah asked curiously.

"Justina recommended Rosina to me," Vivienne explained. "Actually, Rosina started off as a kitchen maid at the castle."

"That's where she's the best, with a knife in her hand," Justina told them. "If I wasn't so squeamish, I'd be in the back butchering meat instead of up here talking to customers."

"With a knife in her hand?" asked Zachariah. "What do you mean by that?"

"Yes," said Vivienne. "Rosina gets squeamish at the sight of blood."

"Why would you say that?" Justina seemed amused. "Rosina used to always be the one to slaughter the chickens back at Mablethorpe as well as when she worked at Gainsborough Castle. I'm surprised you don't know that."

"What?" both Vivienne and Zachariah said together.

"Are you saying that Rosina once worked for Lord Gainsborough?" the sheriff asked her.

"Yes," the girl answered. "Why does it matter?"

"Justina, you told me when I hired her that she came from Theddlethorpe."

"Oh, my lady, please forgive me for that. You see, Rosina

had some awful experience and was very frightened of Lord Gainsborough. She asked me not to tell anyone she worked there, because she ran away and was afraid the man would come looking for her."

"What kind of bad experience?" asked Vivienne.

"I'm not sure," said the girl with a shrug. "Mayhap she was beaten, because when I met her on the road she had blood on her gown and had been hitching rides on the back of carts trying to get as far away from Gainsborough as she could."

"Well, here's the biggest bone I could find for good ol' Grunt." Charles emerged from the back room with a bone wrapped up in brown paper. He held it out and Zachariah retrieved it.

"Lady Vivienne, we need to get going now," the sheriff said softly.

"Yes. It was good seeing you both, but we need to leave," agreed Vivienne.

"Oh, can't you stay for a little longer?" begged Justina. "I would like to get caught up on everything that has been happening at the castle."

"Nay, we really can't," said Zachariah, taking Vivienne by the arm and leading her to the door before she spilled the news about the murder. He didn't need everyone in town talking about it. Especially now that they had a new lead.

They stepped out onto the street and both looked at one another.

"I'm sorry, but I truly didn't know that information about Rosina," said Vivienne. "It doesn't look good for her, does it?"

"Nay, it does not," he said. "But until she's proven guilty, we cannot go around accusing the girl of murder."

"I suppose not. However, I now think my handmaid has been lying to me and I've been a fool to believe her. How are we going to be sure?"

Thunder rumbled in the distance and the sky started to cloud over.

Zachariah looked up at the sky and cursed under his breath. "The first thing I'd like to do is to get my daughter away from your handmaid."

"I can see your concern. However, Adam is there with her."

"Only if he caught Grunt."

The sky flashed with a bolt of lightning, followed by thunder in the distance. A few raindrops began to fall.

"Starah is going to be scared," said Vivienne. "I'm afraid we'd better cut this trip short and head back to the castle right away."

"I couldn't agree more," he told her, eager to find his daughter and hold her tight. Because right now he never wanted to let his precious child out of his sight again.

Chapter Fourteen

Vivienne tossed and turned that night, feeling as if she'd made a mistake by allowing Rosina to sleep in the chamber. What if the girl truly was the murderer? Vivienne could have her throat slit in the night without even seeing it coming. She had wanted to question Rosina about what she'd learned from Justina while they were in town, but the sheriff forbade it. He said word-of-mouth wasn't enough evidence that someone was a killer. He suggested she make Rosina sleep in the great hall with the other servants, but Vivienne refused. At least with her handmaid asleep at the foot of her bed she could keep a close eye on her. Besides, she had no reason to push Rosina out of her room again. She had done so once, telling her to take time to be with Cook. But now Vivienne was wondering if possibly Cook was involved in Lord Gainsborough's death. If so, Rosina wasn't safe around him. Or mayhap they were both involved in this. If that were the case, the two of them together would be twice as dangerous to all involved. Nay, they needed to be kept apart.

Feeling hot and unable to relax, she walked over to the

window and pulled open the shutters to let in the spring breeze. There was a full moon in the sky, shining down on the stillness of the night. In the distance across the courtyard she could see the new wooden frame being built for the kennels, looking like the ribs of a monster encasing the burned-out ruins. The air still smelled acrid from the smoke, but the scent of the blooming flowers in the fields around the castle intermingled with it, bringing back hope that soon things would be right at the castle once again.

"My lady?" came Rosina's semi-muffled voice from her pallet at the foot of Vivienne's bed. The girl sounded very sleepy. Vivienne's actions must have woken her handmaid, and she didn't want that.

Vivienne's heart jumped into her throat. She needed to remain calm or Rosina would realize she was suspicious of her. Her handmaid was very observant. Releasing a deep breath she tried to sound chipper.

"I am just restless, Rosina," she told the girl, realizing after she said it that the handmaid was going to wonder why. "I'm afraid Grunt might get sick on that big soup bone I had Maria give him earlier. He's sleeping in the great hall by Martin. I think I'm going to run down there and make sure that the bone has been taken away from him like I instructed Maria to do after an hour."

"Mmmph," came Rosina's sleepy mumble from under the covers. It was dark in the room but Vivienne saw her turn over the other way, pulling the covers up over her head.

"You stay here. Don't leave the room," instructed Vivienne in a soft voice, hoping to keep the handmaid in her bed so she wouldn't follow her. When Rosina didn't answer, Vivienne realized she must be sleeping.

Just then a movement from outside caught her attention. Vivienne looked out the window to notice a shadowy form of someone sneaking around in the courtyard. The person seemed to come from the keep and was headed toward the smokehouse if she wasn't mistaken. It wasn't a guard, and no one else should be outside at this late hour. She could hear the clock tower from St. Peter's Church in town and it was ringing out the hour of midnight.

Vivienne hurried over to get her cloak, cursing under her breath since she'd forgotten that she had yet to get a new cloak after using hers to cover the corpse. She didn't want to venture out in her night rail, but neither did she have time to dress. It was crucial that she get down to the courtyard quickly before the intruder disappeared. It might be the murderer, and she could possibly catch him before he killed again.

Deciding to borrow Rosina's cloak, she threw it around her shoulders. Then she quietly picked up her weapon belt with her father's sword attached and fastened it around her waist. After pushing her bare feet into her shoes, she quickly headed for the door. She stopped and looked back once more at her handmaid before she left the room. God's eyes, she really hoped Rosina wasn't a murderer. If so, Vivienne knew that would mean that she was being gullible, and she didn't like to be fooled. She also didn't like liars. Either way, she would find out the truth tonight, even if she had to stay awake all night to do it. Before the Gainsboroughs left in the morning, she would present them with the person who murdered Lord Gainsborough, and justice would be served. They wouldn't have to live with not knowing, the way Vivienne had been living for the last seven years.

She opened the door to step out, finding Grunt down on his haunches, sniffing the crack under the door. "Grunt, what are you doing here?" she asked softly. "You're supposed to be sleeping in the great hall with Martin." Grunt didn't usually sleep in her chamber, since Rosina wasn't fond of the dog and Grunt seemed to like Martin much better than Rosina.

The dog dashed past her before she could stop him and disappeared inside the room. She was afraid Grunt would wake Rosina, but didn't have time to get him out of there. Right now she had a killer to catch. With a shrug of her shoulders, she carefully closed the door, leaving Grunt inside the room.

Vivienne tiptoed down the stairs, being quiet as she passed by the kitchens and all the servants who were sleeping by the fire in the great hall. She hurriedly made her way out of the keep, being sure to keep herself hidden in the shadows so the guards on the battlements wouldn't notice her and call out. If she was to catch this murderer she would have to use the cover of night to her advantage. Since the murderer had sneaked into the smokehouse previously to burn Lord Gainsborough's clothes, he or she might be returning now to try to dispose of any more evidence that was possibly left behind. Well, they'd get a surprise tonight, because she was about to greet them with the tip of her father's sword.

She made it over to the smokehouse easily without being seen. Surprised to see no guard at the door again, she made her way closer to the small stone house, trying to find out why. Already the putrid stench of the rotting body assaulted her senses, floating on the air that came through the vents of the gabled roof.

Vivienne's stomach clenched and she thought about heading back inside and waking up the sheriff. But if she did that, his daughter might awaken as well. The poor girl was already scared of simple things like thunderstorms. Vivienne didn't want to take the girl's father away when he was all that made Starah feel safe. Nay, she could do this by herself, she was sure of it.

Determination to find answers kept her moving forward. So

did wanting more than anything to present the killer to the sheriff on her own. Part of her was determined to prove to him that she was capable, crafty, and clever. She wanted him to think of her as an equal partner, not just a big distraction. Then again, why should she even care what he thought of her at all? Nay, she was doing this for another reason entirely. It was to help others in need find answers and regain their peace of mind. Even if she wasn't able to do the same for herself where her family was concerned, it did her heart good to be helping others.

When she got to the door of the smokehouse, she could see that it was open a crack. She also heard the sound of someone moving about inside. This led her to believe that the intruder she saw out the window was now in the smokehouse, possibly destroying any last evidence that she and the sheriff might have missed. Quietly unsheathing her sword, she held it in two hands, sneaking to the door, preparing to enter. Then with one foot she pushed the door open and stepped inside.

"Show yourself!" she yelled, holding the sword steady, even though her hands were shaking. Practicing sword fighting on the practice field with the knights and guards was one thing. Actually having to use it to protect herself was another. The last time she had done that was the night of her parents' murder. The night she stabbed a killer, right before he got away.

Damn it, her stomach was twisting again just like it always did when trouble was near. Just thinking of that horrible night made her feel dizzy and queasy. This couldn't be happening to her. Not now.

Inside the smokehouse, she saw the silhouette of the stranger from the courtyard. It was dark in there and hard to tell, but she could see the figure was covered by a cloak and with a hood covering his head. He was standing by the corpse, and it almost looked as if he were bending over Lord Gainsborough's body that was still laid out on the table. "Put your hands over your head and slowly turn around," she commanded.

"Lady Vivienne?" came a voice from behind her, startling her, since she hadn't expected anyone else to be there. She spun around on her heel to find Leif jumping back, holding his hands above his head. "Nay! Don't hurt me. It's me, Leif, Lady Vivienne," he cried out.

"Leif?" she asked in confusion, her thoughts muddled in her head.

The sound of running feet on the dirt floor of the smokehouse from behind her had her spinning around once again. The figure from inside pushed her, setting her off balance. Vivienne stumbled backward, dropping her sword in order to use her hands to keep from falling. The attacker darted out the door, but bumped right into Leif.

"Ooomph," cried Leif, doubling over as the intruder knocked him to the ground and ran from the smokehouse, heading toward the keep.

Vivienne quickly picked up her father's sword. "I think that is the murderer," she told Leif, darting past him, ready to give chase. "Go to the sheriff's chamber and tell him I need help, quickly." When Leif didn't answer, she got the awful feeling that something was terribly wrong. She stopped and slowly turned around to see him staring at her in the moonlight from his position on the ground. His eyes bugged out and he was curled up in a fetal position, holding his hands to his belly.

"Help ... me," he cried out in a soft voice. That is when she realized the boy's tunic was covered in blood.

"Oh, nay!" She ran to him and dropped to her knees on the ground. Then she noticed the knife sticking out of Leif's side. He had been stabbed by the intruder who ran from the smokehouse. Leif made no sound and wasn't moving. He lay there with his eyes closed, blood oozing from his wound onto the ground.

"God's eyes," she swore under her breath, placing her sword on the ground. She wasn't sure that the boy was not dead. "Help! Someone help me!" she yelled, no longer trying to stay hidden or quiet. The murderer had struck again and this time he had attacked an innocent young man. When was this going to stop?

"Lady Vivienne!" shouted the sheriff, emerging from the dark with Richard right behind him.

"Zachariah," she called out, ripping off the bottom part of her night rail and using it as a compress as she pressed her hands against Leif's body to try to stop the flow of blood. "Someone attached Leif. I think it was the murderer. I'm not sure, but I think Leif is dead."

"Bid the devil," snarled Zachariah, hunkering down and putting his hand against Leif's neck to check for life. "Thank God, he's still alive. But just barely."

"Shall I go for the healer?" asked Richard.

"Yes, please do," cried Vivienne.

"We need to get this boy inside, but I don't want everyone to know what happened," said the sheriff. "If so, we'll have a frenzy of panicking people to deal with and I can't have that right now. Not with the murderer on the loose tonight."

Vivienne looked up across the courtyard, spying the smattering of outbuildings that no one was using at this time of night. "The chapel is the closest. We should bring him there."

"I'll tell the healer to meet you at the chapel," announced Richard, turning to leave.

"Notify the priest as well," Vivienne called out after him. "Poor Leif might need to receive last rites."

There came a moan from the bushes near the smokehouse

and a guard popped up rubbing his head. "What happened?" the man asked.

"Thomas," cried Vivienne, recognizing the guard. "Were you guarding the door to the smokehouse tonight?"

"Aye," he answered with a groan. "Until someone hit me over the head with what felt like a big rock." He rubbed his head again.

"Help me," the sheriff told the guard. "We need to carry this boy to the chapel."

"Is he hurt?" Thomas ran over to help.

"Aye, he's been hurt," said the sheriff. "And if we don't hurry, I'm afraid the boy will die."

Chapter Fifteen

"The healer stitched up Leif and said the boy is in bad shape. He might live but that is only if infection doesn't set in," Zachariah relayed the information to Vivienne a little while later inside the chapel. The room was lit by beeswax candles, making the stained-glass window behind the alter flicker in the dim light. "However, Leif is still unconscious, so only time will tell," the sheriff continued.

Vivienne sat hunched over on a wooden bench. She gazed across the chapel at the wounded boy lying on the floor with the healer hunkered down and Father Benjamin standing over him, saying a prayer. The sheriff and Thomas had carried the wounded boy here, and it didn't take long for the healer to arrive after Richard delivered the message that his help was needed.

"It's all my fault," mumbled Vivienne, watching the priest making the sign of the cross in the air over the dying boy, giving him his last rites. This chapel had always seemed like a place where Vivienne could go to find solace, but not tonight. Tonight, it was a place that only reminded her how precious life really was, and how no one ever knew when their life would be snuffed out suddenly for no good reason at all. "I never should have ventured out in the night," she wailed, feeling the weight of the world on her shoulders right now. "Leif probably saw me and came after me. I'm sure that's why he was even there."

"Why did you go out?" asked Zachariah. "It was a stupid thing for you to do."

"I couldn't sleep and was gazing out the window when I saw an intruder in the courtyard and decided to follow him."

"Follow him by yourself?" The sheriff's voice was angry and condescending. "You couldn't have woken me to go with you? Really, my lady? What in heaven's name were you thinking?"

She shrugged. "I didn't want to wake Starah. Besides, I had my father's sword with me." Her reasons sounded pathetic now, but at the time they had seemed to make good sense.

"Yes, you had your sword," he repeated. "Well, we see how well that protected you now, don't we?"

"It was odd," said Vivienne, wiping the rest of the boy's blood from her hands on a cloth the healer had given her. "The attacker didn't try to kill me. But yet he stabbed Leif so hard that it was almost as if he wanted to kill the boy. It doesn't make sense at all. Leif wasn't even carrying a weapon."

"That's exactly right. You had a sword in your hand, so you were a threat to them. Leif wasn't," Zachariah pointed out. "Besides, the boy was standing in the doorway blocking the attacker's escape. Or so I gather from what you told me."

"Yes. That's right. When you say it, it seems to make sense after all." She sighed deeply. "We were so close to catching the murderer, and now he not only struck again, but he got away with it for a second time. And we have no idea where or who he is. This isn't getting any easier."

"Now, just a minute," he said, sitting down on the bench next to her. The smell of incense filled the air as Father Benjamin swung a small clay pot with holes in it that was used for burning incense during mass. "We don't know it was the same person tonight who murdered Lord Gainsborough," said Zachariah. "This could have been a totally isolated incident entirely."

"Mayhap. But I have a hard time believing that. Don't you?"

The sheriff took a moment to answer. He clasped his hands together and leaned his elbows on his knees before he answered. "Aye. It seems highly unlikely that it isn't somehow connected to the first murder. I just can't figure out how."

"Sheriff Fitch, what were you doing outside in the night?" she asked him. "You never did tell me. Although, I have to say I was more than happy to see you."

"I couldn't sleep either after everything that we learned at the fair today," he admitted. "This case has me stumped and I don't like that. I was standing at the open window thinking and getting a breath of fresh air when I saw the same intruder you did, sneaking through the courtyard. I decided to follow him as well."

"You left your daughter alone?"

"Nay. I had enough sense to stop and post a guard at my door before I decided to go after a murderer. I was determined that tonight I was going to catch him. Or mayhap I should say *her*?"

Vivienne's head snapped upward. "It wasn't Rosina, if that's what you're thinking. I left her sleeping in my room."

"Oh," he said, reaching over and picking up a dagger and holding it up for her to see. "Does this look familiar to you by any chance?"

"Is that the knife that the attacker used on Leif?" Her

stomach lurched, seeing the streaks of blood on it, even though most of the blood had been wiped away.

"It is," he said, turning it over and over in his hand. "Now, we just need to find out whose blade it is. Once we know that, we might actually have an answer."

"Let me see that," she said, causing the sheriff to move the blade closer to her. She leaned forward to inspect it in the dim light, not wanting to touch it. "Oh, no," she said.

"Do you recognize the blade?"

"I do," she admitted. "It is one of the kitchen knives used by the cooks to gut fowl."

"Is there anyone who uses this knife particularly? It seems to have quite an ornate handle for just a kitchen knife to prepare food." The hilt of the blade was wooden, but there were carvings of chickens and ducks on it.

"It is Cook's knife," she told him.

"Are you sure?"

"Positive. I gave it to him myself last year after I borrowed his favorite knife to take fishing and lost it in the lake."

"You fish, too?"

"Yes, of course. I try to learn to do anything I possibly can. I like new experiences."

"I can see that. So, tell me more about this blade." He stared at the knife in his hand.

"I purchased it from a traveling vendor who was a wood carver, actually. I thought it would be perfect with the fowl carved into it. Cook likes it so much that he uses it every day and never lets a soul touch it."

"Then I think we have our accomplice to the murder. It seems two people might be involved just like we discussed."

"Accomplice? Sheriff, you can't tell me that you still suspect Rosina? She's just an innocent girl who sounds like she has had a hard past. Just like me."

"Lady Vivienne, I know you want to believe the best about people who are close to you, but in this business, you need to collect the facts by using your head, not your heart. If you rely on your emotions, you are always going to be led down the wrong path, not to mention be let down by yourself in the end. No one needs that kind of disappointment. Especially not you."

"I wish Leif were conscious so we could ask him what he saw. Mayhap he could help us get his answer."

"What was Leif doing out in the middle of the night?" he asked.

"I wish I knew."

"I thought he had taken to the road again, and was long gone. I am surprised to see him back at Mablethorpe Castle at all."

"I thought he had left as well. I'm sure I don't know why he was here, but there must be a good reason. Did you ask Thomas what he saw while he was guarding the door to the smokehouse?"

"He admitted he fell asleep and that was when someone hit him over the head. He's no help to us, so I sent him back to the smokehouse to guard the door and told him not to fall asleep again."

"I'm sure he won't now. Not after what just happened."

"Lady Vivienne, it would do you good to get some sleep. In the morning I will send for Constable Dorson. I think we have enough proof now who the murderers are. I believe Cook and Rosina are responsible for the murder of Lord Gainsborough."

"Well, I don't know if I truly believe that!" She got to her feet. "I just feel like there is something more that we aren't seeing."

"Perhaps if we sleep on it, we'll come up with more answers by morning."

"Nay. I can't sleep," she told him. "And what if Starah awakes and you're not there? She'll be scared."

"It's all right. I told you, I have a guard posted at her door."

"Which guard?" she asked.

"I have Herman guarding her door until my return."

"Herman? Gainsborough's guard?"

"Yes. He was the first one I saw when I left the room."

"And you trust him?" It was her turn to talk to him in a condescending tone now. "Was that really a good idea? Unless I need to remind you, he was one of two people who didn't have a reasonable excuse for what he was doing during the murder."

"I-I … shouldn't have done that," he admitted, shaking his head and running a hand through his hair. His jaw was clenched. "Damn it, I wasn't thinking straight. How could I have done such a stupid thing!" He jumped to his feet. "Come with me. We'll go to check on Starah together and get a different guard posted at her door. Then we'll stop by your chamber so you can clean up and get changed. We'll go somewhere where we can discuss everything in private. We have the information we need to catch the killer, I'm sure of it. However, I want to make certain everything checks out before I make any arrests. If we work together on this, and hear out each other's thoughts, we might be able to come up with a viable answer after all."

"I'd like that," she answered with a yawn. Finally, the sheriff was going to listen to what she had to say. She planned on listening to him as well, since she knew she usually made decisions with her heart and not her head, just like he'd accused her of doing. There was so much to learn about tracking down a killer. The sheriff had been doing this for a long time, and mayhap she could learn something from him after all. Even if he couldn't find her parents' murderers, mayhap she needed to start trusting him instead of always pushing him away. "I'm ready," she told him, taking his proffered arm as they headed for the door.

"Everything will be all right, Vivienne," he told her, not using her title, and right now she was glad that he hadn't. She needed a friend and a confidant at the moment, not just a professional partner. "Believe me," he said, "we will put our heads together and come up with the answers we need. And by morning we will have our killer, or killers, arrested, and put them behind bars where they belong."

Chapter Sixteen

When Vivienne had gotten back to her room last night, Grunt hadn't been in her chamber. Since Rosina had been sleeping, she didn't bother to wake the girl to ask her about it. It was morning now, and Vivienne opened one sleepy eye to see her handmaid packing her bags.

"Rosina? What are you doing?" Vivienne sat up and yawned.

"Oh, my lady," said the girl, rushing over to the bed. "I don't know how to tell you this, but I don't think I can stay at Mablethorpe Castle any longer."

"Why not?" Vivienne hurriedly got up and started dressing on her own.

"It's all this business with the murder and now that poor minstrel boy being stabbed. I am frightened that someone might come for me next."

Vivienne's head jerked around in surprise. "How do you know about Leif being stabbed? It just happened last night when everyone was sleeping." Vivienne pulled her gown over her head, making sure to keep the ring she wore beneath her clothes hidden.

"I was up early and went down to the kitchens for a bite to eat. The word is spreading amongst the servants already. You know how gossip tends to travel."

Vivienne had been up discussing the case with the sheriff most of the night. She'd only returned to her room and had a few hours of sleep. She'd been so tired that she never even heard Rosina leave the room. She supposed the girl could be telling the truth about hearing the news from others. It was hard keeping a secret in a castle of this size.

"Yes, but this is not gossip, Rosina. What you heard is true. Someone did try to kill Leif last night, and I was almost hurt as well."

"Oh, nay!" She spun around. "Are you all right, my lady?" Rosina was worrying about her again like an old mother hen, just like she always did.

"I'm fine."

"I'm so sorry, my lady. I was sleeping and didn't even know you'd left the room. I should have been with you when you went out to the smokehouse last night."

"How did you know I went to the smokehouse?"

"That's where the minstrel boy was stabbed, or so I've heard. I just figured if you knew about it and said you were almost hurt, then you must have been there too."

"Yes, you are right." Vivienne wondered at first how Rosina knew the incident happened at the smokehouse. It all seemed suspicious. But then again, mayhap word had spread quickly like Rosina said. After all, Richard knew what happened. So did the healer and priest. She wanted to believe the girl was telling the truth, but something inside told Vivienne that Rosina was lying. Perhaps it was just the sheriff's suspicion and trying to convince her that her handmaid was involved.

"Where is Grunt?" she asked Rosina.

"I don't know, my lady. I haven't seen him since yesterday."

Another odd thing for her to say since the dog went into her bedchamber last night when Vivienne left the room and was missing when she'd returned. Grunt wasn't able to open doors on his own. Vivienne's gut twisted harder. God's eyes, she didn't want the sheriff to be right about Rosina. Nay, he had to be wrong! After all, Rosina was sleeping on her pallet when Leif was stabbed. Vivienne refused to believe that the attacker last night could have been her.

"I don't blame you for being frightened, Rosina. Everyone is on edge since the murderer still hasn't been caught." She sat on the bed to don her shoes. "But tell me something. Where will you go where you will feel safer than right here at the castle, with knights and guards watching over you night and day?"

"Well, my lady." She looked to the floor and continued to wring her hands as she spoke. "I saw the Gainsboroughs in the great hall just a short while ago. They are preparing to leave to go back home. They have asked me to return with them. I will be working for Lord Gainsborough as a kitchen maid at Gainsborough Castle."

"Really." Vivienne watched Rosina from the corner of her eye as she unbraided her hair. Then she got up and walked over to get her brush.

"Allow me to do that, my lady." Rosina ran in front of her and took the brush, running it through Vivienne's hair.

"Rosina, where did you work before you came to Mablethorpe Castle?"

"I was living with your last handmaid, Justina—you know that. She took me in when I had nowhere to go."

"I saw Justina at the fair yesterday. She and her husband work for the butcher now."

"Oh." Her hand stilled. "That is nice. How is she?"

"Justina is fine," Vivienne told her. "She is about to birth their first child."

"I'm so happy for her." Rosina put down the brush and walked back over to continue packing.

"I know you once worked at Gainsborough Castle."

Rosina slowly turned around. "I did," she finally admitted.

"Why didn't you tell me this before?"

"I was ashamed. That's why."

"Ashamed of what?"

"I'd rather not say." She closed up her bag, pulling the ties closed. "I hope I will not be leaving you at an inconvenience if I go, my lady. I suppose I should have asked for your permission first."

"Yes. Servants are not allowed to just leave whenever they want. Even though it seems to me that you don't follow the rules where that's concerned."

"I ran away from Gainsborough because I was pregnant," she blurted out.

"What?" Vivienne turned and walked back to Rosina. "What happened?"

"I had an accident and fell down the stairs and miscarried." Tears filled her eyes.

"Rosina, why didn't you tell me this before? I know how hard it is to lose a baby, since I, too, lost a baby at one time." She took the handmaid's hands in hers.

"I didn't know that, my lady. What happened?"

"It doesn't matter. Right now, we are talking about you. Please, tell me more."

"I was ashamed since I was having a child out of wedlock. Lord Gainsborough knew about it, and he was going to dismiss me. He never liked me for some reason. When I saw him here at Mablethorpe, I was afraid. I tried to hide from him."

"Who was the father of your baby?"

"It no longer matters, my lady. He was a stableboy, but he has since died."

"I see."

There was a knock on the door and Rosina hurried over to open it.

"My lady, Sheriff Fitch is here to see you," she reported.

"Good morning, Sheriff." Vivienne strapped on her weapon belt with her father's sword attached. "I am ready to go." She headed to the door.

"Is that really necessary?" he asked softly, looking down at her waist.

"I am not sure what's going to happen today," she whispered back. "I want to be prepared."

"Shall we get started then?"

"Rosina, I'd like to say goodbye to you and the Gainsboroughs before you leave. I will meet you in the courtyard in two hours," she told her handmaid over her shoulder.

"Yes, my lady. Thank you."

Vivienne closed the door and turned to see the bewildered look on the sheriff's face.

"What was that all about?" he asked her. "And did I see your handmaid packing her bags?"

"Yes. Rosina informed me this morning that she is leaving with the Gainsboroughs."

"She's doing *what?*"

"Shhh," said Vivienne with her finger to her lips, looking back at the closed door. "Let's go somewhere to talk where no one will hear us. I think I have some answers we need, but there are still so many questions that are yet unanswered."

ZACHARIAH PACED the ground outside the smokehouse, waiting with Vivienne for the healer to join them. The guard had been dismissed, since the body was about to be moved and the guard was no longer needed.

"Lord Gainsborough's body is already in the coffin and ready to transport," he told her. "We have a very short amount of time to figure out the rest of this before the Gainsboroughs leave to go back home, taking the body with them."

"So you think the healer will be able to tell us exactly what killed Lord Gainsborough?" asked Vivienne.

"I do. Here he is now. Healer, right this way," said Zachariah, opening the door to the smokehouse and stepping inside. They all held rags pressed up against their mouths and noses because of the stench of the rotting corpse.

"What is it you'd like me to do?" asked the man.

"Bartholomew, we need you to look at the corpse and tell us your opinion of what actually killed Lord Gainsborough." Vivienne knew the man well, and he was always able to tell what a person died from just by inspecting them. They should have invited him to do this right from the start.

"I thought you already knew what he died from and that is why you haven't called for me before now," said the healer.

"Yes, we thought so," agreed Zachariah. "I mean, it seemed obvious that the man stuck a dagger in his own chest, hence ending his life. But upon further investigation of some of the man's other wounds, we have some unanswered questions. We would like you to take a look at the dead man's wounds for us."

"I'd be happy to," said the healer, walking over and flipping open the lid of the wooden coffin. The stench filled the air, making Vivienne want to vomit. She took a step back.

"He has a bump on the back of his head," Zachariah pointed out. "As well as a bruised jaw and scratches to his neck."

"Yes, I see that," said Bartholomew, inspecting the body.

"Do you think the blow to the head was the cause of his death?" asked Vivienne.

"Nay, I don't believe so." Bartholomew felt the dead man's head. "It was definitely a hard hit. However, I don't see how that could have killed him. Mayhap just knocked him unconscious."

"Because of the smell of whisky on him, we believe he may have been well in his cups at the time he died," relayed the sheriff.

"Well, then definitely, the hit to his head wasn't the cause of death." The healer kept his gaze focused inside the coffin. "He would have been relaxed enough that it would have hurt him, but done naught more than given him a throbbing headache the next morning."

"I see." Zachariah rubbed his chin in thought. "It also looks to me as if he had a confrontation with someone and was punched in the jaw."

"Yes, it does seem to be the case." The healer continued to examine the corpse. "He has a good bruise on his left cheek."

"Then the person who punched him was right-handed," said Vivienne.

"That's mainly everyone then," mumbled the sheriff. "It is no help at all."

"Those marks on his neck look like scratches from someone's fingernails," added Vivienne. "Perhaps from the close proximity of them, it was from a smaller hand. Like mayhap a woman."

"I believe you are right," said the healer again. "It looks just like that to me, too."

"What about the two stab wounds?" asked Vivienne, lowering her cloth from her face, being curious enough to get closer to look inside the coffin now.

"Well, one is just a surface wound," surmised the healer.

"Surface wound?" questioned Vivienne.

"He means the blade hit flesh, but didn't actually puncture any organs," explained the sheriff.

"That's right," said Bartholomew, running his fingers along the second stab wound. "However, this other wound which is a little higher up is quite deep indeed."

"That was where we found the dagger sticking out of Lord Gainsborough," Vivienne relayed the information. "He was gripping the blade with one hand at the time."

"Hmmm," said the healer, continuing to study the corpse. He felt the chest with both his hands, using his fingers to explore the chest cavity. "It was a deep thrust for sure. It entered the heart. Directly into the center of the heart too. Was there a lot of blood?"

"On his clothes, yes there was," Vivienne told him. "However, someone burned the clothes so there is no longer proof of it."

"I'd say someone knew exactly where to push the blade so the man would die quickly."

"Could someone do this to themselves?" asked Zachariah.

"Perhaps," the healer answered, then slowly shook his head. "However, if the man was drunk as you've told me you believe him to have been, then I highly doubt he'd be able to push a blade into himself with enough force to end his life. Especially one-handed."

"Thank you, Healer. You have been a big help," said Zachariah, closing the lid of the coffin.

"Please, keep this information to yourself for now," Vivienne told him, as the man made his way to the door to leave.

"Of course," he said, stopping in the doorway. "By the way, you'll be happy to know that Leif is already healing quite nicely from that stab wound last night."

"Oh, that is wonderful news," said Vivienne, feeling happy to hear good news right now. "So, he will live then?"

"Yes, I believe so. However, he is still unconscious so he is not out of danger yet. If he can wake up within the next day, he should be able to heal back to normal in a few weeks' time."

"Isn't there something you can do for the boy to wake him up?" asked Zachariah.

"I'm not sure it is good to try to wake him too soon. His body needs to heal. It is better to let him do it on his own."

"That's a shame. We could really use his statement right now to help us identify his attacker. Also, to hopefully put an end to this murder investigation." Zachariah escorted Vivienne to the door.

"Do you believe Lord Gainsborough's murderer is the same person who stabbed the musician?" asked the healer.

"We're not sure yet, but, yes, it is looking that way," the sheriff answered.

"What do you think?" Vivienne asked the man. "Can you tell by the stab to Lord Gainsborough compared to that of Leif's wound if the same person did it?"

Zachariah chuckled. "Nay, Lady Vivienne, that is impossible."

"I'm afraid he's right," said the healer. "Especially since different blades were used. However, I can tell you that Lord Gainsborough's murder seems to have been intentional. Leif was stabbed quickly and the attacker wasn't aiming to kill. Or at least it doesn't seem that way. I can't be sure."

"I surprised the attacker," Vivienne told him. "I had my father's sword aimed at him so he became frightened and ran. Leif was blocking the door, and because of that he was stabbed."

"We don't know that the attacker hadn't planned to kill Leif all along," the sheriff pointed out. "It is all just speculation.

After all, there was no reason for either Leif or the attacker for being at the smokehouse in the middle of the night."

"Yes, the sheriff is right," agreed Vivienne.

"Well, I do hope you figure out who did these stabbings," said Bartholomew. "Everyone inside the castle walls is very scared and upset. They seem to be becoming careless, and more accidents are happening as well. I think even the hounds are upset."

"What do you mean by that?" asked Vivienne.

"Well, that page boy, Martin, was scratched by one of the kennel groom's dogs this morning while giving the hound tallow, it seems."

"Oh, nay. Is Martin all right?" asked Vivienne.

"Yes, it is just a bad scratch on the hand. It seems that your dog is upset too, Lady Vivienne.

"Grunt is upset? How so?"

"The kitchen maid, Maria, said Grunt wanted a bone, and when she didn't have it with her, he scratched her arm looking for it."

"Grunt did that? I don't know why Maria wouldn't have just given the dog the bone. She had it on her, because I gave it to her last night."

"She had other scratches on her as well that she wanted me to look at, but they seemed to be at least a few days old. The one on her thigh was actually starting to get infected, so I am glad she didn't wait any longer before coming to me for a tincture."

"Her thigh?" asked Vivienne.

"Yes, it was quite high up, too."

"That doesn't sound like something Grunt would do," said the sheriff.

"My lady, I don't like to be spreading gossip, but it didn't seem like a scratch from a dog."

"What kind of scratch was it?" she asked.

"It's probably nothing. I shouldn't have said anything, I'm sorry."

"Nay. It might be important to the investigation," Zachariah urged him on. "Please, tell us."

"Well, I can't be sure, but the girl seemed to have some bruising in the groin area as well."

"Bruising? Are you saying she was beaten?" asked Vivienne. Zachariah cleared his throat and she looked over at him.

"My lady, the girl likes to show cleavage and flirt with the men," the sheriff pointed out. "Perhaps it was from some ... shall I say ... some vivacious coupling?"

"I believe you might be right," said the healer with a nod.

"Oh, I see." Vivienne felt suddenly embarrassed. She knew Maria was a flirt, but she really didn't think the girl went around having rough sex with all the kitchen help.

"Will there be anything else, my lady? Sheriff?" asked the man.

"Bartholomew, you often use plants from my herb garden for healing," said Vivienne.

"Yes, I do, my lady. And I thank you for your generosity. It has brought about many positive results in healings in the past."

"Well, right now, I have a lot of herbs flourishing in my garden. I think if we could possibly make a tincture from some of the stronger smelling ones, like peppermint, lemon balm, rosemary, and perhaps clary sage, we might be able to put it under Leif's nose. The strong aroma might help him to regain consciousness faster. What do you think?"

"I suppose it wouldn't hurt to try," the man answered.

"Then come with me to my herb garden." Vivienne left the smokehouse, and the men followed her out the door. "We can make up a tincture in no time."

"Lady Vivienne," said the sheriff from behind her. "If I

must remind you, we have yet to discuss our new findings. Remember, the Gainsboroughs are leaving within the hour and taking the corpse with them. If we are going to expose the murderer before they depart, we don't have much time to figure out the details."

"You're right," she told him. "Bartholomew, can you make the tincture without me?" she asked.

"Of course I can, my lady. I know the herbs like the back of my hand."

"You can do so in the kitchen. If anyone gives you trouble, tell them you are doing this for me, and they should leave you alone."

"Yes, my lady. Thank you," said the healer with a bow, before turning and heading to the herb garden that was situated behind the main keep.

"Do you still think your handmaid is innocent?" asked Zachariah.

Vivienne let out a big puff of air from her mouth. "To be honest, I'm not sure what to believe anymore. However, I must say I am starting to think you might be right and that she's been fooling me for a while now. It breaks my heart to think someone like Rosina could actually murder a man, but the signs all seem to point in her direction."

"Because of what Justina told us in town?"

"That is part of it. I confronted Rosina this morning about once working at Gainsborough."

"What did she say?"

"She admitted it was true and said she didn't mention it to me because she was ashamed," Vivienne told him.

"Ashamed of what?" This took the sheriff's interest.

"It seems while she was there, she became pregnant out of wedlock."

"So, she has a baby? I didn't know that."

"Nay. She fell down the stairs and had a miscarriage."

"Who was the father?" asked Zachariah.

"She said a stableboy, but he is dead now."

"What does any of this have to do with why she left there?"

"Rosina said Lord Gainsborough knew about this and he was going to dismiss her. It seems he was mean to her or didn't like her."

"That's odd," said Zachariah, seeming to be in deep thought. "I thought Lord Gainsborough liked anyone who wore a skirt."

"So did I."

"Oh, I just remembered something." Zachariah snapped his fingers. "I need to get my daughter from the chambermaid whom I paid to watch her. I'm not sure what to do with Starah, since it is crucial we close this investigation, and we have very little time to do it."

"I'll get my aunt to watch her if you'd like," offered Vivienne.

"If you wouldn't mind, it would really help."

"I'll have Martin and Grunt stay with her too. That should keep Starah occupied."

"All right, let's go then. I have a few things yet I'd like to talk over with you. Then I think we need to bring out into the open what we've learned."

"So you really believe we've found our murderer?"

"Yes, I do. Don't you?"

"I suppose so." This was so hard for Vivienne. She didn't want to see anyone be imprisoned. Then again, if someone took another's life than it was only right that they should pay.

"Now, the only thing that is troubling me is finding the murderer's accomplice."

"You mean the person who stabbed Leif? Because Rosina was in my chamber sleeping at the time."

"Not only that, but don't forget someone burned down the kennels as a distraction so the actual murder could take place," the sheriff reminded her.

"I think we must be overlooking someone who is right in front of our noses."

"The guard from Gainsborough, mayhap?" asked the sheriff. "After all, he seems to be staying in the background while all this is happening."

"True, and he has no one to vouch for his whereabouts during the fire," she added.

"I think we should go find him and ask him a few more questions." Zachariah held out his arm to escort her back to the keep and this time Vivienne accepted him.

"This is quite a lot of work, isn't it?" she asked with a sigh.

"No one said being a sheriff was an easy job."

"Being a sheriff's partner is quite difficult as well."

"Partner?" He chuckled. "You mean assistant, don't you?"

"Mayhap for now," she said, giving him a sly smile, hoping that once they solved this murder, her days of being an investigator would not be over.

Chapter Seventeen

"**I**'m nervous," Vivienne whispered to Zachariah a short while later, as everyone gathered in the courtyard of Mablethorpe Castle at their request to hear what they had to say.

The Gainsboroughs already had the coffin on the back of the wagon, and Rosina had her bag in the back, as she sat in the hay waiting to leave and start her new life back at Gainsborough Castle again. Herman was atop the bench seat to drive the wagon, while Lady Gainsborough and Lord Wilfred stood at the side, looking more than ready to go.

"There is nothing to be nervous about," Zachariah assured her. "We are here to expose a killer, and to bring about justice for a man's murder."

"Are we ready to start then?" asked Vivienne, her heart about beating out of her chest. Grunt ran up and licked her hand. Martin and Starah ran after the dog to catch him. "Take Grunt to the little patch of grass and sit down and wait for the announcement," Vivienne told the children. Her aunt came forward, collecting the children and pulling them away.

"We are waiting for Constable Dorson to arrive to make the arrest and take the murderer away," explained the sheriff.

Vivienne quickly scanned the people filling the courtyard. They were all still and remained silent with just whispers here and there. They all looked frightened and she didn't like that. Maria and Cook stood side by side. When she glanced down, she saw Cook's fingers wrap around Maria's. Vivienne's uncle looked anxious and angry as usual. He wasn't happy with the idea of announcing the name of murderer in front of so many. However, the sheriff told him it was important that everyone was there for this, so he had no choice but to agree.

"Announcing Constable Dorson, my lord and lady," came the voice of the herald as the constable rode into the courtyard, followed by another constable on a horse as well, and a guard driving a wagon with an iron cage in back, big enough to lock up a person. Or murderer, as the case would be.

"Oh, Zachariah, I don't think I can go through with this," Vivienne whispered so no one could hear what she said, especially since she hadn't called him Sheriff.

"Let me do it then, sweetheart. You just try to relax."

Vivienne felt dumbstruck. Did he just call her sweetheart? Her head told her to hit him for using such an endearment with her. It was improper and inappropriate. So why then was her heart telling her that she rather liked it? That she felt special standing next to the sheriff. Like she was truly his partner. Or mayhap his sweetheart, as he'd said?

Quickly shaking the silly thought from her head, she decided it meant nothing and was just something he said to all women. Her stomach tightened and her nerves made her legs shake. She was really nervous about exposing the killer. Or was it that she was nervous being with a man who called her sweetheart? Either way, she wanted this to be over as soon as possible.

"I need everyone standing over here please," announced the sheriff. "Rosina, Herman, please get out of the wagon and join us."

"What?" Rosina looked up in fear. All Vivienne wanted to do was to run over and protect the girl. To tell her everything would be all right. But would it really?

As soon as they'd joined them, the sheriff continued.

"As you all know, Lord Gainsborough's death a few days ago was none other but murder."

There were gasps from the crowd. Low, frightened murmurs went back and forth between them. "A young man, a jongleur, was also attacked last night about midnight." More small talk was heard from the crowd. "He was stabbed and fights for his life right now in the chapel, with the priest standing over him and giving him his last rites."

"My children are frightened. It's not safe for them," cried a woman.

"My family can't sleep nights knowing there is a killer right here at the castle," shouted a man.

Several children started crying, and their mothers pulled them closer to them or picked them up in their arms.

"Everyone please calm down," commanded Zachariah with his hand in the air. "I know it has been hard, but there is no need to live in fear anymore. We have finally been able to identify the murderer."

"Who is it?" called out one of the kitchen workers.

"I bet it's the same person who started the fire in the kennels," shouted someone else.

"Lord Mablethorpe, my son and I are leaving," announced Lady Gainsborough, taking Lord Wilfred's arm. She turned to go back to the wagon, but Vivienne's uncle stopped her.

"Nay, Lord and Lady Gainsborough, you will stay put until the sheriff dismisses you."

"Lord Gainsborough," repeated Vivienne, thinking it odd to hear Lord Wilfred called that, but it was his title. It was just that whenever someone said Lord Gainsborough, she figured they were talking about the man's father. A sudden thought flitted through her brain, and she turned to look over at Martin. Hadn't Martin claimed he saw two ghosts at the smokehouse the night the deceased's clothes were burned? If she weren't mistaken, Martin had said one of the ghosts looked like Lord Gainsborough. He hadn't been talking about the dead man after all. It was clear to her now that Martin had meant Lord Wilfred all along.

"Sheriff," she whispered, tugging on his sleeve. "I need to tell you something."

"Not now, Lady Vivienne," he said back. "I am about to expose our killer."

"Who is the murderer?" someone shouted. "We want to know."

"Yes, please tell us, Sheriff, so we can all get back to our own business," grumbled Lord Mablethorpe.

"I first must explain how we've come to this conclusion," the sheriff told them.

"We?" someone else called out. "Are you talking about Lady Vivienne?"

"Yes," said Zachariah. "Lady Vivienne has been working with me on solving this case and has proven to be a great asset indeed."

"A woman is working with the sheriff? That is mad," complained a man from the crowd.

"Please, keep all comments to yourself."

Zachariah looked over at Vivienne and nodded. It was her turn to speak. As much as she wanted to remain quiet, she had to speak up right now if she wanted to gain the respect of others. This was an important day for her. Today, people wouldn't think she was just a crazy, high-spirited fool. Now they'd know she was serious and bringing about justice to help those in need. No matter how silly her actions seemed to be.

"Thank you," said Vivienne, gaining the courage from the sheriff's gaze that she needed. She stepped forward to speak her piece as well. "We believe that the night that the kennels burned, the murderer used the distraction to corner and kill Lord Gainsborough."

"That's right," said the sheriff. "Through questioning everyone, we came to the conclusion that even though some of you had others to confirm your whereabouts, some of those stories were actually lies."

"What does that mean?" asked Vivienne's uncle. "That the murderer had an accomplice?"

Zachariah looked over and exchanged glances with Vivienne. They only had proof of one murderer, even though they both had suspicions there might have been two people involved and working together. She prayed the answer would come to them fast, since they were about to put both their reputations on the line.

"Allow me," she said, speaking loudly so the entire crowd could hear. "The deceased's body had a lump on his head and a bruise on his jaw. This told us that he'd had a confrontation with someone that turned into a fight."

"That's right," added the sheriff. "He also had scratches on his neck that looked like a woman had made them."

"So the murderer is a woman?" someone asked.

"Quiet, please. Let them explain," shouted Lord Mablethorpe, taking control of the situation.

"We believe that Lord Gainsborough had been drinking heavily the night of the murder," said Vivienne. "The smell of whisky on him was strong."

"That made him vulnerable and unstable on his feet,"

added the sheriff. "It was the perfect opportunity for the murderer to strike. That is, when no one was watching, since everyone's attention was on the fire."

More gasps came from the crowd.

"I recently saw a side of Lord Wilfred that was not shy but vengeful and filled with rage," stated Vivienne, not able to look the man in the eye when she said it.

"My son is not a murderer!" shouted Lady Gainsborough. "This is preposterous. Lord Mablethorpe, I demand you do something about this nonsense at once!"

"Hold on now. No one's accused your son of murder yet, so please stay quiet, my lady, or you'll be refrained," the sheriff threatened.

"Lord Wilfred told me himself that he didn't want to be betrothed to me, and neither did I him." Vivienne looked around to see Adam watching her intently, hunkered down petting one of his hounds. Herman sidled up next to Rosina, who was wringing her hands like crazy. "I saw a rage within him on the practice field that told me even though he was a timid man, as most of us knew him to be, he was also capable of hurting or striking someone if he wanted to do so."

"Lord Wilfred, we believe you told your father that night during the fire that you wouldn't marry Lady Vivienne, and he didn't take it well. Am I right?" asked Zachariah.

"He never listened to me," spat Lord Wilfred. "He always belittled me and made me feel unworthy of being his son."

"Wilfred, please. You don't have to say anything." His mother grabbed his arm to pull him back, but he pushed her away and stepped forward.

"My father was drunk that night, it's true," said Wilfred. "And he started to come after me physically. I punched him in the jaw and he fell and hit his head against the wall. I didn't mean to kill him, honest I didn't. It just all happened so fast, and I didn't know what to do."

The crowd went wild.

"Quiet!" shouted Zachariah, holding his hand in the air once again. "The healer verified that the blow to Lord Gainsborough's head was not what killed the man."

"It's not?" asked Wilfred, seeming confused and a little relieved at the same time.

"Nay. We believe that Maria was accosted by Lord Gainsborough just after that, and she fought for her life when he tried to rape her," announced Vivienne.

"My husband did what?" gasped Lady Gainsborough. "How can you say such a thing?"

"It's true, Lady Gainsborough." Maria let go of Cook's hand and slowly stepped forward. "Your husband asked me to bring him wine under the stairs. When I did, he tried to rape me."

"There was spilled wine on his clothes and on his fingers," Zachariah affirmed. "As well as Maria's scratch marks on the dead man's neck. She is telling the truth."

"So she killed him, then?" asked a woman in the crowd. "I'm confused."

"Nay, it wasn't her." Cook bellowed.

"He did it! We know he did. Have him arrested at once," called out Lady Gainsborough, pointing an accusing finger at Cook.

"I will not ask you to refrain from speaking out again, Lady Gainsborough," warned the sheriff, nodding and sending one of his constables to her side. The woman looked at the constable and quickly shut up, obviously not wanting to be hauled away.

"I heard Maria's screams while I was gutting a rabbit in the kitchen," explained Cook. "I was way behind in preparing the meal for the feast. I wanted the food ready and not raw or burnt when everyone came in from fighting the fire. Hearing Maria's screams, I came running to her aid with my knife still in my hand."

"Then he did kill Lord Gainsborough," said Herman. "Lady Gainsborough is right."

"Nay!" shouted Vivienne. "There were two stab wounds to the dead man's chest. The first one is where Cook's blade went in but it hit flesh only and wasn't the killing force."

"Then I didn't kill him?" Cook sounded so relieved, as if he thought it had been him.

"Cook, why don't you tell us everything in your own words what happened that night?" asked the sheriff. "And speak loudly so everyone can hear."

"Of course, Sheriff. I'd be happy to." Cook cleared his throat and then continued. "I was going to my sweetheart's aid, that is true." His gaze flashed over to Maria. "I was just doing what any man would do if he knew the one he loved was about to be taken against her will."

"We understand," said Vivienne. "But you didn't stab the man on purpose, did you?"

"Nay, it was an accident," admitted Cook. "But how did you know that, Lady Vivienne?"

"You are a big, strong man who kills game to cook it. If you meant to kill him, you would have sunk that blade deep into his heart," Vivienne told him. "And that wasn't the case here at all."

"Lord Gainsborough tripped on the toe of his damned long shoe after Grunt jumped up on him," explained Cook. Grunt barked, hearing his name. "I had been holding the blade and Lord Gainsborough fell against it, I swear it is the truth. Then he fell to the ground bleeding. I was so scared that I grabbed Maria and we ran to the kitchen, not knowing what to do."

"But there was someone who gave you an answer, wasn't there?" Zachariah looked at Cook and Maria.

"I ... I ... yes," said Cook.

"We were told not to say anything because we'd be arrested for killing a nobleman, but she swore she would help us by making it look like Lord Gainsborough took his own life," Maria spoke up next.

"She?" asked Adam, getting to his feet.

"Yes," said Zachariah, looking over at Vivienne. "Would you like me to announce it?"

"Nay," said Vivienne, feeling so sad right now that she wasn't sure she wasn't going to cry. "Rosina, please come forward."

"Me, my lady? Why?" The girl's body shook as she wrung her hands together.

"Because, when you took Lord Gainsborough's dagger and stabbed it right into his heart that night, that was the final blow that actually killed him."

"Rosina, nay!" screamed Wilfred. "Please don't tell me that is true."

Rosina's face suddenly changed and became evil-looking. Vivienne swore this wasn't the same girl who had been her sweet, innocent handmaid for the past six months.

"Your father not only tried to rape Maria, but he raped *me* when I worked for him in Gainsborough," Rosina cried out.

"What?" gasped Lady Gainsborough. She stumbled backward and Herman caught her.

"My father did that to you?" Wilfred's meek voice was back.

"Yes," Rosina snarled. "He found out about us, Wilfred. He knew we were in love and wanted to be together." This set the crowd wild, and both the sheriff and Lord Mablethorpe had to calm them down now.

"Your father not only raped me, but got me pregnant, thinking that was enough to pull us apart forever." Tears flowed from Rosina's eyes. "He pushed me down the stairs and I lost the baby. Then he threatened to kill me if I didn't leave, because he didn't want his son marrying a servant."

"Rosina, I had no idea why you left our castle. Why didn't you tell me?" Wilfred looked heartbroken. Vivienne felt a little like that as well.

"Rosina was once a kitchen maid, and knew right where to stab an animal—or even a human—through the heart, so they'd die quickly," the sheriff continued. Vivienne was glad because she was feeling choked up right now and couldn't speak if she'd tried. "She did it out of revenge. Rosina wanted Lord Gainsborough to pay for what he had done to her."

"Rosina, you deceived us," snapped Lady Gainsborough. "You wanted us to believe that Wilfred killed his father, when you did it all along!"

"She knew she could control you that way," explained the sheriff. "And you, Lady Gainsborough, would do anything to protect your son. Even if he had really killed your husband."

"That girl told me Cook was going to sneak into the smoke-house to burn my husband's clothes and steal his jewels," Lady Gainsborough spoke up next, spilling her secrets. "So I went out that night, dismissing the guard, planning on getting my husband's jewels back before that bald-headed fool took them."

"I made the comment one night when I was in the kitchens that I might have Grunt sniff Lord Gainsborough's clothes to help find the murderer," Vivienne said aloud. "Rosina, you heard me, and that is why you knew you couldn't let that happen."

"He deserved to die for what he did," snarled the girl, her eyes blazing with fire.

"You also hid behind me on the stairs and in the kitchens,

because you didn't want Lord Gainsborough to know you were there."

"Yes, I killed Lord Gainsborough and only regret that I hadn't done so much sooner."

"Constable, restrain her," Zachariah said, nodding to Constable Dorson who walked over and held on to Rosina's arm.

"Rosina made us think we killed him, too," cried Maria. "We did whatever she said because we thought she was protecting us."

Suddenly, things became all too clear to Vivienne. "It was you sleeping in my room, pretending to be Rosina the night Leif got stabbed, wasn't it, Maria?" she asked the kitchen wench. "That is why Grunt was at the door whining to come in. He knew you had his bone earlier and he was trying to get it back. He wouldn't act that way around Rosina. She never liked Grunt, and was sometimes even mean to him."

"It was me, my lady, I am sorry," admitted Maria, wiping her eyes. "I didn't want to deceive anyone. I was frightened, and thought Cook would be going to the dungeon or be executed for accidentally killing a man."

"Rosina, it was you in the smokehouse, wasn't it?" asked Vivienne to her handmaid. "You tried to kill Leif. Why?"

"I had to kill him," she spat. "Leif overheard me and Wilfred talking after that day at the fair," said Rosina. "The musician was sleeping in the gallery, and awoke and heard that I'd made it look like Lord Gainsborough killed himself so Wilfred wouldn't be blamed for the murder of his father."

Lady Gainsborough talked to the sheriff next. "Rosina told us if we gave that musician money, he'd keep his mouth shut and leave and never return. Then my son would be in the clear and no one would ever know that he killed his own father."

"So you told Leif to meet you in the smokehouse that night

where you were going to pay him to keep his mouth shut?" asked Vivienne.

"I was supposed to go," Lord Wilfred spoke up. "But at the last minute, Rosina insisted on meeting him with the money instead. She said it would be safer if anyone saw, so I wouldn't get caught. Foolishly, I believed her."

"Search her," ordered the sheriff. Sure enough, Constable Dorson pulled a handful of coins from the girl's pouch. It was a bigger amount of money than any servant would ever see in a lifetime.

"Everything was going as planned until you interrupted," spat Rosina, glaring at Vivienne. "You threatened me with that stupid sword pointed right at me. What was I supposed to do? I had no choice but to run, but the jongleur was blocking the door."

"So you decided to kill him too?" asked Vivienne. "Rosina, I thought I knew you better than that."

"I always planned on killing Leif. I was going to hide his body and keep the money for myself and never tell the Gainsboroughs, but my plans changed when you arrived, Lady Vivienne. I had to kill him and leave him on the ground while I tried to escape."

"But why did you want to kill him?" asked Vivienne. "You were paying him off."

"I couldn't take the chance he'd talk in the future," said Rosina. "Or demand more money. Besides, I deserved that money, not him! I had to shut him up forever. I did it to protect Wilfred because I love him."

"I thought I loved you too, Rosina, but not anymore," said Wilfred, sadly shaking his head. "I'm sorry, but I no longer feel the same way about you."

"How could you stab Leif and just leave him there to die?" asked Vivienne, still shocked that her handmaid did this. "He did nothing at all to hurt you. I just don't understand."

"I figured if I killed Leif, you fools would all be so busy looking at him that I could get away without being caught. I used Cook's knife to do it, too." She smiled proudly. "I knew someone would recognize it and that he'd be blamed for both murders in the end. I had everything figured out perfectly. And I would have gotten away with it too, if it wasn't for you having to get involved in the murder investigation, Lady Vivienne. You ruined everything!"

"I didn't do anything but help to bring about justice," said Vivienne, no longer feeling bad for the girl. She raised her chin and spoke loudly. "Rosina, you did some horrible things and now you will have to pay for them. Mayhap even with your life." Vivienne wanted the girl to pay, but in her heart, she still didn't want Rosina to be executed. She supposed the sheriff was right saying that she always made decisions with her heart. Well, in this case, she had to make decisions with her head instead. Rosina murdered a man. Mayhap two, since they still didn't know if Leif would even live. As sad as it was to see this happen to Rosina, the girl had to be punished for her actions in whatever way the law decided. In the end, justice would be served.

"Put her in the cage and take her away," commanded the sheriff with a wave of his hand.

Vivienne's heart broke watching Rosina be hauled away, not able to push aside the good memories she'd had with the girl. Everyone had a good side as well as a bad one, she decided. But Rosina's bad side was so vengeful, greedy, and hateful that now she would have to pay for her mistakes, and Rosina had no one to blame but herself.

"What is going to happen to us now?" asked Cook, holding Maria close to him in a protective hug.

"Well, you were an accessory to a crime, knowing what Rosina did and not saying anything," answered the sheriff.

"We were frightened for our lives," cried Maria. "We thought we killed a nobleman, but we didn't do so after all. Let us go free. Please, Sheriff, I beg you. I am pregnant with Cook's baby, and we want the chance to get married and raise a family together and start life anew. We don't want to die."

"I only tried to protect her. I swear, neither of us ever once even thought about trying to kill Lord Gainsborough," said Cook. "Doesn't that count for something?"

"Oh, my," said Vivienne, feeling as if she couldn't breathe. Was this ever going to get any easier? She cared for these people and thought of them as family. She didn't want to see Maria and Cook punished for something they didn't do. All she wanted was for them to be able to marry and raise children and be happy ... everything she'd once wanted in life as well.

"Yes, and what about me and my son?" Lady Gainsborough demanded to know. "We didn't kill my husband either. You cannot lock us away. It's not fair."

"One question at a time," shouted the sheriff. "As for Cook and Maria, I think I will leave their fate up to Lady Gainsborough, if she wants to press charges or not, since this has to do with her deceased husband."

"Mother, let them go. They didn't mean to harm Father," said Wilfred. "Father tried to rape Maria, and would have gotten away with it if all this hadn't happened."

Lady Gainsborough pursed her lips together and scrunched her face while thinking of what to say. "My husband's behavior was abominable, and even though he is dead and got what he deserved, I am ashamed to say I was ever married to him. My son is Lord of Gainsborough now, and he doesn't want them punished, so I will not protest."

"Mayhap not, but I will," bellowed Lord Mablethorpe. "I

can't have servants in my household that I can't trust. I'm afraid I'm going to have to let both of them go."

"Let us go?" gasped Maria. "But this is our home, Lord Mablethorpe. We have nowhere else to go. How will we live? How will we survive?"

"That is not my problem." Vivienne's uncle stubbornly crossed his arms over his chest and set his jaw, looking in the other direction.

"Gilbert, please," said his wife under her breath. "They are both so young and have never caused us any trouble before now."

Vivienne had to do something fast to help Maria and Cook. When her uncle made a decision, he didn't easily change it. But she wasn't about to let him throw Maria and Cook out with nowhere to go.

"Uncle, if I promise to be responsible for their future actions, will you allow Maria and Cook to stay here at Mablethorpe Castle and continue working in the kitchens?" asked Vivienne.

"Without being punished for their actions? Nay, never," he growled.

"Oh, I didn't say they wouldn't be punished." Vivienne grinned. "I think a few months of the two of them cleaning out the stables together, as well as the kennels and the mews might make them think differently about not coming to me or you or Lady Mablethorpe with their troubles and concerns next time."

"Yes, my lady, we promise to come to you from now on. It won't happen again," said Maria with a curtsy.

"Cook?" asked Vivienne. "What do you have to say?"

"I say you are too kind, my lady, as always. And also that I'd better get used to smelling and shoveling shit, I guess." That made the crowd laugh, breaking the tension in the air.

"Oh, all right," agreed her uncle. "But mark my words, if I feel I can't trust either of you, out you go!"

"Thank you, Lord and Lady Gainsborough," said Cook with a bow.

"We won't let you down," added Maria, holding tight to Cook's hand as she curtsied.

"Now, as for you, Lord and Lady Gainsborough," said the sheriff. "Since it was not by your hand that Lord Gainsborough died, I do not feel you should be punished for it. It is hard enough losing a loved one. We all know that."

"I agree," said Lady Gainsborough. "Now, can we please leave this godforsaken place and go home to bury my husband?"

"Not yet," said the sheriff. "I said you wouldn't be held accountable for the murder, but you still had a hand in deceiving many people, including me. You kept secrets that should have been brought to the surface."

"I was only trying to protect my son," sniffed the noblewoman.

"And I was only trying to be with the woman I loved." Wilfred turned with sad eyes to look at Rosina. The constable had tied her hands together and was leading her to the cage.

"We understand that, Lady Gainsborough," said Zachariah. "But the fact still remains that both of you did something wrong, and it can't go unnoticed."

"Are we going to be imprisoned as well?" Wilfred's eyes stayed focused on Rosina, who was put in the cage and the door locked behind her. She sat with her hands tied together, and her head down.

"I think a steep fine would be sufficient," decided the sheriff. "However, the amount will be decided on by Lord Mablethorpe, since he had to house and feed all these people during the course of the investigation. "Lord Mablethorpe, please come to me with your list of expenses when you have them."

"That's all you are going to do about them?" snapped Lord Mablethorpe. "It hardly seems fair."

"Your expense sheet's amount will be paid by the Gainsboroughs ... in triplicate," said the sheriff. A slow smile crossed Lord Mablethorpe's face. "I will also send a missive to the king, explaining what has transpired here, and he will decide if any lands or holdings, or perhaps even the castle itself will be taken away from the Gainsboroughs because of these unfortunate events."

"That sounds fair to me," said Lord Mablethorpe. "John," he called to his steward. "We need to make an expense list at once."

"Aye, my lord," came John's reply.

"Nay!" shouted Lady Gainsborough. "That is not fair. My son is supposed to inherit all my husband's holdings."

"Get them out of here," instructed the sheriff, giving his constables the order. "Send them back where they belong."

His constables escorted the Gainsboroughs to their wagon.

"Wait! What about my kennels?" Adam came rushing over to them. Grunt saw him and ran over with his tailing wagging. Martin and Starah were right behind the dog. "Who burned down the kennels? That person needs to be punished. My dogs were nearly killed!"

Zachariah looked over at Vivienne, and shrugged. That was one thing they had yet to figure out, but Vivienne thought she knew the answer.

"I think it might have been an accident, Adam, and not a ploy to be a distraction to a murder after all," she told him.

"An accident? How?" Adam wanted answers and she couldn't blame him.

"Mayhap there is someone here besides me or the sheriff

who can answer that," she said. "Martin? Do you know anything about it?"

"Him?" The sheriff spun around. "Lady Vivienne, I don't understand," he said softly. "I hope you know what you're doing."

"Let the page boy explain." Vivienne nodded. "Go ahead, Martin."

"I did it, I'm sorry." The little boy looked down and kicked at the dirt. "I just wanted to feed the dogs some tallow to get them to like me, the way I do with Grunt. I climbed up on the gate in the kennels to give it to them and I fell and dropped the tallow and the candle. The candle fell in the hay and it started a fire. I was scared when the big flames shot up, so I ran to the castle to get help."

"You should have told us what really happened instead of keeping it to yourself," scolded Vivienne, but in a kind voice so as not to cause the child to cry.

"I know. I'm sorry." He kicked at the dirt some more. "I just didn't want to be punished. I was afraid if I told Lord Mablethorpe what happened, he wouldn't let me pet the hounds or play with Grunt anymore. I knew I was in big trouble. I didn't want the kennels to burn down or any of the dogs to die, honest I didn't. I love all the hounds!" His big blue eyes looked up at her, silently begging for her help.

"I know you do, Martin." Vivienne smiled at the child and put her hand on his shoulder. "Grunt and all the dogs love you, too. But you still should have at least told me what happened. I would have understood."

"You're right. I'm sorry," said the boy, dropping to his knees and throwing his arms around Grunt's neck in a big hug, trying hard to hold back his tears. "Please, don't take me away from Grunt or the other dogs."

"Well, at least you did the right thing now by coming forward," the sheriff told him.

"Adam?" asked Vivienne. "If Martin promises to help you get things back in order in the kennels and to assist you in feeding the dogs and looking after them when he isn't busy being a page, would you forgive him for his mistake?"

"Well ... I suppose so," said Adam with a chuckle, reaching out to ruffle the boy's blond hair. "I think the hounds would miss Martin if he didn't visit once in a while. I'm just glad no one was really trying to kill the dogs after all, and that none of them died in the fire."

"Me too," came Martin's muffled voice, since his mouth was against Grunt's fur.

Vivienne looked up at her uncle, waiting for his approval of her plan. He nodded slightly and her aunt smiled.

"Martin, what do you say?" asked Vivienne.

Martin looked up with his wide blue eyes and ever so slowly the corners of his mouth turned up into a wide grin. "It'll be hard, but I think I can do it, my lady. Thank you." He looked over at Starah and took her hand. "Come on, Starah. Me and Grunt want to show you the new kennels." He ran away with the sheriff's daughter at his side and Grunt barking and leading the way.

"I think I'd better watch it or that page is going to steal away my daughter's heart someday," mumbled Zachariah, laughing heartedly.

"Everyone go back to what you were doing," called out Vivienne's uncle, taking her aunt by the hand and heading back to the keep. "Matter of fact, let's all have some wine and ale. I think it is well needed by all."

"Thank goodness, this is all over," commented Lady Mablethorpe.

The wagon with the cage holding Rosina rolled out of the courtyard. Rosina's eyes met Vivienne's, and this time the girl's goodness shone through, but it was too late. Justice had been served and her life would be much different now because of her decisions. Rosina lifted her hands that were tied together and waggled her fingers at Vivienne, silently saying goodbye. Forever. Vivienne felt so choked at the moment that she couldn't have said a word if she tried. With her eyes still locked with the handmaid's, she raised her hand to wave back, but instead she slowly lowered it back to her side and just nodded. Then the wagon rolled over the drawbridge and it was gone. Vivienne would never see Rosina again. The Gainsboroughs left, with Herman driving their wagon that held the corpse of Lord Gainsborough in the back, encased in the wooden coffin. Finally, the man would be buried back home where he belonged.

"I'm not sure anyone is going to really miss Lord Gainsborough, but a part of me still feels sorry for him, as well as for Rosina," Vivienne told the sheriff.

"How so?" he asked.

"Lord Gainsborough was a pathetic man who only thought about himself and had no one who really loved him."

"He laid the foundation for his own life and this is the way it played out," explained the sheriff. "Sometimes all we can do is accept the hand that life deals us, no matter if we like it or not."

"I suppose you're right. Rosina, on the other hand, found someone she loved, but her revenge kept her from ever being with Wilfred in the end."

"Yes, that's true."

"Zachariah, isn't it funny how thinking with one's heart can make people miserable in the end, after all? It doesn't seem it should be that way at all."

"Ah, I see you are thinking with your heart right now, or you never would have just called me Zachariah."

She smiled at him and they started walking to the keep together.

"What will happen to Rosina now?" asked Vivienne. "Will she be executed for murder?"

"I don't know," Zachariah answered. "I suppose there will be a trial to decide that, but the truth is, she confessed. Rosina is guilty and will get what she deserves in the end."

"She said she did it for love. For the love of Lord Wilfred."

"Hah! I sincerely don't think any kind of relationship between the two of them would have ever worked out."

"I suppose not."

"At least not while Lady Gainsborough is alive, anyway."

"I guess justice will be served after all, and no matter what the heart says, that is all that matters in the end."

"I agree," said the sheriff.

"Lady Vivienne!" Father Benjamin came running over from the chapel.

"What is it, Father?" asked Vivienne. "Is Leif all right?"

"He is better than all right, my lady. He has woken and is asking for food. It seems the herbal tincture you had the healer make worked! It helped the boy to regain consciousness."

"That is wonderful news. Thank you, Father," said Zachariah. "I'll be sure to stop by soon to get a statement from Leif about the stabbing. Of course, he'll have to have some kind of punishment too, since he was going to accept a bribe to keep quiet about the murder."

"The healer wants to move him into the keep," said the priest. "He says Leif shouldn't leave here for at least a few weeks. Until his wound is healed."

"Tell Leif he is welcome to stay indefinitely," Vivienne told the priest. "And Sheriff, I will come up for a just punishment for Leif as well."

"My lady?" The priest looked at her in confusion. "Did you say indefinitely? Really?"

"Sure. Why not? We could always use another musician here at the castle. I mean, with all the gatherings my uncle plans, we'll need lots of entertainment."

"I will let him know," said the priest, bowing and heading back to the chapel.

"Do you really need another musician, or is it that you are thinking with your heart again?" asked Zachariah. "Somehow I don't believe your uncle will agree to it."

"I like Leif, and he has nowhere to go. I want him to stay and make Mablethorpe his home from now on. Don't worry, I'll talk my uncle into letting him stay."

"You do like taking in strays, don't you, my lady?"

"I suppose I do," she answered. "I just hope that there is someone else out there who feels the same way as I do, thinking with their heart instead of their head. Someone who might have found my brother or my son and taken them in as well."

"We'll find your answers, Lady Vivienne, don't you worry. I promised you I wouldn't give up searching and I mean it. No matter how long it takes."

"Thank you, Sheriff."

"Sheriff, excuse me." Another constable from town rushed through the gate, heading over to meet them.

"What is it, Constable?" asked Zachariah.

"I am sorry to interrupt, but we are having trouble in town."

"Again? What kind of trouble?" he grumbled.

"It's that rat catcher again, called the Pied Piper. Everyone is up in arms about him."

"Constable, do what you can. I will look into it when I return on the morrow."

"Aye," said the constable, hurrying away.

"Did you say you'll return on the morrow?" asked Vivienne, not sure why Zachariah wasn't doing his job and leaving right away.

"Yes, that's right. I've been told I work too much," he said with a wink. "I'm going to take the rest of the day off to spend it with Starah. Mayhap a picnic is in order." He looked up at the sky, taking in a deep breath of fresh air. "After all, it is a sunny day, so there is no chance that a storm will cut it short this time."

"What a nice idea," agreed Vivienne. "I think your daughter would love that."

"Perhaps you'd like to join us? And bring Martin and that hound of yours with you? After all, Starah seems to adore all of you and it would make the outing more special. Don't you agree?"

Her eyes interlocked with his and that feeling of being safe and happy again filled her heart. "Yes, I think that would be in order, Sheriff Fitch. Of course, I am answering from my heart as well as my head this time, if that's all right with you."

They both laughed at that.

"Then, if you'll allow me to escort you, Lady Vivienne?" He held out his arm, and she gently placed her hand upon it, not able to look away from his handsome face.

"I'd be honored," she said in a breathy whisper. "And you can just call me ... *partner* from now on."

If there was anything else she could have said at that moment, it would probably have been better. The smile in his eyes faded and he seemed to put up that wall between them once again.

"Too much? Too soon?" she asked with a giggle.

"I'll race you to the kennels to get the children," he said, taking off at a run.

"Sheriff, this isn't fair. I'm not wearing my breeches and boots!" She picked up her skirts and sped after him, knowing that any game he wanted to play, she'd be able to win in the end.

From the Author:

I hope you enjoyed *Murder at Mablethorpe Castle* and will take the time to leave a review for me. As many of you might know, I normally write romance and this is my first endeavor with writing a murder mystery.

As a child I adored reading the Nancy Drew and Hardy Boys mysteries, and just couldn't seem to get enough. I would spend so much time at the library, having to use my wagon to haul home all the books I checked out to read. They were exciting, mysterious, and always held my interest. Those books made me want to read the next one in the series to find out what happened to Nancy Drew or Frank and Joe Hardy and all their friends. I was a voracious reader from a very early age. Of course, that might have something to do with me becoming a writer. I want to share that same way I felt reading books with my readers.

For those adults who enjoy romance murder mysteries, be sure to read my historical *romance* murder mysteries, **Summer's Reign**, **Ruby**, **The Baron's Bounty**, and even my contemporary small-town romance murder mystery called **Doubting Thomas**.

There is a slow-burn romance going on between Sheriff Zachariah Fitch and Lady Vivienne Harlowe, and only time will tell if they get together for anything other than solving murders. As for Lady Vivienne's backstory and what happened with her family, don't think I forgot to tell you what happened. But you're going to have to keep reading each book in the series to find out, since the answers will slowly rise to the surface with each new book.

As you've probably already noticed, hints have been given as to where and what Harlowe and Fitch will be off to investigate next. And yes, it involves that horrible street in town with the rundown houses and all the rats called Rotten Row. There is a rat catcher that everyone refers to as the Pied Piper, and he has a dark side to him that is about to come out and throw the entire town into a frenzy. It'll be up to Harlowe and Fitch to solve another mystery and bring things back to order.

You won't want to miss Book 2 in the series that is called **Murder on Rotten Row**.

Stop by and visit my **Website** at http://www.elizabethrosenovels.com. You can follow me on **Amazon, Bookbub, Goodreads, Facebook** and **Bluesky** and **Twitter**. I also have a **Private Readers' Group** on Facebook that I invite you to join.

Thank you,

Elizabeth Rose

And now, I'd like to leave you with an excerpt of one of my favorite murder mystery romances that is called *The Baron's Bounty*. My Scottish heroine has an obsession with shoes, and can identify people by the way they walk. My hero is English, a widower with a child, and also a Baron of the Cinque Ports. Oh, and I want to add that my heroine is sent as a proxy, kind of like a placeholder, to marry the man for her cousin, who will arrive in England later.

Enjoy!

The Baron's Bounty — Book 2 in The Barons of the Cinque Ports Series

The horse's reins were tangled in the brambles at the edge of the cliff. As she reached out to untangle it, she heard some low voices, but couldn't decipher what the people were saying. Startled, she jumped backward when she heard the loud sound of a thud and breaking branches. Something—or someone—fell from the top of the cliff, hitting on the rocks and roots along the way down.

Also by Elizabeth Rose

Mystery Series:

Harlowe & Fitch Historical Mystery Series

Medieval Series:

Below the Salt

Legendary Bastards of the Crown Series

Seasons of Fortitude Series

Secrets of the Heart Series

Legacy of the Blade Series

Daughters of the Dagger Series

MadMan MacKeefe Series

Barons of the Cinque Ports Series

Holiday Knights Series

Highland Chronicles Series

Pirate Lords Series

Highland Outcasts

Medieval/Paranormal Series:

Elemental Magick Series

Greek Myth Fantasy Series

Tangled Tales Series

Portals of Destiny

Contemporary Series:

Tarnished Saints Series

Working Man Series

Western Series:

Cowboys of the Old West Series

And More!

Please visit http://elizabethrosenovels.com

About Elizabeth

Elizabeth Rose is an award-winning, bestselling author of over 100 books and counting. She writes medieval, historical, contemporary, paranormal, and western romance. Her books are available as EBooks, paperbacks, and some audiobooks as well.

Her favorite characters in her works include dark, dangerous and tortured heroes, and feisty, independent heroines who know how to wield a sword. She loves writing 14th century medieval novels, and is well-known for her many series.

Elizabeth loves the outdoors. In the summertime, you can find her in her secret garden with her laptop, swinging in her hammock working on her next book. Elizabeth is a born story-teller and passionate about sharing her works with her readers.

Please be sure to visit her website at **Elizabethrosenovels.com** to read excerpts from any of her novels and get sneak peeks at covers of upcoming books. You can follow her on **Twitter, Facebook**, **Goodreads** or **BookBub.** Join Elizabeth's **newsletter** so you don't miss out on new releases or upcoming events.